Moondance

Linda K. Hopkins

MOONDANCE

Chapter 1

Darkness hung over the ground like a pall as Melissa stumbled blindly through the forest, lurching between shadowy trunks and swerving around bushes that seemed to materialize out of nowhere. Barbed branches clawed her face and arms, leaving angry welts in their wake. Protruding roots, intent on hindering her escape, sent her to her knees, leaving them scratched and bleeding. She gasped for breath as the blood pounded furiously in her ears while her chest burned with each breath. Sweat dripped down her forehead, covering her brow. Fear had slickened her palms, and her legs trembled as she careened between the trees. Behind her, her pursuer flew with seeming effortlessness over the ground, its enormous paws making no sound as it closed the gap between them. From the corner of her eye she saw the huge cat drawing alongside her, its bright green eyes shining eerily in the dark. Her foot caught the rough end of a stump, and she flung out her hands as she tumbled to the ground. The panther leaped toward her as her screams tore through the air.

Melissa jolted upright in her bed, her eyes wide as she searched her room in terror for the beast. Rigid fingers gripped the sheet, straining the fabric until it was close to ripping. Her heart hammered in her chest, the memory of reaching claws and hot breath on her neck still too close to dismiss. She loosened her hold on the sheet one aching finger at a time until it fell from her grip. A cool breeze blew through an open window, and she shivered as it brushed over her damp skin. Pulling in a deep breath, she willed her heart to slow its racing, and finally the dream ebbed as the creature slunk back to the edges of her mind. She looked around the room, reassuring herself that nothing lurked in the shadows. A flash of green made her freeze, but it was just the light from her laptop, and she laughed shakily. The sound broke the silence, making her a little bolder. "There's nothing here," she whispered, then said it again, a little louder this time, to make sure that any creatures lurking in her room knew it as well.

The clock beside the bed read half-past four. Fumbling in the darkness, Melissa found the switch for the bedside lamp and turned it on. She blinked in the sudden flare of light as she untangled her feet from the sheet and tentatively placed them on the floor, pushing away the last tendrils of the dream. The panther had become a recurrent visitor in the nighttime hours – stalking her between the city high-rises in broad daylight or chasing her over the rugged terrain of the Rocky Mountains at dusk. Sometimes snow lay thick on the ground, the jet-black fur of the panther a stark contradiction to the brilliant white, while other times huge drops of rain spat from the sky, sliding down the panther's sleek pelt as it stalked her through the shadows.

She headed to the kitchen and flipped on the light. Everything looked exactly as it had the night before, easing away more of the dread that still pooled in her stomach. She took a tin of coffee from the cupboard and spooned some into a filter as she thought about the dreams. They had started a few years back, but had become more frequent in recent months – in fact, she mused, around the same time she had started on a new project at work. "Repressed fears," she could hear Dr. Phil saying, and she smiled sardonically as she filled the coffee machine with water and switched it on. But perhaps the fear idea wasn't that ludicrous, since the timing of the dreams *was* strange. Perhaps the panther represented her fear of failure. This project was, after all, her chance to finally prove herself to her company. To Leander Garrett.

Melissa had started working at Quigley Ramsbottom Consulting, or Quigs, as it was affectionately known among its employees, as a summer intern in her first year of university, then moved into a permanent position after earning her business degree. Her job wasn't romantic – as a junior analyst she wrote job descriptions, analyzed pay grades and compared benefit programs for Quigs's client companies, producing data for the consultants who worked directly with clients. Melissa noticed that when she talked about her job with friends and family, their eyes would glaze over and they'd change the subject, but she didn't mind the work. Of course, it wasn't what she wanted to do forever – her ambition was to join the ranks

3

of consultants at Quigs – so when she was asked to join a team in which she would work on a project for a specific client, she thought she was finally moving in the right direction. But things have a habit of not quite working out as expected, and although she'd been working with the team for six months, she had not once met anyone from the client company. As for impressing Leander Garrett – well, he barely even noticed her.

She sighed as she watched the brewing coffee drip into the pot. Lee Garrett was the wonder child of Quigs. Like Melissa, he had been hired by the company straight out of university, but there the similarities ended. In the ten years he'd worked with the firm, Lee had quickly earned promotion after promotion and was highly regarded by the partners. So much so that if you wanted to get anywhere at Quigs, it was Lee you needed to impress. And that was the problem. No matter how hard she worked or how many hours she put in, Lee did not pay her the slightest attention. And when he did speak to her, his manner was decidedly abrupt. "I need those numbers by noon, Ms. Hewitt." "When can I expect the completed analysis, Ms. Hewitt?" "I need a coffee, Ms. Hewitt." It was frustrating – there was no one else that he addressed so formally. She filled a mug with coffee and returned to her room to open her laptop. Since there was little chance of getting back to sleep, she might as well finish the data analysis report Lee expected for the weekly team meeting that morning. She opened the file and studied a column of numbers.

When she entered the boardroom later that morning, Lee was already seated at the large mahogany table that filled most of the room. Papers were spread over the smooth surface, but his attention was on Caro, seated beside him. Her chair was angled toward his, and she smiled as she leaned closer. Several years older than Melissa, Caro had been working at Quigs a few months when Melissa had started as an intern. Single and unattached, she worked hard and played hard, much like Lee.

They ignored Melissa as she sat down. "Come on, Lee," Caro was saying. "You know I'm right." She ran a finger along his forearm. "He'll listen to me."

Lee smiled blandly. "Sleeping with him isn't the solution."

Caro leaned closer with a sultry smile. "You sure about that?" she said softly, staring at him.

Melissa quickly looked away. Caro and Lee hadn't *slept* together, had they? From the corner of her eye, she saw Lee pull away, and she shot him a quick look. He was staring at her, his green eyes dark and narrowed, his expression grim. She felt the heat rise in her cheeks as she focused her gaze on the pile of papers in her hands.

"I have the report you wanted," she said. She passed him the document and he flipped it open to the first page.

"These aren't the numbers I asked for."

"I did some extra analysis. The data you want is in the next section."

He turned to the next page. "Very well. I'll have a closer look at this later."

Tracy and Kasper, the last two members of the team, entered the room.

"Let's get started," Lee said. "We have a lot to get through."

Lee did not look at Melissa again for the rest of the meeting, and her mind wandered as the discussion moved on to points beyond her involvement. Despite Lee's aloofness, Melissa could not help admiring his good looks. With his dark green eyes and swarthy features, he was regarded by the women in the office as the most handsome man in the company. She studied him now as he talked to Kasper. His black hair was cropped, except for a single strip drawn into a ponytail and twisted into a knot. The style would appear ridiculous on most men, but it gave Lee a sensual, provocative look. Heavy eyebrows covered his deep-set eyes, and although it was still early, a faint five o'clock shadow lined his upper lip. Alluring and a little dangerous, thought Melissa, despite the white collared shirt and silk tie he wore. Clothes that did little to hide his muscular arms, strapping chest and slim waist. She dragged her attention back to the meeting as it drew to a close.

"So Kasper, you and Tracy will go through the proposal we're making about executive benefits, and Caro, come see me in my office with the notes from the last client meeting and we'll review to ensure nothing's been missed." Lee looked around the table, waiting for their nods of acquiescence. "I'll get Mary to post the next meeting in your calendars." Melissa gathered her papers and headed out the door, careful not to look at Lee as Caro whispered something in his ear.

She was at her desk later that day when Kasper stopped to peer over her shoulder. "What are you working on?" he asked.

She groaned. "Lee wants me to rerun some numbers using the average instead of the median. Since when do we use average numbers?"

"I think Lee likes to give you a hard time. He doesn't seem particularly fond of you."

Melissa snorted. "You think!"

"Sometimes people act like that to hide their true feelings. Perhaps he's secretly in love with you." He snickered.

"We're not in kindergarten, Kasper."

"But seriously, I think he likes you even less than he likes me."

"What do you mean?"

"It's clear that Caro's his favorite. Haven't you seen how he hangs on her every word?"

It was more like the other way around, Melissa thought. There were times when she had the distinct impression Lee merely tolerated Caro's fawning.

"I haven't really noticed."

"Of course you haven't," Kasper said sourly. "At the next team meeting, see how he gives her all the good work, and leaves me the crappy stuff."

She frowned. "O-kay." She wished Lee would give her half the work he gave Kasper. She watched as he walked away, then pushed herself from her desk. A coffee was in order.

Her desk was in a large common work area, next to the window overlooking the river. The space was shared by all the analysts, allowing little chance for privacy. At the far end of the office was a small kitchen, and behind that were consultant and management offices. Ignoring the other analysts, Melissa headed across the room, around the corner and past the reception area where Mary sat answering the phone. The elevators were just through the heavy glass doors, and she pushed them open and pressed the DOWN button. Although there was a coffee machine in the kitchen, she preferred to buy hers from the little coffee shop downstairs. The elevator doors were already sliding closed when a man in his early fifties dashed through,

7

carrying a briefcase slung over his shoulder. He was from out of town, but Melissa recognized him as Patrick Ramsbottom, senior partner in the firm. He gave a self-deprecating shrug at his inelegant entrance.

"Melissa Hewitt, am I right? I've heard some good things about you." Surprise must have registered on her face, because he continued with a small smile. "Leander Garrett can't stop singing your praises."

"Really?"

"He's very impressed with you. He says you're a hard worker with a bright future."

"Oh …" Melissa said faintly.

He furrowed his brow. "'Diligent, thorough and personable' are the words he used."

"Personable?"

"Or maybe he said 'friendly.' Whatever it was, he definitely has a high regard for you." They reached the ground floor and the doors slid open. "Keep up the good work, Melissa." He strode out as she followed in bewilderment. Surely Patrick must be mistaken – it couldn't have been Lee who'd said such things. But she couldn't help smiling as she recalled the conversation. Diligent, thorough and friendly. Someone, whoever it was, had taken notice of her hard work.

Melissa's good mood lingered throughout the afternoon, and she was still smiling when she unlocked the door to her apartment that night. She had worked late, taking the last bus out of downtown Calgary, and picked up something to eat on her way. It was a beautiful spring evening, and she'd alighted from the bus early and walked the last few blocks home. She flipped on the lights as she stepped through the door, chasing away the shadows. As apartments went, hers was tiny, with a single bedroom, a compact kitchen and a small living room, but it was all the space she needed. A narrow deck opened off the living room, and if she stood on her toes and peered around the corner, she could just see a glimpse of the Rocky Mountains – the best mountain view she could afford. It took only an hour to drive to the mountains, and on hot summer weekends she drove to Kananaskis or Banff National Park and spent the day hiking, choosing trails away from the throngs of tourists that crowded the sites so popular on postcards and calendars. In the winter, she packed up her skis and made for the slopes, spending her hard-earned money on outrageously priced passes. Sometimes one of her friends joined her, but as often as not she went to the mountains alone. And it was worth it, she thought, when she stood on top of a peak and looked out over an immense snow-covered landscape. Nothing in the world could compare with the utter stillness at the top of a snowy mountain, where the stresses of city life seemed a million miles away.

She dropped her purse on the table and headed into the kitchen to pour herself a glass of wine before stepping onto the deck. A brightly colored bistro table and a few potted plants, wilting in the unseasonal spring heat, made the small space seem more homey. It was twilight, but the air still retained the heat of the day, and she leaned back in her chair and closed her eyes as murmurs of conversation spilled from open windows and drifted around her, mingled with the shouts and laughter of a few boys as they kicked a soccer ball around a small patch of weedy grass that separated her block from the next. The sounds slowly dissipated as the light faded and the boys were called inside, and windows were closed for the night.

Her mind wandered back to the conversation she'd had

with Patrick in the elevator. Was it possible that the man who couldn't even deign to notice her had actually spoken of her so highly? She took a sip of wine. The relationship between her and Lee hadn't always been this cool. When she had first started her internship at Quigs, six years before, they'd been good friends. They both loved the mountains and had quickly discovered they had similar tastes in music. Heading downstairs to get coffee together had soon led to long lunches, where the time slipped by so quickly they had to race back to the office to avoid their absences being noticed. Conversation had come easily and was interspersed with much laughter. But then Lee had gone to Toronto for a three-week project, and when he'd returned, he was a different person. Gone were long conversations over lunch, replaced with an icy aloofness. He barely acknowledged her presence, and his interactions with her became strictly professional, to the point where he addressed her as Ms. Hewitt. He spoke to her only when necessary, with a look and a tone that suggested he did so under compulsion. She'd tried, at first, to find out what had brought about the change, but when her attempts to talk to him were repeatedly rebuffed, she'd finally given up. When she returned to Quigs the next summer, it was as though they were complete strangers.

But she missed Lee and the easy friendship they'd had. The conversations and laughter. And she wondered, for the umpteenth time, what had changed. How he could have come back so different. And which one was the real Lee. Sometimes, in unguarded moments, she felt his eyes on her, and when he brushed past her in the passage, it was almost as if he did so on purpose; but then she'd see his cold, distant expression, and she knew she'd been mistaken. Still, it added an air of unreality to the situation, and she found herself imagining at times that it was all just a show. As though they were acting roles in a play, presenting an air of indifference to the world, while secretly their friendship continued. It was just a silly notion, of course, but it made it that much harder for her to get him out of her mind. For a few short months he had been her friend, and then he was gone.

The stirring of a cool breeze finally brought Melissa to her feet. Only a faint smudge of light still hung on the horizon, while a single street lamp at the end of the pathway cast a dim glow on the surrounding buildings. Melissa picked up her glass, but before she headed inside a dark shape against the wall made her pause. She peered into the shadows, her eyes intent, and when a pair of green eyes turned to her, she stumbled backward. They held hers for a moment, then blinked into darkness as the creature rose and disappeared around a corner. For a single instant, one foolish moment, she was sure it was the panther from her dreams. She laughed nervously. There were no panthers around Calgary, and even a cougar would not venture this far into the city. It was just a cat – a very large, very black cat, but still just a cat. The wine glass in her hand was shaking, and she took a long, slow breath before heading back inside and into the light.

Chapter 2

Melissa was seated in the boardroom one week later, waiting for the rest of the team to arrive for the weekly meeting. She was the first one at the table, and she reviewed her notes as she waited for the others. The door opened and Lee entered the room. He paused for a fleeting moment, then closed the door behind him.

"Morning, Ms. Hewitt," he said as he dropped his notes on the table and took a seat.

"Morning. I'm not sure where everyone else is."

"It's just us. Let's get started."

Melissa glanced around in confusion. "Just us?"

"The others are needed on another project, so we'll wrap this up without them." He was studying his notes, but he glanced at Melissa when she didn't respond. "We already have everything we need. It's just a question of pulling it all together into a presentable form. You've written reports before, haven't you?"

"Yes. But what about the client meetings? Will you go on your own?"

Lee leaned back in his chair, his gaze finally meeting hers. "I could. Or you could come with me."

"Me? With you? But I've never attended a client meeting before."

"Then now's a good time to start, isn't it? You know the data, probably better than anyone else on the team, and you'll be writing the report. Isn't this what you want?"

"Yes, of course. And I'm ready. I was just taken by surprise."

"You'll do fine. We have a meeting scheduled with Mr. Hong next Friday, so I expect a finalized report by Wednesday." He rose and walked out the door without waiting for her agreement and after a moment, Melissa hurried after him, her mind spinning. From junior analyst to writing the final report and attending client meetings – this was the chance she'd been waiting for. The opportunity to show Lee what she was really capable of. She hurried to her desk, her mind already picturing the charts and diagrams she'd include in the report.

When Friday morning rolled around, Melissa took her time choosing an outfit. The pantsuit was too earnest, and her long skirt not earnest enough. She finally settled on a black-and-white print dress paired with a black jacket. Not a power suit, but still professional. She scraped her hair into a bun and slipped her feet into a pair of black kitten heels, then picked up the report and left her apartment. Although she could list the numbers it contained without even glancing at the page, she had brought it home to run through the data one last time. When she saw Mr. Hong later that day, she'd be able to tell him anything he wanted to know about his company. She reached the office a short while later, smiling at Mary as she walked past reception.

"Hey Melissa," Mary called, scratching through a pile of notes on her desk. "I have a message for you." She pulled out a piece of paper and adjusted her glasses on her nose, squinting as she deciphered the writing. "Lee says he'll meet you at, uh, Mr. Hang's office at one."

"Mr. Hong's? Lee's not coming in?"

"No. He said he'd be in meetings all morning and will meet you at the client's."

"Thanks, Mary," she said, pushing away her disappointment. She'd hoped Lee would be there to encourage her before her very first client meeting, but then again, he'd probably just ignore her.

Melissa arrived at the offices of Hong Industries a few minutes before one to find Lee waiting for her outside the building. He watched as she stepped out the taxi, his eyes lingering on her for a moment. "Nervous?" he asked as they walked into the office tower.

"Maybe a little," she admitted. "I don't know what to expect."

"It gets easier each time," he said. "You'll do fine." They were ushered into Mr. Hong's office a few moments later, and the small man hurried around his desk, his hand extended in greeting.

"Welcome, welcome," he said with a brief bow. He pulled out a chair. "Sit, please. I'm most eager to hear your report."

Melissa sat down and handed him a thick document, then opened her copy to the first page. "Let's start with management," she began.

Two hours later, they left the offices of Mr. Hong, who

was clearly a satisfied client. "Well done, Ms. Hewitt," Lee said as they stepped into the sunshine. "You did an excellent job. I'm impressed, although not particularly surprised."

"No?"

"No. I knew you'd do well."

"Really?" Melissa said, not bothering to keep the wry tone from her voice.

Lee stopped and faced her. "I'm well aware of what you're capable of, Melissa."

She remained silent, squelching the retort that rose to her lips. It hadn't escaped her notice that he'd used her first name, and she wondered what it meant. Had presenting the client report given her some new status? Or had it just slipped out?

Lee sighed. "Look, why don't we go for a drink? I think you've earned it."

Melissa frowned. "I, uh, I have to be home early tonight."

"It's only three-thirty, and we won't stay long. You'll be home in time for whatever hot date you have this evening."

"You've barely spoken to me in six years, and now you want to go for a drink?"

"To celebrate a job well done," he said. "We all need to do that from time to time."

Melissa nodded slowly. "Okay," she said as she slid into a waiting taxi. "Let's go celebrate."

Lee directed the taxi to a pub near the offices and they arrived after a short ride. They weaved their way past the bar and out to the patio, and she removed her jacket as she took a seat at a small table. Across from her, Lee loosened his tie and rolled up his sleeves as they gave the server their orders. His arms and the back of his hands were covered in a light dusting of dark hair, and Melissa could see the start of a tattoo that stretched up his inner arm.

He leaned back in his seat. "So now that the meeting's behind you, you can think about the weekend. Are you going hiking?" Melissa glanced at him in surprise. "I remember how much you enjoyed the mountains. Has that changed?"

"No," she said. "I just hadn't expected you to remember."

"I remember everything you told me," he said. She frowned and traced the pattern on the tabletop with her finger. "So, are you hiking?" he repeated.

"I haven't decided."

"Do you go with friends?"

"Sometimes." She looked up to meet his gaze. "But I enjoy the peace and solitude."

"You shouldn't hike alone. There are dangerous things out there."

"Like bears?"

"And cougars."

"Cougars don't come near people."

"Unless they feel threatened."

The server returned with their drinks, and Melissa took a sip, watching Lee over the rim of the glass. "Why this sudden concern?" she said.

"There've been cougar sightings on some of the hiking trails lately." He lifted his drink. "Why doesn't your boyfriend go with you?"

Melissa leaned back in her chair and looked at him narrowly. "I don't have a boyfriend."

"Why not? You're attractive and pleasant enough."

"What a flattering commendation."

Lee frowned. "That came out wrong. But I expect there are plenty of men lining up to date you."

Melissa raised an eyebrow. "You're asking me about my dating life?"

"Yes." Lee's mouth lifted in a slight smile. "So tell me what you look for in a man."

"Tall, dark and handsome." She said the words flippantly, then flushed when she realized that she was describing Lee.

"Tom Cruise?"

"Ugh, no! He's too … slick. Besides, he's not tall."

"Then who?"

"Well …" Melissa thought for a moment. "Hugh Jackman."

"Wolverine."

"Les Miserables."

"Oh, yes – you enjoy musicals! So why don't you have a boyfriend?"

"I just haven't met someone I want to be with. What about you? You have a girlfriend, don't you?"

"No."

"What about the girl at the last Christmas party? What was her name?" She'd had long, blond hair, a dress that barely covered anything, and four-inch-high stilettos. She'd clung to Lee all evening, but now that Melissa thought about it, he hadn't returned the attention.

"You mean Amber? It wasn't anything serious."

"And the woman from the previous year?"

He frowned. "I don't remember."

"Black hair, red dress."

"Ah, yes. I know who you mean. I'm surprised *you* remember."

Melissa snorted. "She was difficult to forget." The

17

woman had climbed onto the table after a few drinks and shown off more than her dancing skills. "So why don't you have a girlfriend? You're good-looking and – what was the word? – pleasant."

Lee's lips quirked. "I just don't."

"So you can ask me personal questions, and I can't ask you?"

"That's right." Lee drained his glass and placed it in the center of the table.

"Hmm." She took another sip of her drink.

"So if you don't have a hot date, what are you doing tonight?"

"I volunteer at the Children's Hospital."

"Really? What do you do?"

"Hang out with the patients. A lot of them are alone. There's one girl – Emma – who was in a car accident a few months ago. Her mother and baby brother were both killed, and she was seriously injured. Her dad farms out near Lethbridge, so she doesn't get to see him much."

"That's pretty rough. How did you meet her?"

"An old friend of my mom's works at Children's. She thought I could help Emma since my dad was killed in a car accident."

Lee stiffened. "Killed? When? What happened?"

"Drunk driver. Four years ago. He died on impact."

She watched the server weaving between the tables, but could feel Lee's eyes on her. He leaned closer. "I'm really sorry, Mel," he said. "I wish – I wish I'd known."

Melissa bit her lip. Her sister had already moved to Vancouver when Dad died, and she'd been alone in Calgary. She could have used a friend.

"It was a long time ago now."

There was a moment of silence, then, "Can I come with

you to the hospital one day?"

Melissa looked at Lee in surprise. "If you want."

"Thank you." He watched as she finished her drink. "Ready to go?" he asked.

They walked the few blocks back to the office in silence, but Melissa could not help glancing at Lee beneath her eyelashes. For just a few hours, he'd been the man she remembered. The guy who'd held her hand when she'd related the details of her mother's death from cancer. Who was interested in a little girl in hospital, and concerned about the loss of her father. Could he still be hidden away in there? she wondered. Or had it just been a mere flicker of his former self? By Monday would he be back to his usual, detached formality, all intention of visiting Emma with her forgotten? It would be interesting to see.

CHAPTER 3

Melissa was still thinking about her conversation with Lee when she drove to Children's Hospital later that evening. She could not understand why, after six years, he was suddenly interested in talking to her. She tapped the steering wheel with her finger. It didn't make any sense. The memory of the afternoon taunted her, reminding her of the friendship she had lost, and the rhythm on the steering wheel quickened. She reached the hospital a short while later and eased into a parking space in the underground lot before striding into the brightly painted building.

"Hey kiddo," she said with a smile as she entered the six-year-old's room.

"Hi Mel," Emma said. She lay against the white sheets, a light sheen of sweat covering her forehead.

"Bad day, hey?"

"Pamela was being mean." Emma had been trapped in the car after the accident, her skull fractured, both arms broken, and her legs crushed by the mangled steel as she waited to be rescued. Numerous surgeries had saved the limbs, and Pamela was helping her relearn how to use the damaged muscles.

"I heard that," Melissa glanced up to see Pamela's smiling face at the door. "If you're not careful, I'll show you how mean I can really be."

Emma pulled a face, but Melissa could see the grin she was hiding. "You're such a meanie, you can't be any meaner than mean!"

"Can't I?" Pamela said as she walked toward Emma with her fingers wriggling in the air.

"No! Don't tickle me!" Emma shrieked, pulling the sheet over her head as Melissa laughed.

"Don't believe a word she tells you," Pamela said to Melissa. "She's doing a fantastic job, and she'll soon be running and jumping with all her friends."

"Oh, I know," Melissa said. She smiled as Pamela left the room and turned to the girl. "Okay, Em, how about we read a story?"

"Will you lie down next to me?"

"Of course." Melissa took a book from a pile on the nightstand and waited as Emma scooted over in the bed before climbing on beside her. She opened the book to the first page and began reading. "*Beauty and the Beast*," she read as she wrapped her arm around Emma's shoulders. "'There was once a very rich merchant...'"

Melissa was up early the next morning, eager to get to the mountains before the crowds. After the dreariness of winter, the warm spring temperatures drew people out like bees from a hive. She kept to the speed limits as she drove – her little Honda Civic was an old lady and did not like to be pushed too hard. She arrived in good time, and only a few other cars dotted the parking lot. She stopped to read the notice on the sign board at the head of the trail. *Warning. Cougar sighted in this area. Remain on trail at all times. If a cougar is encountered, do not approach!*

Ah, she thought, so that was why Lee was concerned! The image of a black panther rose in her mind, and her hands turned clammy as she pushed it away. It was just a dream – there were no panthers in Canada. And as long as she kept to the trails, the chances of encountering a cougar were slim. She looked around to see some other hikers further ahead on the path, then adjusted her backpack, and pressed in her earbuds as Bruno Mars crooned through her iPod. She followed the trail as it led past a waterfall and through a meadow before it reached a pristine alpine lake. The frigid glacier water, blue-green in the sun, was spectacularly beautiful, and Melissa sat down against a tree to eat her packed lunch. Jays squawked in the trees around her and squirrels hopped between the branches, scolding the birds. It was midafternoon when she picked up her backpack and started the hike back to the parking lot.

The rest of the weekend disappeared all too quickly, and before she knew it, Melissa was on the bus heading in to work on Monday morning. The warm weather had given way to cold, dreary rain, and Melissa was shivering when she stepped into the office. She was in earlier than usual, but Lee had still arrived before her. He greeted her in the passage.

"Morning, Ms. Hewitt. How was your weekend?"

Melissa paused. Lee had actually greeted her, although

he was back to the old formalities. "Fine, thank you. I survived my hike in the mountains."

"So I see," he said. He gestured toward his office. "Do you have a moment?"

"Of course," she said, following him. He closed the door behind her and motioned for her to sit down.

"The company has tickets for next week's performance of *Phantom of the Opera*. Are you interested in going?"

"I thought tickets were for clients."

Lee shrugged. "There are plenty of other events for clients. And no one is using these."

"Who else is going?"

"Me," he said.

"You?" The word tumbled out before Melissa could think.

"It's not a date," he said testily. "I'll just be in the seat beside you." He paused. "Consider it a reward for a job well done."

"Sorry," she said, "I didn't mean it like that. It's just ..." As her voice trailed off, Lee lifted his eyebrows questioningly. "You barely speak to me, and now you'll be sitting next to me at the theater."

"Yes." He crossed his arms and leaned against his desk. "So do you want the ticket or not?"

"Of course."

"Mary keeps them at her desk, so I'll ask her to give it to you."

"Okay." Melissa waited a moment, wondering if there was anything else, but when Lee walked around his desk and sat down, she knew she'd been dismissed. She paused as the door. "Thank you," she said, before quickly leaving the room. She made her way to her desk and sat down, her mind spinning as she stared at her computer screen.

Lee was out of the office for the rest of the week, and when Friday arrived and Mary still hadn't given her the ticket, Melissa stopped by the reception desk. "Did Lee say anything to you about tickets for *Phantom of the Opera*?"

"Let me think. *Phantom of the Opera*," Mary mumbled as she glanced over her desk. "Oh, yes! Lee took both tickets on Monday before he left."

"He did?" Melissa frowned. "He didn't give you something for me?"

"For you? I don't think so."

"Okay. Thanks."

She headed back to her desk. Was Lee just messing with her? Had he found a client who wanted the tickets and not bothered to tell her? She grabbed her wallet and headed to the elevator. A cup of coffee was definitely in order. Her phone buzzed with a message from Lee as she entered the coffee shop. He must have been reading her mind!

Sorry about the ticket, it read. *Was going to give it to you before I left on Monday, then forgot. I'll pick you up at seven tomorrow.*

Melissa frowned, skeptical. *We can meet outside the theater*, she texted back.

The reply came a moment later. *Might not find you. Easier if I pick you up.* She was still reading when another message arrived: *We'll be saving the environment if we just use one vehicle.*

She sighed. Who could argue with that? *OK*, she wrote. *See u at 7.*

Melissa stood in front of the mirror at ten minutes to seven the next evening, critically examining her outfit. She had chosen a red dress with a halter top and wide skirt that reached to her knees. The color made her blue eyes sparkle, and her long, dark brown hair lay glossy and shining on her shoulders. Her phone buzzed: *Meet me downstairs when you're ready*, it read. She headed downstairs to see Lee idling his black pickup truck at the curb. He climbed out as she stepped through the doors, and she ran her eye over him appreciatively. He wore a black sports jacket over a crisp, gray button-up shirt, open at the neck, and a pair of black pants.

"Ms. Hewitt," he said as he opened the passenger door for her. She smiled and climbed in, breathing in the rich smell of leather.

"You look very nice, Melissa," he said as he slipped into the seat beside her.

"Thank you. You look rather dapper yourself."

"Dapper?" He chuckled. "Well, thank you."

They fell silent as Lee weaved his way through the traffic, heading past the gleaming high-rises of downtown Calgary to the theater on the other side of the river. He turned into the parking lot beside the arts center and maneuvered his large truck into a free space. "Shall we?" he asked.

"We shall."

The lobby was crowded, and they pushed their way through the throng of milling people without pausing and made their way into the theater. The orchestra was tuning in the pit as Melissa and Lee found their seats near the front.

"Good seats," she said.

"Took me forever to get them arranged."

She smiled and rose as other patrons squeezed past to reach their places. A few more minutes passed before the first haunting notes of the orchestra swelled through the air, and the curtains rose to show an auctioneer bringing down his gavel. Melissa settled into her seat as the show began, and everything but the unfolding story faded from her mind.

Melissa was humming when they left the theater three hours later, the last bars of music still swirling through her mind. They got into Lee's truck and he joined the line of vehicles turning out of the lot. Above them, the sky was a black canopy with a sprinkling of stars and a silver scimitar hanging overhead.

"The moon's so bright," she said, peering through the windshield. "Do you think it's waxing or waning?"

"Waning. Still fifteen more days."

She looked at him questioningly. "Fifteen days?"

"Till it's full."

"How do you know?"

"The moon affects plant growth. Gardeners watch the lunar cycles to determine the best time to plant."

Melissa raised her eyebrows in surprise. "You're a gardener?"

They pulled up at a red light. "No, but my mother is. When I was a kid, she made me keep track of the phases of the moon. After a while, you just know."

"And do you creep into Fish Creek Park to howl at the moon when it's full?" she asked with a grin.

"No."

The word was curt, and Melissa shifted uncomfortably. "Do your parents, uh, live in Calgary?"

"Kamloops."

"My sister's in Vancouver."

He glanced at her. "Yes, you told me before. My brother's on the Island at UVic." Lee pulled his pickup into a space in front of Melissa's apartment building. "I'll walk up with you," he said as she opened her door.

"Ah, a gentleman."

He shrugged. "If you want." He climbed out of the truck and met her on the sidewalk. "It's just mannerly to make sure someone gets home safely."

"You think I'll be accosted in the passage?" she asked in amusement.

"You never know who, or what, may be lurking about."

The words were low, and Melissa felt a sliver of fear. "There's nothing dangerous here," she said.

Lee leaned closer, his mouth at her ear. "Are you so sure, Mel?" he said as a shiver swept through her. He pulled back and met her gaze. "Still, it's the gentlemanly thing to do."

He walked beside her, taking the heavy building door from her hand when she yanked it open. They reached her apartment a few minutes later. "Do you want to come in?" she asked.

He glanced down the passage. "I should get going. But can I come to the hospital with you next Friday?" Crossing his arms, he leaned his shoulder against the doorpost as Melissa looked at him in surprise. "You didn't think I was serious about going, did you?"

"Not really. Why *do* you want to come?"

"I think you're doing a great thing, helping injured kids."

She eyed him dubiously. "And you want to help, too?"

"You sound surprised."

"I am surprised. But if you really want to come, I won't stop you."

"Maybe we can get something to eat afterward."

Melissa wrinkled her nose. "Cafeteria food should only be eaten in extreme circumstances."

"I wasn't thinking from the cafeteria. I'll book a table somewhere."

"At a restaurant?" she said disbelievingly.

He laughed. "Yes, Mel. At a restaurant." He leaned closer and dropped his voice. "Tonight wasn't a date, but this definitely will be."

She pulled back to look at him. "You're asking me on a date?"

"Yes. Are you saying no?" His gaze met hers, and Melissa's heart skittered for a brief moment.

"I'm not sure. Will you still be talking to me the next week?"

He drew in a sharp breath as he looked away. "I deserve that, I suppose," he said. He turned back at her. "I'm sorry I was so—"

"Rude?"

He winced. "Yes."

"Why were you?"

"I can't explain."

"Can't or won't?" He met her gaze but remained silent. "Will you start treating me like that again?" she finally said.

He took a deep breath. "All I can promise you is next week."

Melissa looked at the floor. Could she take a risk on so little? She nodded slowly and lifted her eyes to meet his. "I'll go out to dinner with you."

He smiled imperceptibly. "Thank you," he said, before turning and walking away.

CHAPTER 4

The next week passed by quickly, and it was Friday when Lee cornered Melissa in the kitchen. Apart from a few passing words, they had not spoken all week.

"Are we still on for tonight?" he asked.

She crossed her arms as she looked at him. "Well, you're still talking to me, so I think we're good."

"I've made reservations. Nothing too fancy, so don't dress up."

"Jeans?" Calgary *was* the home of the Calgary Stampede, where jeans were often regarded as formal wear.

"Sure. I'll pick you up at six."

She nodded as Caro walked into the kitchen. She stopped a few inches from Lee and danced her finger along his arm. "Joining us for drinks tonight?" she said.

"Not tonight, Caro."

"Why not, baby?" Caro leaned closer, closing the small distance between them.

A wave of irritation swept over Melissa. "Yes, go. I'm sure you'll have fun."

Lee's eyes narrowed as he took a step back. "I have other plans tonight," he said, looking at Melissa. "Plans I'm not willing to change."

Melissa stared at him for a moment. "Good," she said, before walking out of the room. She heard Caro murmur something, but when she glanced over her shoulder, Lee was walking away and Caro was glaring at his retreating back.

Lee picked her up promptly at six, and they were at the hospital by six-thirty. As they neared Emma's room, Melissa turned to Lee. "She has good days and bad days, so she might be a bit grumpy."

Lee followed Melissa in as she opened the door. "Hey, Em," she said. Emma was playing on a tablet, which she dropped onto her bed when she saw Melissa.

"Mel! I was waiting for you." She looked at Lee. "Is this your boyfriend?" Melissa groaned inwardly. "No, kiddo. This is my friend, Lee."

"Do you also read to kids like me?" she asked him.

"This is my first time, but I'm a pretty good reader," Lee said.

"Good. 'Cause Mel kinda sucks at reading." Melissa widened her eyes in surprise. "You speak all strange when you do the boy voices," Emma said. She looked back at Lee. "I bet you're really good at being a boy."

Lee laughed. "The best."

A pile of books stood on the stand besides Emma's bed. "So what do you want to read tonight?" Melissa asked.

"Dunno. You choose."

Melissa glanced questioningly at Lee, who selected a book from the pile.

"How about *The Jungle Book*?" he said, holding up a volume with a beautifully decorated cover.

"Yes. Then you can be Bagheera." Emma said with a giggle. She looked at Melissa. "And you can be Mowgli."

Melissa smiled. "Cool. I like Mowgli." She sat down beside Emma and turned to Lee. "Come on, Bagheera," she said. "Start reading."

Lee opened the book to the first page. His voice was smooth and clear as he read of how Mowgli's fate was discussed by the jungle council until Bagheera arrived. "'A black shadow dropped down into the circle,'" he read. "'It was Bagheera the Black Panther, inky-black all over, but with the panther markings showing up in certain lights like the pattern of watered silk. Everybody knew Bagheera, and nobody cared to cross his path; for he was as cunning as Tabaqui, as bold as the wild buffalo, and as reckless as the wounded elephant. But he had a voice as soft as wild honey dripping from a tree, and a skin softer than down.'"

Melissa shivered, thinking of the creature that stalked her dreams. That panther, too, was inky-black all over. Would its fur be softer than down? Lee paused to look at her, his expression unfathomable.

"Don't stop," Emma said, tapping Lee on the knee.

He returned to the book and continued reading. "'Mowgli loved better than anything else to go with Bagheera into the dark warm heart of the forest, to sleep all through the drowsy day, and at night to see how Bagheera did his killing.'" Melissa's mind drifted as Lee's voice washed over her as he continued to read, and she jumped when he touched her arm. "Come on Mowgli," he said. "Your turn." He handed Melissa the book and pointed at a line.

"Um," Melissa cleared her throat. "'What is man that he should not run with his brothers?'" she began. "'I was born in the Jungle. I have obeyed the Law of the Jungle, and there is no wolf of ours from whose paw I have not pulled a thorn. Surely they are my brothers!'"

She passed the book back to Lee, and he picked up the story where she had left off as Bagheera explained why it was so important for Mowgi to return to the man village. Melissa watched him, her mind wandering as he read. This was the Lee she remembered. Considerate and kind. By the time they were ready to leave, Emma's eyes were drooping.

"Sleep well, little sister," Lee said as he laid the book on the side table.

"Will you read to me next time?" Emma asked Lee.

He glanced at Melissa questioningly, and she gave a small shrug. "I'd love to read to you again," he said.

"Good night, Em," Melissa said, leaning forward to kiss her on the forehead. "See you next week."

"Night-night, Mel."

"I think you made Emma's day," Melissa said as they left the room.

He smiled. "No, she made mine."

"So, where are we going?" she asked as they walked through the hospital to the parking lot.

"River Café."

"I thought you said we weren't going somewhere smart," Melissa said in dismay.

"You look fine," Lee said, taking in her jeans, pretty blouse and heeled ankle boots.

The restaurant Lee had booked was on a small island in

the middle of the river, and he parked in a lot at the base of a pedestrian bridge that led to the island. The sun was beginning to set as they walked over, and the bridge swayed beneath them, but it was the view that took Melissa's breath away – a ribbon of gold that wound around the island. Lee stood beside her as she leaned against the bridge railing. "It's beautiful," she said.

"Yes," he said, but his eyes were on her. She blushed and turned away, and a moment later he followed her onto the path that led to the restaurant. It was busy with joggers and cyclists, who skirted the pair as they walked alongside the river. A slight breeze stirred the air, rustling the leaves of the tall trees that shaded the lawns, but it wasn't cold. Up ahead the restaurant glittered with fairy lights; they were reflected in the river, making the scene appear even more magical.

Within minutes of arriving they were seated at a table overlooking the river. A small candle flickered between them, and Melissa watched as the light played over the planes of Lee's face.

"So you're coming to visit Emma again?"

"If you don't mind."

"I think she'd be mad at me if I didn't bring you. Thank you for coming."

"It was my pleasure," he said.

The waitress arrived at the table, notebook outstretched. "Oh, I, er ..." Melissa glanced at the menu. "Salmon."

The girl turned to Lee. "Top loin steak, double portion, rare, no vegetables," he said. "And a bottle of Melbec." Melissa stared at him in shock. "What? Don't you drink wine?"

"No vegetables?"

"They don't agree with me."

"You never eat vegetables?" she said incredulously.

"Only to please my mother," he said, a grin lurking at the edge of his mouth. "And since she's not here …" He left the sentence dangling.

She leaned back in her seat, her eyes narrowed, as he laughed at her. "My metabolism is a little unusual," he said, "but I'm in perfect health. So, are you hiking tomorrow?" he asked as the wine arrived. The food arrived twenty minutes later, and Melissa shuddered slightly as she saw the blood pooling around Lee's steaks. He grinned. "Would you like to try some?"

"How can you eat that? Is it even cooked?"

"The outside is. The rest is heated through."

"You could just eat it fresh off the carcass," Melissa said caustically.

Lee smirked and took a large bite. "Mmm, delicious."

They lingered over their meal, passing from one topic to another with barely a pause in the conversation. When they were finished, they wandered along the river in the moonlight before finally heading back to Melissa's apartment. As before, Lee left the truck to walk her to her front door.

"Thank you for a wonderful evening," she said as they reached the door to her apartment.

"I'll see you on Monday, Mel."

"Do you want to come in for a drink?"

"I really should go. If I stay, I'm not sure I can act sensibly."

"Sensible is overrated."

He smiled wryly. "Maybe. But we work together."

Melissa tapped her foot on the ground as she tamped down the flare of annoyance. "That's an excuse."

"Probably," he said, "but still relevant."

She stepped back and crossed her arms over her chest. "You should stop toying with me," she said, anger coloring her tone. "Clearly I'm just a distraction."

Lee's eyes narrowed, and he leaned closer, closing the gap she had just created. "You're far more than a distraction, Mel," he said hotly. "And that's just the problem." Their gazes collided until he strode away, flinging open the door to the stairwell and disappearing around the corner as it swung closed. Melissa leaned against the door jamb, her heart pounding, before turning into the apartment and flinging her purse onto a chair.

"Fine," she muttered beneath her breath. "If that's the way he wants it, that's fine by me. He's an idiot anyway!" Did he think he could flirt with her when he felt like it, then push her away when it suited him? She kicked off her boots and made for the shower. Perhaps if she scrubbed hard enough, she could wash away the memory of his smile, his gorgeous face and the way he'd looked at her on the bridge.

Melissa was walking through a jungle. In the distance wolves were howling, and she increased her pace. The canopy of leaves overhead was dense, and more than once she glanced around, trying to discern a path in the thick undergrowth. Danger lurked in the jungle, but if she could reach the village, she'd be safe. A creature roared behind her, and she spun around, stumbling slightly at the sight of the enormous tiger pacing closer.

"You think you can escape?" the tiger asked.

"I'm not afraid of you," she said.

"Ah, but you should be," he said with a grin that showed his huge teeth. "You don't belong in the jungle."

"She belongs with me," said another voice from behind.

Melissa turned to see a panther, its tail swishing through the air. Bagheera, she thought with relief. She moved closer to him until she could feel the fur of his powerful flank against her legs. He looked at her, his gaze a bright green. "I'll take you to the village," he said. She placed her hand on the panther's coat and walked away from the tiger as his roar of frustration split the air.

Chapter 5

Melissa had just arrived at her desk on Monday morning when Lee approached. If she hadn't known better, she would have said he was nervous, but that was impossible. Lee was never nervous. She crossed her arms and stared at him as he leaned against her desk.

"What do you want?" she said, her voice low.

"To apologize. I was rude and angry."

Her eyes widened in surprise. "Why?"

"Why am I apologizing, or why was I angry?"

"Both."

"I like you, Mel. That scares me a little."

"And you've never liked someone before?"

He smiled faintly. "I've always kept a tight rein on my emotions. I've never allowed a situation to get beyond my control."

"And this is beyond your control?"

He leaned closer. "*You* are beyond my control," he said. "You're not like other women I know."

"Women like Caro?"

"Women like Caro are easy to deal with. They take what they want and expect you to do the same," he said.

She lifted her eyebrows. "So why are we even talking?"

"Those relationships are empty and shallow, and I'm tired of them. I want something more."

She laughed dryly. "You really have a way with words, Lee."

"Will you give me another chance?"

"We still work together, remember?"

He glanced around. Kasper had arrived at his desk and was watching them curiously. "We'll take it one step at a time and figure it out as we go along."

She leaned back in her chair and looked at him, considering. "You can't control me."

"I know."

"And you can't keep pushing me away."

He rubbed his jaw with his fingers. "I know."

"Can you trust me, Lee?"

He stared at her a moment. "I don't know," he finally said.

"I guess that's better than no," she said. "At least you're being honest."

"Does that mean you'll go out with me again?"

"I'm not sure. I need time to think."

She watched him walk away thoughtfully. She had enjoyed their date until he'd left her at her front door. Could she give him another chance?

She knocked on his door near the end of the day and poked her head around the corner. "Have a minute?"

"Of course."

"Come over for supper tonight."

"At your apartment?"

"Where else?"

"I'm not sure—"

Melissa held up her hand, cutting him off. "What were you saying about another chance?"

Lee gave a wry smile. "What time?"

"Seven."

Melissa pulled the dish out of the oven as her apartment's entrance buzzer rang on the dot of seven. She'd made a chicken and mushroom casserole, wondering as she added the ingredients if mushrooms fell into the vegetable category before deciding that they didn't. She opened the door and drew in a ragged breath as she took in his black jeans, black boots and black t-shirt. She opened the door wider, and he stepped inside. "I brought some wine," he said, holding out a bottle of Pinot Grigio.

She led him into the tiny kitchen and rummaged in a drawer for a corkscrew, which she handed to him before taking two glasses from a cabinet in her living room.

"I hope you eat chicken." She placed the casserole on the table. "All the greens are in the salad."

"You didn't have to do that. I would've eaten it."

"I know," she said as they sat down. "Are you coming to the hospital with me on Friday?"

"If you don't mind."

"I don't mind." She passed the casserole dish to Lee and watched as he piled the chicken on his plate. She had made extra – a lot extra – but it didn't look like she would have any leftovers. He noticed her watching and stopped with an embarrassed smile.

"I'm sorry, you probably wanted this to last a few

meals."

"I saw how much you ate the other day. I'm just fascinated by how much you eat. Do you have a standing order at the meat counter?"

"Actually, I usually hunt my own meat."

"What, a few buffalo a year?"

He looked up from his plate and caught her eye. "A dozen will do," he said, his expression surprisingly serious.

She laughed and took a forkful of food. Her eye fell on the image inked on his arm, and her breath froze.

"You have a tattoo of a panther," she said. It stalked up the inside of his forearm, its face turned back in a savage snarl.

"Yes." He glanced at her. "You don't like it?"

"No, it's just …" She blinked, pushing away the memory of the panther chasing her through her dreams. "It looks a little vicious."

Lee studied it for a moment before replying. "It reminds me of who I am."

She frowned. "Who are you?"

"Someone with an inner beast."

"We all have our demons," she said softly.

He looked up and met her gaze. "You're right," he said. "I just don't want to forget mine." He grabbed the bottle of wine and topped up her glass. "So tell me your favorite places to hike."

They finished the meal talking about the mountains, until Melissa brought up the following Saturday. "I thought it would be fun to go picnicking," she said. "Want to join me?"

Lee frowned. "Saturday? I … I'm not sure."

"Oh, okay," she said lightly, swallowing her

disappointment.

"Where did you want to go?"

"Bow Valley. But it's fine. Another time, maybe."

"Look, Mel, it's not that I don't want to—"

"Really, Lee, it's fine."

"No, it's not!" He ran his hand over his face and swore softly beneath his breath. "I'll come with you," he finally said.

"Don't do me any favors." She winced at her tone, more caustic than she intended.

"I'm not. I want to come with you. There are just some things I need to sort out."

"Are you sure?"

"Yes. And I think they have barbecue pits, so I'll bring the meat."

"Okay." She rose from the table and began to clear the dishes.

Lee joined her, and the tension eased as they worked together. They moved into the living room when they were done, and Lee perused the titles on her shelves. "*Pygmalion*," he said, pulling a slim volume from the shelf.

"*My Fair Lady* is my most favorite musical."

He flipped open the book. "'You see this creature with her kerbstone English,'" he read with a flourish, "'the English that will keep her in the gutter to the end of her days. Well, sir, in three months I could pass off that girl as a duchess at an ambassador's garden party.'"

Melissa rose to her feet and flung out her arms. "Oh, 'wouldn't it be loverly?'"

Lee laughed. "You and my mother would get on well. She adores musicals. She made us watch one with her every weekend."

"Oh no," Melissa said with a grin. "How did you

survive?"

"It was traumatic. I've been in therapy for years."

"No wonder you're scared of relationships."

Lee took a step toward her. "Just one," he said. His eyes caught hers, and Melissa's teasing response died on her lips. She stared at him, catching her breath as he gently brought a finger to her face and slid it down her cheek. He leaned forward and very lightly brushed his lips over hers, before stepping away. "Thank you for the dinner, Mel," he said. "I'll see you tomorrow." He turned to the door before she could say a word, and then was gone.

Melissa drove Lee to the hospital on Friday evening. He shuddered slightly as he opened the passenger door, closing it cautiously as it squeaked on its hinges.

"Are you sure it's roadworthy?" he asked as she pulled into the traffic.

"Of course," she retorted.

"We'll take my truck to the mountains tomorrow."

They read more of *The Jungle Book* with Emma that evening, and Melissa dropped Lee outside his apartment afterward. He had a few things to get done if he was going to be out the next day, he explained, but he would pick her up promptly at ten the next morning.

She stood in front of the mirror at ten o'clock the next morning and smoothed down the short yellow sundress that she wore over a pair of boy shorts as she waited for him to arrive. A packed cooler was ready at the door, with a blanket folded on top. Another ten minutes passed before the buzzer rang.

"Sorry I'm late," Lee said as she opened the door. "I had something to take care of."

"I wondered if you were standing me up."

"Nope. Shall we go?" He reached for the cooler.

It took an hour to reach the picnic area at Bow Valley, and when they arrived most of the spots near the parking lot had already been claimed, but they found a site overlooking a small pond farther away from the crowds. Lee placed the cooler on the picnic table and dropped a stack of firewood beside the barbecue before walking to the pond and gazing out across the brilliant turquoise water. The water reflected the mountains in the background, which distorted when a soft breeze blew across the surface.

"I love it here," Melissa said, joining Lee at the edge of the pond. He glanced at her, then back at the mountains.

"It is nice. I usually stick to the area around the cabin."

"You have a cabin? Where?"

"Past Turner Valley."

"Really? I often hike around there. Is it close to one of the trails?"

"It's pretty far from the road. You'd have to follow the river to reach it by foot." He turned from the pond. "I'll start the fire. It's the one thing I learned to do as a Boy Scout."

"You learned just one thing?" Melissa said in amusement.

"I only did it for a few months."

"You didn't enjoy it?"

"I did, actually. My father wasn't too happy about the camping trips."

"Why not?"

Lee was silent a moment. "He thought it was a waste of time," he finally said. "Wanted me to play hockey instead."

"But you didn't enjoy hockey?"

"I did. And since it didn't leave time for camping, it was a good thing I dropped Scouts."

Melissa watched as Lee stoked the growing flames. "So how often do you go to the cabin?"

"As often as I can."

"So *that's* where you go hunting."

"It is, actually. But that's not the only reason I go."

"Let me guess. You take your friends for male bonding time."

Lee smiled wryly. "No. I've never taken anyone there."

"Never? What about your family?"

"The cabin was built by my grandfather, but my father hates the place, and it's too remote for my brother's tastes. Grandpa left it to me when he died, because he knew I was the only one who'd want it."

"When did he die?" Melissa asked gently.

"About ten years ago, shortly after my grandmother passed away." Opening the cooler, Lee pulled out a large container with two enormous steaks. "How do you want yours done?" he asked, gesturing at the meat.

"Dead."

"Very dead or a little dead?"

"Ugh," groaned Melissa. "Just as long as it's cooked all the way through, I'm happy. But I won't eat all of that." Lee sliced off a small section, then glanced at her, eyebrows raised.

"Perfect," she said.

He slapped the meat onto the grill, then removed his less than a minute later. She opened a bowl of salad and placed it on the table as she waited for her steak to cook. The picnic spot was in a small clearing surrounded by trees, and she lifted her face to the sun's warming rays. Above them, chickadees hopped from branch to branch, their *dee-dee* chirps mingling with the shouts and laughter of other day trippers. The setting was peaceful, and Melissa felt the stress of the week slip away as the fresh mountain air filled her lungs.

They lingered in the sun long after the meal was done, chatting and laughing. Lee had seemed distracted at first, but relaxed as the afternoon wore on, and it was he who suggested they do a short hike. They stowed the cooler in his truck, then studied the map of trails. They chose one that followed the perimeter of the ponds before heading into the surrounding mountains.

"Should we be worried about cougars?" Melissa asked Lee as they walked.

"Cougars won't trouble us," he said. "So as long as you're with me, you're safe."

"Are you the cat whisperer?" Melissa asked with a grin.

Lee threw her a quick look, his expression strange. "Something like that," he said.

The trail passed through an alpine meadow, where wild flowers splashed gaudy colors against a sea of green before leading into a forest, where jays and squirrels vied noisily for attention. The view opened up at the summit of the mountain, and Melissa could see people far below, strolling around the ponds.

The day had grown hot, and Melissa eagerly screwed the cap off a bottle of water and, tipping her head back, drained the contents in one gulp. She blushed when she saw Lee watching her. "My sister tells me that that's very unladylike," Melissa said with an embarrassed laugh.

"You're very ladylike," Lee said. "Beautiful and alluring."

Melissa arched an eyebrow. "Alluring?"

"Definitely. I want to hold you in my arms and kiss you

thoroughly."

Melissa felt herself flushing. "You have my permission to do so."

The ghost of a smile tugged at Lee's mouth, then was gone. "It's probably not a good idea," he said. He turned back on the trail. "We should keep going." When she didn't start walking, he stepped past her. His body brushed against hers, and Melissa froze. The touch had been light, but it had zipped through her like lightening. He stopped, then in one fluid movement turned back and brought his hands to her face. He pressed his lips to hers, firm and hot, but before she'd even registered what was happening, he stepped away and strode down the path. She brought her fingers to her lips as she stared at him. Had that just happened? she wondered. It had to be the shortest kiss she'd ever had, but she'd felt it all the way to her toes. He was increasing the distance between them, and Melissa ran to catch up to him.

"What was that?" she said when she finally caught up.

He glanced at her over his shoulder. "I think it's called a kiss."

"It was so short, I wasn't sure."

"I shouldn't have come today."

"Seriously? What's that supposed to mean?"

Lee was silent for a moment. "I thought I'd be in better control."

"What are you talking about, Lee? Better control of what?"

"Myself."

"Okay, I'm confused. You think you shouldn't have come because you gave me one very tiny kiss?"

"I couldn't stop myself. And believe me, I would love a much longer, deeper kiss."

Melissa shivered. "Hmph. Well, if you ask me, you seem very much in control."

They walked in silence for a few minutes until Lee stopped and turned to face her. "I'm sorry, Mel. I know I'm acting strangely. I'm just not myself today." He paused. "I've really enjoyed spending the day with you. I just have other things on my mind."

"What kinds of things?"

"Personal stuff." He took her hands in his, and she looked down. The hair on the backs of his hands seemed thicker than before, a trick of the light and shadows. "Will you give me a chance to redeem myself? How about we stop for ice cream on our way back?"

She cocked her head. Whenever things seemed to be going well with Lee, he'd do or say something to push her away. But he had apologized, and was clearly trying to make up for it. "You think you can buy me off with ice cream?"

"Double chocolate ice cream with fudge swirl?"

"Well ..."

"And sprinkles on top?"

"Fine. But it'd better be a large."

He grinned. "The biggest we can get."

It took a short while to reach the end of the trail, and they were soon driving to the closest town. They pulled up outside the ice-cream parlor and took their places at the end of a long line. Already the shadows were growing longer, but that did not deter the seekers of frozen sweets. Finally, cones in hand, they found an empty bench at the edge of the parking lot and sat down. The sun was sinking below the mountains, painting the sky a soft shade of pink. To the east the moon hung low in the sky, a silver disk behind the jagged peaks.

"It's almost full," Melissa said as they headed back to the truck. She glanced at Lee, surprised to see him staring at the moon with narrowed eyes. "What's wrong?" she said.

"Nothing. It'll be full tomorrow."

The sky grew darker as they drove, and the moon was hidden behind trees that lined the road, but then they were gone and the landscape spread before them. The moon had risen higher and hung in the sky like a huge, gleaming orb, almost a complete circle.

"It's beautiful," she whispered. Lee's hands were clenched tightly around the steering wheel. "You okay?" she asked.

He glanced at her. "Of course."

She looked back at the moon. "It's a marvelous night," she began, the lilting sounds of Moondance filling the truck. She looked at Lee, who was glaring silently at the road. He glanced at her, then joined in with a sigh.

"A fantabulous night …" They reached the end of the song and lapsed into silence as Melissa watched the landscape slipping by. She could see the city lights in the distance, brightening the sky like a beacon. Beside her, Lee began singing again, his voice low and soft.

"'Fly me to the moon,'" he crooned, smiling when Melissa joined in, her voice harmonizing with his. She blushed when they reached the end of the verse.

"You sing really well."

"I told you my mother loved musicals. What I didn't tell you is that she made me sing all her favorite songs with her. She likes all the old romantics."

"Then how about this one?" She lifted her voice in another song.

"'That's amoré,'" he joined in.

They sang the rest of the way home, finding as many moon-related songs as possible. Lee laughed when she started singing in French. *"Eau de clair de lune ..."*

"I think you mean *'Au clair de la lune.'"*

"Whatever."

He pulled up in front of her apartment block. "Will you come inside?" she asked.

"I shouldn't."

"Please?"

His jaw clenched and unclenched. "Okay. But just for a moment."

He followed her as they made their way upstairs, and when they reached her front door, he hesitated for a moment before stepping inside.

"A drink? Coffee?" she asked as she dropped her purse on a side table.

"Just some water, please."

She filled a glass and brought it to him. "I had a great day," she said.

"I did too. I'm sorry I was a bit ..."

"... strange? Offish?"

He smiled. "Yes."

"I'll forgive you if you kiss me."

"Mel," he groaned. "Don't tempt me."

"Why not?" She moved closer, until just inches separated them. "I know you want to." And she wanted him too. She wanted to feel his hands on her skin, and his lips on hers. All the distance Lee had put between them for so long no longer mattered, because she knew that the man who took her for dinner and read stories to a hospital-bound kid was the real Lee. And she knew, no matter what, that they belonged together. It was this surety that gave her the confidence to move closer.

His arms snaked around her waist, but he hesitated for a moment before bringing his lips to hers. His tongue teased her lips, and when she opened her mouth to him, he pushed her against the wall, deepening the kiss. His hands slid up her back and tangled in her hair, wrenching out the band that held the ponytail in place. "Mel." He moaned her name. His lips slid along her jaw to her ear, and then back to her mouth, demanding more, and she pulled him closer, wanting as much as he would give. He pulled back a moment later, and Melissa sucked in her breath.

"Your eyes," she whispered. Instead of their usual forest green, they were shining brightly, like neon lights outlined in gold.

Lee hands dropped to his sides before her next heartbeat, and he took a step backward, his expression hardening as his eyes snapped shut. "I have to go," he said. He spun around and strode to the door, yanking it open and disappearing around the corner. When she ran to follow him, he was gone, the stairwell door swinging closed behind his furious exit. She leaned against the wall. What was that? she wondered. His eyes had been as bright as lights, and in the moment before he closed them she was sure … she shook her head, trying to dismiss the thought. It had just been a trick of the light that made his pupils seem more elongated than usual. It was quite impossible. But that still didn't explain why his eyes had shone so strangely. And nothing explained why he'd rushed away in such a hurry.

Chapter 6

Melissa tossed all night, finally falling into an unsettled sleep in the early hours of the morning, then waking again before the sun had fully risen. Birds were chirping outside the window, and after a few fruitless minutes of trying to get back to sleep, she gave up the effort and padded to the kitchen in search of something to eat. She brewed a pot of coffee and powered on her laptop. When the green power light came on, she stared at it for a moment before opening Google. She typed in "neon green eyes," and came up with results about eye color. Hmm. Not helpful. She tried "eyes that change color," and read the Wikipedia result at the top of the page: 'Certain emotions can change both pupil size and iris color.' She poured herself a cup of coffee as she thought about it. Could Lee's eyes have brightened because he was feeling certain emotions? She sat back down and read some of the other results, finding emotions a common factor in the articles.

Cupping her mug in her hands, she paced around the apartment. Lee's eyes must have brightened because of the kiss. But that didn't explain why he'd left so quickly. Unless her words had broken the mood and brought him back to his senses. After all, he'd been annoyed with himself when he kissed her in the forest. Thoughts spun through her mind, becoming more tangled, until eventually she found a piece of paper and pencil, sat down and started writing. *1*, she wrote. She circled the number a few times as she collected her thoughts. *Didn't want to kiss me,* she wrote beside the number. *Not interested (but why kiss me?) or can't handle close relationships?* She took another sip of coffee before continuing.

2. Usually dates shallow women (he says).

3. Pulls away when he feels ... he's getting too close? I'm getting too close? Too much emotion? Threatened?

4. Scared of commitment.

She underlined the word *scared* a few times, and drew a box around *commitment*. She studied the list for a moment, then added below: *Scared of what? Why?* She studied her notes. They provided no answers, only more questions, and after a few minutes, she scrunched up the page and threw it into the garbage.

Lee wasn't in the office on Monday, and when Melissa asked Mary about it, she learned he'd flown to Vancouver the night before for some rushed meetings with potential clients and wouldn't be back until the next week. She checked her phone regularly, wondering if he'd try to contact her, but apart from one email, asking her to gather some data, she heard nothing from him.

On Friday, she went to the hospital to visit Emma.

"Where's Lee?" the little girl asked, sitting up as Melissa walked into the room.

"He's not coming, kiddo."

"Why not?"

"He's away at the moment."

"But he'll be here next time, right?"

Melissa sat down on the edge of the bed and took Emma's hand. "I'm sorry, Em, but I don't know if Lee'll be coming again."

Emma frowned. "I thought he liked coming."

"He does, but he's got other stuff to do."

"Like what?"

Melissa shrugged helplessly. "Just stuff … work stuff. He's out of town at meetings a lot."

Emma's eyes narrowed. "You fighted, didn't you. It's your fault he's not coming!"

"No, we didn't fight," Melissa said, striving to keep her voice calm. "I just know he's very busy."

"He said he likes visiting me! He only wouldn't come 'cause you told him not to."

"Why don't we read more of *The Jungle Book*?" Melissa said brightly.

Emma shook her head. "No. I don't want you to read that stupid book." She lay on the bed and turned toward the wall. "Just go away."

Melissa watched her helplessly for a moment, then rose to her feet. Leaning over, she kissed the girl on the forehead. "I'll see you next week, 'kay? Love you, Emma."

She gave her one last, lingering, look, then left the room and made her way to the common area, where children who were well enough could leave their beds to play games and watch TV. A group of kids were building a puzzle when she stepped into the room, and she joined them at their table with a forced smile.

Melissa saw Lee as soon as she arrived in the office on Monday morning. He was standing with Caro near reception, laughing at something she was saying, his head bent close to hers. His back was to Melissa, but as the door swung closed, his head snapped up like a dog sniffing the air, and he turned to look at her. She gave a tentative smile, but he turned back to Caro. Something tightened in her chest as she walked past him and headed to her desk. His look had been cool, like that of a stranger. The same expression he had given her a thousand times over the past six years. She slipped into her chair and darted another look at him across the room, watching as he walked towards his office. Had he decided to push her away again? How was it that he could change so easily from being the funny, caring person she knew him to be to some distant stranger? And more importantly, why? She was sure that he felt something for her. She switched on her computer and tried, unsuccessfully, to push Lee from her mind.

It was close to lunchtime when she saw him again. He held a stack of papers in his hands and was examining them as he walked, but he looked up before reaching her.

"Melissa," he said.

She stopped, waiting for him to say more, but he was silent. "You owe me an explanation," she finally said.

He sighed, then flicked his head toward his office. "Come," he said. She followed him in and closed the door, but didn't take a seat. Nor did he, and they watched each other cautiously across the desk.

"What explanation do you think I owe you?" he asked.

"Why did you leave like that the other night?"

"Like what?"

She dropped her voice. "You were kissing me, Lee. And then you just left."

"Yes, and?"

"And … you didn't give me any explanation. You didn't even say goodbye. I've heard nothing from you since."

"Why would you? It was just a friendly day out. I could tell you were reading more into it, though, so I left."

She stared at him incredulously. "What is wrong with you? *I* was reading more into it? Wasn't it *you* who said you wanted to kiss me?"

"It was you who invited me out," he reminded her, "and I kiss many women."

"I see," she said. "So you're as shallow as all the women you usually date?"

"Exactly! I probably should have warned you to stay away from me."

"You're unbelievable," she said. She turned toward the door, then stopped. "You know, you could at least have the decency to tell me the truth."

Lee frowned. "And what do you think that is?"

"That you're scared of being with someone that you feel something for."

"You think I feel something for you?" He laughed harshly. "You mean nothing to me, Ms. Hewitt."

She felt as though she'd been punched in the stomach. "What are you scared of, Lee?" she whispered.

He snorted. "Absolutely nothing."

"Then why do you keep running away?"

"You have no idea what you're talking about," he said, his voice a snarl. He walked around the desk, and came to a stop before her. His face was a few inches away, his lips twisted into an ugly grimace. "You have *no idea* who or what I am."

She stepped backwards, and felt her back against the wall. "So what are you?" The words wavered slightly. "A serial killer? A terrorist?"

"Don't be ridiculous!"

"Fine. Whatever!" She placed her hands on his chest and pushed him away. Something flickered in his eyes, but he stepped back and lifted his brows sardonically. "Be careful who you throw yourself at next time, Melissa."

She bit down on her lip and pushed past him, flinging the door open and stumbling out. How could she have thought there could be something between them? He was such a jerk!

She headed for the elevator, and a moment later was outside. She was trembling, and her breath came in short gasps. She was furious at Lee, but even more so with herself. She'd allowed herself to feel something for him. To think that perhaps he was someone special, forgetting how he'd ignored her for years. She was such an idiot! She walked, not thinking about where she was going, until she reached the river. Lunchtime walkers and joggers were out in full force, enjoying the warm, sunny weather, while mothers splashed with their children in the shallow paddling pool close by. Farther down the river was the restaurant where she and Lee had gone for supper, and she headed in the opposite direction, walking past a family of ducks as they waddled into the water. She sat down to watch and slowly pushed Lee from her mind. He was like a loose cannon, ricocheting from one wall to another – she was better off without him. Her heart clenched at the thought, but she was resolute. He'd pushed her away one too many times, and she was done with him, once and for all.

By the time she finally headed back to the office, her head ached, but she felt a lot calmer. She had made a decision, and even though it hurt, she would not cede control of her emotions to a man who crashed through her life like a wrecking ball.

"Where did you disappear to?" Kasper asked as she sat down at her desk.

"I had a bit of a headache," she said. "I needed some air."

"Lee came looking for you. He wants you to look at some numbers for an office clerk."

"He can take his numbers and shove them," she said angrily. Kasper's eyebrows rose, and she sighed. "Never mind. Thanks for the message. I'll run the numbers now."

Kasper gave her a keen look. "Did you and Lee get in a fight or something? Because he was as angry as you."

"No, of course not."

"Good. Because none of us want to be caught in the middle of some disagreement."

"No disagreement, Kasper. Actually, Lee and I understand each other very well."

"Good." He began walking away, then returned to her desk. "Look," he hissed. "It's Dave Timmins."

Melissa glanced over her shoulder at the man in question. "Yes, so?"

"He left Quigs months ago. Resigned. Moved to another job. And now he's back!"

"Seriously? You're upset that he came back? He's not even on our team."

"Well, clearly he doesn't have Quigs's interests at heart."

Melissa turned back to her computer. "I think you're

overreacting just the slightest bit, Kasper. It's really not an issue."

"It is to me," Kasper groused. Melissa ignored him as he headed back to his desk.

The rest of the week dragged by, and when Friday finally rolled around, Melissa felt as though she'd lived through a month of Mondays. She had avoided Lee as much as possible, but she could not help seeing him across the office or sitting near him in meetings. She'd felt his gaze on her a few times, and in unguarded moments, she could almost trace a mix of wistfulness and a little bitterness in his expression, but when his eyes met hers, it hardened to its usual look of disinterest. His attention only made her more annoyed. Did he think she'd fall apart? She finally escaped the office on Friday evening and made her way home with relief. She stepped into her apartment as her phone buzzed.

"Melissa!" Lauren's voice came through the receiver. "Where have you been? I tried calling you earlier, and you didn't answer."

"I just got home from work. And my phone's been on mute."

"You work too much. Which is why I'm calling. Nick has a conference next week, so I was wondering if you wanted to come and keep me company."

"Well …"

"Oh, and Nick said he'd pay for the plane ticket."

Melissa pondered. Nick was a great brother-in-law, and it had been a while since she'd last seen her sister Lauren and the kids. "I'll have to check with my work, but if it's okay with them, I'd love to come."

"Great! So when will you know?"

"It's Friday night, Lauren. I'll speak to them Monday

morning."

"Oh, come on! I'm sure your boss checks his email on the weekend."

Melissa sighed. "Fine. I'll send an email and let you know."

"Yay!" Lauren said, laughing. "The kids will be so excited."

"Don't say anything till I know for sure," Melissa warned, but Lauren wasn't listening.

"We'll go to Granville Island and Capilano Bridge. And the aquarium, of course."

"Sounds good. I'll speak to you soon, sis. Give my love to the kids."

"You can do that yourself in a few days."

"And say hello to Nick – and thanks for the ticket."

She ended the call and stared at the phone reflectively. A few days away seemed very appealing. She opened her email and typed in Lee's address. Although Norm was the office manager, as project manager, she needed Lee's approval. Her fingers hovered over the keyboard as she considered the words, then started typing.

Chapter 7

Lee responded to Melissa's email right away. *Approved.* That was it. One single word.

She called Lauren back and listened to her excitement for a few minutes before cutting her off.

"I have to go, Lauren. I'm off to visit Emma at the hospital. I'll see you next week."

"Okay. Nick said you'd get an e-ticket. I'm so excited – we'll have so much fun!"

Melissa smiled as she ended the call. Even though she was the younger of the two, she'd always been the more level-headed, less excitable sister. Their mother had been diagnosed with pancreatic cancer when Melissa was sixteen and Lauren was nineteen. There had been surgery, then chemotherapy, but they could not stop the cancer that spread like an insidious parasite through her body, and she'd died almost one year to the day after receiving the diagnosis. The family had been devastated, but it was Melissa who'd held things together, meeting with the funeral home, planning the reception with the help of her mom's friends and slowly clearing out her mother's clothes and belongings. It had also been Melissa who'd held Lauren as she sobbed through the night, Melissa who'd sat with Dad as he stared for endless hours at photos, Melissa who responded to all the heartfelt condolences. And it had been Melissa who'd finally dragged Dad and Lauren from the house and insisted they start living again.

When Dad died, Lauren had already moved to Vancouver, and Nick had been there to help her through the worst, but still, Melissa had spoken to her on the phone almost every day for months, and still spoke to her at least once a week. There weren't many opportunities to visit, however, so it would be nice to spend a few days with Lauren and her family.

The e-ticket was in her inbox when Melissa awoke, and on Monday morning she was on the plane for the short hop over the mountains. Soon she was heading through Vancouver airport to the arrivals lounge. She smiled when she saw Lauren standing at the railing, waving one arm furiously in the air, while the other clutched little Josh. "Over here," she shouted. She threw her arm around Melissa and pulled her into a hug. "It's so wonderful to see you! It's been *ages* since you were last here." She looked down at the little girl clinging to her legs. "Look, Grace, it's Aunty Mel," she said. "You remember her."

Melissa dropped to her haunches and smiled. "Hello, Grace."

"Hello," she said shyly, swinging around her mother's legs.

"You've grown so big, you must be eating a dinosaur every day for breakfast." Grace giggled and Melissa took her by the hand as they headed out of the terminal. "So, what's the plan for today?" she asked as Lauren maneuvered the car through the stream of traffic racing down the highway.

"Have you had breakfast?"

"If you count airplane pretzels and coffee."

"Okay, breakfast first. Who wants pancakes?"

"Me!" the kids both shouted.

"You're such a mom," Melissa said in amusement.

"I know," Lauren agreed contentedly.

The days passed quickly as Lauren dragged Melissa around Vancouver, determined to show her all the sights, ignoring Melissa's protests that she had seen them before. Stanley Park, the aquarium and Granville Island were at the top of the list. In the evenings they chatted in the kitchen as Lauren made supper, and Melissa played with the children until it was time for them to go to bed. As soon as they were asleep, she and Lauren made their escape to the garden, drinks in hand.

"So, have you met someone yet?" Lauren asked Melissa on Friday evening as the last rays of sun disappeared behind the trees. The children had just gone to bed, and Nick was expected back within an hour.

Melissa twisted the wine glass in her hand. "No," she said. She looked up to see Lauren looking at her shrewdly.

"Who is he?" she asked.

"No one. There's no one."

Lauren was silent for a moment. "I know you, Mel," she finally said, "and I know when you're lying. I'm your sister, so tell me what you're hiding."

"I'm not hiding anything," Melissa protested. "There was someone at work, but it didn't work out."

"What was wrong with him?"

"There's nothing wrong with him," Melissa said with a sigh. "Apart from the fact that he's a total moron."

Lauren lifted an eyebrow. "Ah! One of those."

"Exactly."

Lauren took a sip of wine. "Good thing you found out sooner rather than later."

"You're absolutely right."

"You still have feelings for him, don't you?"

"No. Of course not. The guy's an idiot! It's just that, well, we actually got on really well … when he wasn't being an idiot."

"What you need, sister dearest," Lauren said, "is to meet some other men. Tomorrow you and I are going out."

"What? No! What will Nick say?"

"Nick won't mind – especially if there's a chance you'll meet someone."

"Lauren, I live in Calgary. I don't want to meet someone in Vancouver."

"Okay, I get it. But at least you can see what you're missing. And get your mind off this guy."

"I don't have anything to wear."

"That's a terrible excuse. You know I'm happy to lend you something."

Melissa sighed. "Fine. But just for a few hours."

"Of course! Don't want Nick to think I've abandoned him."

Nick walked into the house an hour later, and when Lauren told him the plan, he was enthusiastic. He talked about it the following morning as they trailed around the local farmers' market. "If you meet the right guy, you could move to Vancouver," he said. "Lauren would love it if you were closer."

"I'm not moving to Vancouver," she protested. "And I'm definitely not interested in meeting someone here."

"Couldn't you at least pretend that you want to be closer?" Lauren said.

Melissa sighed again. "You know how much I miss you, Lar," she said. "But my life's in Calgary. I enjoy living close to the mountains."

"I know," Lauren said, matching Melissa's sigh. "But who knows what the future will bring, right? Besides, we have gorgeous mountains here too."

Melissa rolled her eyes as Lauren linked their arms with a laugh.

After a search through Lauren's wardrobe, Melissa – with some urging from her sister – settled on a short black dress and three-inch-high black booties. When she was dressed, she was made to sit in front of the mirror so Lauren could curl her hair and do her makeup. By the time she was done, Melissa had to admit she looked pretty good. Nick whistled when she walked down the stairs. "You'll be breaking hearts this evening," he said.

"Yeah, right," Melissa said, but she still smiled. "We really don't have to do this," she said to Lauren when she came downstairs.

"Yes, we do. Remember when Mom died, and you had to drag me out of the house? Well, now it's my turn to drag you out. You need to start living, Mel. You spend far too much time working and being alone."

"I like being alone."

"I know. And that's the problem. If you don't start getting out, you'll be alone forever."

"Sounds fine to me."

"Come on, baby sister. Let's get you out."

The club was already buzzing with people when they arrived, and bright flashes of light hit the sidewalk every time the door opened. A line of people snaked around the corner, all waiting to gain admittance.

"Really?" Melissa said. "We have to line up for this?"

"Don't be so miserable." Lauren dragged her to the end of the line by the arm. "It'll all be worth it in the end."

When they finally made it through the doors, the place was packed. "I'll get us some drinks," Lauren said. She waved toward a collection of pub tables at the far end. "See if you can find us a table."

Melissa pushed her way through the darkened room, but as she moved closer, she could see all the tables were taken. She took up a spot near the wall and looked at the dance floor. Music was blaring from the speakers, and she watched as the dancers moved to the beat.

"Hey, you want to join us?" a voice called out. Melissa glanced around to see two guys standing at a table. "There's plenty of space," said one of them.

"Uh, no, thanks—" Melissa began, but Lauren's voice cut her off from behind.

"We'd love to! Thanks. This place is so packed." She placed the glasses on the table. "I'm Lauren, and this is my sister, Mel."

"Hi," Melissa said, waving her fingers.

"Jordan," said the first guy, smiling at them, "and this is Jake."

Jordan and Jake, Melissa thought. Cute.

"You girls been here before?" Jordan asked.

"I come sometimes with my husband," Lauren said.

Melissa smiled. Smooth.

"But this is Mel's first time," Lauren added. "She's visiting from Calgary, and is *very* single." Melissa shot Lauren a glare, but she just smiled sweetly. "You guys like to dance?"

Melissa groaned inwardly.

"Of course! That's why we're here," Jake said, looking at Melissa. "Come on."

She sighed, and with one last, long drink, followed Jake to the dance floor. She studied him as they danced, aware that she was enjoying the same scrutiny. Unlike Lee, his hair was dirty blond, worn back from his forehead. A narrow mustache lined his upper lip, and he had a thin goatee on his chin. He smiled easily, and she could see he had deep laugh lines like Lee. Not bad looking.

"So you live in Calgary?" he said when he was close enough to make himself heard.

"I do."

"Pity! You should move to Vancouver. I've lived here all my life, and there's no place like it. I go down to the beach all the time to surf. Do you surf?"

"No. Not much beach around Calgary."

He grinned. "Of course not! I don't just surf, of course! In the winter I snowboard. I guess you could snowboard around Calgary."

"Yes, but I ski."

"Oh, skiing's for nerds! And girls. Boarding's much better! I board every weekend in the winter, and I'm pretty good too, even if I say so myself."

"Hmm."

"I've even won a few competitions."

"Really?"

"Yep! Should've been on the Olympic team, but, well, you know, things didn't work out."

The music changed to something slow. "I think I need a drink," Melissa said.

"I'll get it." Jake led the way to an empty table. "Wait here."

"So, what's he like?" her sister asked, sidling up beside Melissa.

"You are in so much trouble."

"Me? Why?"

"You were practically begging him to dance with me!"

Lauren grinned. "He looks very nice."

"Jordan's pretty cute."

"I'm a married woman." Lauren said primly.

Melissa burst out laughing. "Like that would stop you from noticing."

"Okay, he's not bad, but Nick is much better."

"Spoken like a good wife."

Jake returned with the drinks. He heaved a sigh of relief when he reached the table without spilling, and handed Melissa her glass. "So tell me more about yourself," he said.

"Not much to tell," she said. "I work in HR."

"Really? Me too."

Lauren rolled her eyes. "I'm going to get a drink."

"Where do you work?" Jake asked, paying Lauren no attention. As soon as Melissa mentioned Quigley Ramsbottom, his eyes lit up. "Seriously! I've been to a few of the conferences you guys put on. In fact, I was at one just a few weeks ago. Pat Ramsbottom was doing a presentation on market trends. And Leander Garrett was talking about stock options. He's in the Calgary office, isn't he? Do you know him?"

Melissa ground her teeth. "I know him."

"He seems pretty awesome. Really knows his stuff. My

manager wants to get him in to do some work for us sometime."

"Oh."

"Do you work with him much? I mean, even I learned a thing or two from him. You must be learning a helluva lot from the guy."

"I've done some work with him," Melissa said through gritted teeth.

"Hey, I sometimes go to Calgary for meetings. Why don't we get together next time? Go out for lunch or something. Maybe Leander could join us."

Melissa placed her drink on the table. "You know what? I don't think that's such a great idea. But I'm sure Lee would be happy to, you know, hang out, meet up, go for a date, whatever."

Jake frowned. "Look, I just thought it would be a fun idea. He doesn't have to come."

"Jake, I'm sure you're a really great guy, but I'm just not interested."

"Fine! Whatever!" He threw back the last of his drink. "But you're really missing out, you know!"

"I'll take my chances," Melissa said dryly. "And just for the record," she called out after him as he headed back to the dance floor, "Lee's a total idiot!"

"What was that about?" Lauren asked, coming up to the table, drink in hand. "First tiff, already?"

Melissa groaned. "I think you married the only nice guy there is."

"Nick is pretty amazing. But there's someone out there for you, I know it."

"You know what? I think I'd rather just remain single. Now drink up, and let's dance some more."

They stayed until midnight, dancing together or with

some of the guys who asked, before sliding into a waiting cab outside the club. "Tell me it wasn't all bad," Lauren said, as she slammed the door closed behind them.

"Actually, I had a pretty good time."

"Despite Jake?"

"He showed very poor judgment of character, but he wasn't my type anyway."

"So tell me I was right to drag you out."

"You were right to drag me out," Melissa parroted obediently.

"I'm glad you had fun tonight." Lauren wrapped her arms around Melissa and gave her a brief hug.

Melissa's flight left Sunday morning. It had been good to spend time with Lauren and the kids. She had done a decent job of forgetting about Lee until Jake had brought him up. He wasn't the only one to show poor judgment of character, she thought. She had been just as guilty. Still, she was done with Lee and his issues, and it was time to move on, maybe even get a new job. She'd been at Quigs for three years, and three years before that as an intern, and although she hadn't planned to leave anytime soon, it would be good to expand her horizons and get some new experience. And it would be much easier to get over Lee if she didn't see him every day.

As the plane soared over the Rockies, Melissa thought about who might have the inside scoop on which companies were hiring. Her mind ran through her contacts, before settling on one. It was time to catch up with Cynthia.

Chapter 8

Melissa and Cynthia had been in the same business management course in the first year of university, and they'd become good friends over the next few years. They had lost touch for a while, but when Cynthia moved to Calgary, they had quickly reconnected. Cynthia worked in human resource management in one of the large oil and gas companies in town and had plenty of contacts in the HR world. If anyone would know of a possible position, it would be her.

Melissa texted her that evening, and they agreed to have lunch the next day.

When Melissa arrived at her desk the following morning, Kasper was waiting for her. "Hey, Mel," he said, before she'd even turned on her computer. "Did you have a good trip? Glad you're back because you and I have some work to do."

"We do?"

"Yep. AB Trucking has a small project they want done, and we're the ones doing it."

"You and me? No one else?"

"Correct. You and me. I've already read through their reports. We're meeting the CEO tomorrow afternoon. Let's go to the meeting room – we have a lot of work to cover."

"So who decided to give us the project?" Melissa asked as they sat down at the boardroom table.

"Lee."

"Lee?" Melissa could not keep the surprise from her tone.

"Apparently he was impressed with how you managed the meeting at Hong Industries." There was a trace of bitterness in his tone that Melissa ignored as she wondered why Lee had given her the project – was he trying to appease a guilty conscience?

"Well, let's get started."

They worked together until noon, and Melissa rushed to the restaurant to find that Cynthia was running late. She was shown a table, and she sat down to wait, taking the chance to compose her thoughts. Cynthia arrived a few minutes later.

"I'm so sorry – I couldn't get away," she said.

"Not a problem," Melissa said, waving away her apology. "How are you doing?"

"Well … I'm married!"

"What? Who? When?"

Cynthia held out a hand with a glittering diamond ring, waiting as Melissa examined it. "Richard Kelly. He was at university with us. Remember him? Tall, dark blond hair?"

"Uh …"

"Well, he moved to Calgary after school, and we bumped into each getting coffee."

"But married? Already? Couldn't you just move in together?"

Cynthia shrugged. "I know that's what most people would have done. But we wanted it to be permanent. I mean, if we're going to live together, promising to love each other forever shouldn't be a big deal."

"No, I guess not." She paused as the waitress returned for their orders. "So, tell me about the wedding," Melissa said. It was silly, but she felt a little hurt that she hadn't been invited.

"Oh, we didn't have a big wedding. Too many family complications – especially his sister. We went to Las Vegas and told the family afterward."

"Wow! So what's with his sister?"

"Well, for one thing, she really doesn't like me. She's big into animal rights, the environment, that sort of thing. And because I work for oil and gas—"

"Ah, you're the enemy."

Cynthia grinned. "You could say that. Richard said he wouldn't put it past her to organize a protest at the wedding. She's pretty big with PETA. So what about you? Seeing anyone?"

"Nope. Too busy for a relationship."

"And how's work going?"

"I'm thinking it's time to make a move."

Cynthia's cocked an eyebrow. "I thought you loved Quigs."

"I do. But I want some different experience. I'm not sure I want to be a career consultant."

"Hmm. Well, you're not going to believe this, but I was speaking to Annika Bootsveld at Mercer Engineering this morning. One of her analysts left a few weeks ago, so she's looking to fill the position. She's still doing interviews."

"Seriously? That's … amazing! I knew you'd be the right person to speak to!"

"I hope that's not the only reason you wanted to meet!" Melissa laughed. "Of course not."

Melissa phoned Annika Bootsveld as soon as she left the restaurant, and within minutes an interview was arranged for the following morning. Melissa arrived at eight o'clock precisely, waiting nervously as the receptionist announced her arrival.

"Melissa, so nice of you to come on such short notice." Annika approached Melissa with her hand outstretched. Short and plump, she looked more like a grandmother than a businesswoman, but she had a reputation of being hard-nosed and smart.

"Ms. Bootsveld—"

"Annika, please. Now come along. We'll talk in my office." She led Melissa down a short corridor. "So you work with Lee Garrett," she said as they sat down. "I'm surprised you'd want to leave." She leaned forward with a grin. "He's such a hunk!"

Melissa shrugged. "He's okay."

"Well, let's talk business. Did you bring your résumé?"

Melissa handed over a sheaf of paper and sat in silence as Annika read through the history of her life. The older woman made a few notes, then chewed her pen reflectively. "Mmm. Good, good. Yes. Okay." She looked up at Melissa. "I just have a few questions for you."

By the time they were finished, it was already nine-thirty. "It was a pleasure to meet you, Melissa," Annika said. "I'll be narrowing down the candidates in the next few days, and will be in touch afterward."

"Thank you," Melissa said, shaking Annika's hand. The interview had taken longer than she'd expected, and she rushed back to the office. She and Kasper were meeting the CEO of AB Trucking that afternoon, and they still needed to finalize the report. She was breathless as she flew past reception and hurried to her desk. There was no sign of Kasper, and she dropped into her seat with a sigh, quickly powering up her computer.

"Where've you been?" Melissa's heart sunk as she turned to look at Lee. He met her gaze with a frown as he waved the paper in his hand. It was the report she'd been working on with Kasper.

"I had an appointment," she said. "Of a personal nature." She met his gaze squarely.

"That's not acceptable, Ms. Hewitt. You're meeting with this company today, and you're not ready."

Melissa glanced at Kasper's desk. "Where's Kasper?" she said.

"He was in a car accident this morning. Nothing serious," he added when Melissa gasped. "But he needs to sort things out with insurance. I told him I'd handle his side of the meeting."

"You're coming to the meeting with me?" she asked incredulously.

"Yes. Do you have a problem with that?"

Melissa rose to her feet. She was a few inches shorter than Lee, but she pushed herself to her full height and looked him straight in the eye. "I'm a professional, Lee," she said, "so if I have to work with you to get a job done, then that's what I'll do." She reached for the report in his hand. "Now, if you'll excuse me, I have some things to finish before our meeting this afternoon." She sat down and turned her back to him as she opened the report. She could feel him standing behind the chair, but she still shivered when he leaned over her to whisper in her ear.

"That's what I like about you, Mel. You never back down." His breath tickled her ear, and then he was gone. She closed her eyes and took in a deep breath. The man was like a see-saw – up, then down. Hot, then cold. Any trepidation she felt about leaving Quigs vanished – the sooner she could get away from Lee, the better. She pulled out a file and slapped it down on the desk, then turned to her computer.

Lee was waiting for Melissa outside the offices that afternoon, and they climbed into a taxi in silence. Melissa tapped the report in her lap, her finger rapping an incessant rhythm as the cab pulled into the stream of traffic.

"I don't like this any more than you do," Lee said.

"Then why're you here?"

"We're professionals, Melissa. It's not acceptable to cancel an appointment when I could easily go in Kasper's place."

"I could've gone alone."

"I suppose you could have."

"You don't think I can do it."

Lee shrugged. "On the contrary. I know you can."

"Then why are you here?"

"Perhaps I enjoy watching you."

Melissa felt a flare of anger. "Stop it! Stop playing games with me," she said.

"I don't play games, Melissa. You think I'm messing with you? I'd just hurt you more if I allowed things to go on between us."

"Because you feel nothing for me."

He narrowed his eyes. "Yes," he said. "Because I feel nothing for you."

Melissa turned back to the report and opened it to the first page, searching for a distraction. The taxi driver had the radio playing softly, and she tapped her foot to the music as the lyrics of 'I Will Survive' filled the car. She grinned inwardly, and hummed with the tune. Like Gloria, she would neither crumble because Lee had said goodbye, nor lay down and die. Beside her, Lee snorted softly, and her smile grew wider.

Take that, Leander Garrett.

Somehow, Melissa made it through the meeting. Lee had explained upon their arrival that he was filling in for Kasper, then sat back and let Melissa take the lead. She was relieved when he left her at the door after the meeting to make her own way back to the office. The song she'd been humming earlier came back to mind as she waited for a cab. I will survive, she thought. As soon as she had another job, she'd move on from Lee and forget all about him.

Kasper was back in the office the next morning, and Caro and Tracy gathered around as he described how he'd been rear-ended by a truck on his way to work the previous day.

"That's too bad," Caro sympathized. "And you've only had your car a few months."

"I know," he groaned. "And insurance won't pay out the full amount."

"Well, at least you weren't hurt," Melissa said.

"Yeah, right, if you call whiplash not getting hurt."

"Poor you," said Tracy. "I had whiplash once, and the pain was terrible. I had to take painkillers every day, and it gave me stomach aches, and then …"

Melissa walked back to her desk, tuning out the

conversation, and sat down to work. She was just finishing up for the day when Annika called.

"Melissa." Her voice sounded friendly. "I would like to offer you the job. I'm sure you'd like some time to think it over, so get back to me when you're ready."

"Thank you." Melissa drew in a breath to steady her voice. "I'll call you in the morning."

"Excellent."

She stared at her screen for a few minutes as the reality of what she was doing slowly sunk in. She was leaving Quigs! For the first time, she wondered whether she was doing the right thing, but she pushed the thought aside. If she stayed, she'd be thrown together with Lee time and again. At least this way, she could get him out of her system once and for all. She shut down her computer and gathered her things to leave. As soon as she was home, she'd type up her letter of resignation.

Melissa knocked on Norm's door the next morning before stepping inside. She held her letter of resignation, neatly typed and folded into an envelope. Norm glanced up as she entered.

"Morning, Melissa. What can I do for you?"

"I've come to give you this," she said, handing him the envelope. He stared at it for a moment, then looked up to meet her gaze.

"What is it?"

"My notice."

"I see." He leaned back in his chair. "I thought you enjoyed working here."

"I do. But I think it would be good for me to get other experience."

"Lee's been talking about giving you more project

work."

He had? "I still think this is the best move for me right now."

"Would you consider returning in the future?"

"I would." She thought of Kasper's derision when Dave returned – would he feel the same if she was the one returning?

"Good. Then tell me where you're going."

Melissa spent the next ten minutes telling Norm about her new position. He knew Annika well, he said, and was sure she'd learn a lot. As she left the room, she was relieved at how smoothly the meeting had gone, but her good feelings evaporated when she saw Lee leaning against the opposite wall with a frown.

"I need to speak with you," he said. He leaned into Norm's office. "Give me a moment, Norm. I'll be right back."

"Take your time," Norm called as Lee grabbed Melissa by the arm and led her into his office a short distance away.

"Don't touch me," she said, wrenching herself from his grasp.

"You're leaving. Why?"

"How do you know?" she demanded.

"I heard you talking to Norm."

"That's impossible. The door was closed."

"Are you leaving because of me?"

"You think this is about you? That's ridiculous." She turned from him, but he caught her arm and yanked her back.

"So you're throwing your career away on a whim?"

"I'm not throwing my career away," she hissed. "This is a good opportunity. It has absolutely nothing to do with you."

"Really? Tell me, would you have accepted another offer a few months ago?" He smiled mockingly when she remained silent. "I thought not."

"You're right when you say it would be a mistake to be together, Lee. You're no good for me whatsoever. So leave me alone."

He dropped her arm and stepped away. "I should never have taken you for a drink. I should've stayed away."

She laughed grimly. "Yeah, you really should have. But it's a bit too late for that, now isn't it?"

CHAPTER 9

Melissa headed for the mountains early Saturday morning. The sun shining through the windshield was already hot, and as the mountains grew closer, she felt the stress of the week melt away. She pulled into a nearly empty car park and breathed in the fresh mountain air. The trail she'd chosen was steep, switchbacking through a forest of pine and spruce before breaking into the open near the summit. An hour and a half later, she reached the top and dropped her backpack to the ground to drink in the view. To the west, mountain ranges stretched into the distance, while in the east, the foothills gave way to open prairies. No one else was about, and only the cry of an eagle broke the silence. At times like this, she thought there must be something else out there – some higher power – that had created such beauty. It was too incredible to be the result of a cosmic accident. As children, she and Lauren would attend church with their grandmother whenever they stayed the weekend, and a verse drifted through her mind: something about God being the maker of heaven and earth. Standing on the mountain peak surrounded by the sweeping panorama made her feel very insignificant, and yet awestruck to be a witness to such beauty.

Her eyes were on the view ahead instead of the trail when she started her walk back, and she missed seeing the animal standing in her path. A sudden blur was her only warning before she fell into the dirt, her arm securely gripped in the mouth of a large, tan cougar. She screamed, and for the briefest moment, its grip slackened before it dug it's teeth even deeper into her flesh. With her free hand she hit the creature in the ribs, and it snarled and shook her arm, ripping it even more. She scrabbled her hand over the dusty ground and her fingers curled around the smooth bark of a stick. Heaving it into the air, she swung at the creature, catching it on the ribs. The cat loosened its grip, and she pulled her arm away and scrambled backward before pushing herself hurriedly to her feet. Her skin was ripped and bloody, but she barely noticed as she grabbed the branch again and swung it through the air in the direction of the cougar. It snarled and darted away from the crude weapon, its olive-green eyes watching her intently, and Melissa gripped the branch more tightly.

A crashing sound came from the trees, and then, suddenly, a flash of black rushed through the air, slamming into the cougar and sending it flying. She stumbled back as a huge black cat, bigger by far than the cougar, fought her attacker. Her mouth went dry as she realized it was a panther – just like the one from her dreams. Tan and black blurred together as snarls and growls ripped through the air. Blood spurted over the dirt; the cougar yelped but met the panther with bared teeth. The black cat didn't even pause as it lunged for the cougar's throat, ripping open the side of its neck. The cougar stumbled to the ground, then rose and fled.

The panther watched as the cougar disappeared between the trees, then slowly turned its bright green gaze on Melissa. She stared back, frozen with fear, as the creature looked at her. It glanced at her arm, bloody and dirty, and she stepped backward, holding the injured limb to her chest as she gripped the stick. The cat followed her movement, then with a flick of its tail turned and vanished through the trees. Melissa stood frozen, watching the place where it had disappeared. Voices reached her a moment later, and a middle-aged couple appeared on the path. They stopped when they saw her, their eyes wide as they took in her ripped and bloodied arm.

"Oh my," the woman gasped.

"What happened? Are you all right?" said the man.

"A cougar." Melissa's throat was dry, and the sound came out in a rasp. She swallowed and gripped her arm tighter. "There's a cougar," she said. "It attacked me." She was shaking now, and the tears started to flow as she sank to a rock beside the path.

"Where?" the man said, glancing around.

"It …" Melissa gulped back her tears. "It ran off."

"Which way?"

"Enough, Steve," the woman said. "She needs help, not an interrogation."

"The cougar may still be around!"

Melissa shook her head. "I don't think so. It was—" she was about to say "chased off," but something made her change her mind. "I hit it pretty hard, and it ran away."

"Still," Steve said, "it could come back."

"You're not helping," the woman snapped. She looked at Melissa, and her face softened slightly. "I'm Joan," she said. "Let's have a look." She took Melissa's arm and carefully examined it. Multiple rips and bites had torn the flesh right to the bone, and her lips tightened in horror. "It needs to be cleaned and bound." She swung her backpack off her shoulders and dug inside for a moment before pulling out a water bottle and a bright red bandana. "Give me your arm." She opened the water bottle, and grasping Melissa's wrist, dribbled water over it. Melissa bit her lip as the water sliced through her wounds. Using the bandana as a makeshift bandage, Joan wrapped her arm and tied the corners into a knot.

"Can you get down the mountain?" she asked.

"I ... I think so."

"Then let's get you up." She slipped her arm beneath Melissa's and helped her rise, then gently pried the stick from her grasp. The ground swayed, and Melissa closed her eyes.

"How do you feel?"

Melissa took in a steadying breath. "I'm okay."

"All right. We need to get you to a doctor. We'll take it slow."

She placed her arm around Melissa's waist and turned to Steve. "Lead the way," she said.

They warned people of the danger as they slowly made their way down the mountain and arrived back in the parking lot an hour later. Melissa's arm was throbbing with pain, and she felt faint and nauseated. "Where's your car?" Joan asked.

Melissa glanced around, then stopped when she saw a black F-150 parked a short distance away. Leaning against the cab, arms folded over his chest, was Lee. He walked over as Melissa stared at him. "Are you all right?" he asked. "What happened?" His eyes were clouded with concern.

"Do you know this woman?" Steve asked, and Melissa could hear the relief in his voice.

"I work with her." Lee took her arm, carefully unwrapped the makeshift bandage and examined the gashes in silence as a wave of dizziness washed over her. "She needs to sit," he said, holding her by the uninjured arm.

"She was attacked by a cougar," Joan said. "She needs to see a doctor."

"I'll take her." He rewrapped her arm with the bloodied bandana.

Joan frowned. "Melissa? Do you know this man? Are you okay if we leave you with him?"

Melissa looked at Lee, who met her gaze with a now stony expression, all previous concern wiped away. Another wave of nausea washed over her. "It's okay," she whispered.

Joan glanced between them, still hesitant, and Melissa smiled weakly. "Really, it's fine. Lee will help me."

"Lee?"

"Leander Garrett," Lee said brusquely. He put his hand beneath Melissa's elbow and guided her to her car. "Let's go," he said.

"Your truck?"

"I'll pick it up later." He slipped off her backpack and searched for her keys as she watched.

"What are you doing here anyway?" she said as he opened the door for her. He helped her into the seat then climbed in the driver's side. Her head was throbbing and she leaned it against the headrest as her stomach churned.

"I was with a friend from Wildlife Services when the call came through about an attack. I offered to come out instead."

"But ... how did they know?"

"Someone must have called."

"But ..." The burning pain in her arm stopped Melissa from saying more. Something didn't make sense, but she didn't have the energy to figure it out.

They arrived at the hospital a half hour later, and Lee led her through the doors of the ER. "I'll wait out here," he said.

"You don't have to stay," Melissa told him.

"You need someone to get you home."

She dropped her head and cradled her arm against her chest. It was too much effort to argue. A nurse called her name a short while later and she followed her to a small, curtained room. The nurse tutted when she saw the rips in her skin. "We need to clean it out before we can stitch it," she said.

Melissa endured the next hour with gritted teeth as dirt was washed from the wounds and her skin stitched back together.

"You're lucky your injuries aren't any worse," the doctor said. "You'll have some scars, but no permanent damage. You know, it's extremely rare for a cougar to attack a human like that. And you say it ran away when you hit it?"

Melissa studied the patterns on the ceiling. "That's right," she said. Omitting the panther from the story hadn't really been a conscious decision, but for some reason, she wanted to keep that part of the attack to herself. The more she thought about the events, the more it seemed to her that the panther had been protecting her from the cougar, just like the panther in her dream had protected her from the tiger. It seemed the least she could do was protect its privacy. Black panthers were rare enough that people would be searching for the animal if they knew it existed.

"Wildlife Services are in the waiting room to ask you some questions," the doctor said. "I said they could see you when you're done. Do you have someone to take you home?"

Melissa nodded.

"Very good. We're almost done here, then you're free to go."

A short while later Melissa was escorted to the waiting area, where a uniformed park warden was talking to the pretty girl at the admitting desk. The girl gestured in her direction, and the man strode toward her.

"I'm Sean Rosseau," he said. "Are you the person who was attacked by the cougar?"

"Melissa Hewitt," she said.

"I just have a few questions for you, Ms. Hewitt." He glanced around the room. "Are you here on your own?"

"No." Melissa nodded toward Lee, seated in the corner.

"Let's sit down," Rosseau said, leading her to a seat near Lee. "Now start at the beginning, and tell me everything that happened."

Melissa repeated the story she'd told the doctor.

"The cougar just ran off?"

"I hit it pretty hard." Lee was watching her intently as she spoke.

"Very well. We already have rangers searching the area for the cougar. We cannot have it attacking anyone else. We'll let you know when we find it."

"Thank you," she said.

"So the cougar just ran off," Lee said as he drove her home.

"Mmm," she mumbled. She was leaning her head against the seat back, her eyes closed.

"Do you want to tell me the truth?"

She forced her eyes open to look at him. "What do you mean?"

"That's not the whole story, is it?"

"Are you accusing me of lying?" she demanded.

"Are you?"

She stared at her reflection in the window. "There was a panther," she finally said.

"A panther?"

"Yes." She frowned. "Isn't that strange? Where do you think it came from?"

"What happened?"

"It attacked the cougar."

"I see." Lee was silent a moment. "Why didn't you tell Rosseau?"

"I didn't want them searching for it."

"Why not?"

"It protected me, so I guess I'm returning the favor. From what I've heard, panthers are pretty rare. If people heard about it, they'd hunt it down."

He was silent a moment. "You were protecting the panther by keeping it a secret?" he finally said.

"Yes."

"Hmm." He drove in silence for a while as Melissa closed her eyes again.

"Were you scared?"

"Of the cougar or the panther? They both terrified me. I thought the panther might return to finish me off."

"But it didn't."

"Who knows what would have happened if Joan and Steve hadn't arrived."

They lapsed into silence, and Melissa dozed.

When they arrived at her apartment, Lee helped Melissa from the car, then swept her into his arms when she swayed from dizziness. He still held her keys, and he unlocked the door to her apartment while holding her, and carried her to her room.

"Do you have painkillers?" he asked as he placed her on her bed.

"The doctor gave me some," she mumbled. "In my bag."

He was back a moment later with two tablets and a glass of water. "You need to rest," he said.

"Thank you, Lee."

He stared at her a long moment. "Goodnight, Mel. I'm flying to Toronto tomorrow, so I won't see you till I'm back."

He disappeared through the door, and a moment later Melissa heard the lock click into place. She rolled over onto her good arm and closed her eyes as the events of the day slowly slipped away.

She was hiking. She hummed as she walked, but when a huge cat sprang onto the path in front of her, she stopped. She hadn't noticed it sitting on the branch above her, and now it was too late to run. It stared at her, its green eyes bright in the shadows beneath the trees. The animal was completely black, from nose to tail, and its head was level with her waist. It paced closer, its footfalls barely making a sound, and slowly circled her, its tail swishing across her legs. She stood, frozen in place, as it sniffed her hand and brushed against her side. "Lee," she whispered, "help me." She wanted to scream, but the sound caught in her throat. A soft growl rumbled in the chest of the cat. "I warned you," Lee's voice blew through the trees, "stay away from cougars." The scream gathered in her chest, and she spun around in an effort to escape. The panther pounced a moment later, its front legs wrapping around her waist, but as she fell, it twisted in the air and took the weight of her fall. She scrambled away, and the panther disappeared.

CHAPTER 10

When Melissa awoke the next morning, her arm was burning with pain. She swallowed some more painkillers and lay back down, but sleep evaded her. After a few uncomfortable minutes, she padded through to the kitchen and made some coffee. She stared at her phone for a long moment, then picked it up and dialed Lauren's number. She listened wearily as Lauren fussed; she wanted to fly out on the next available flight, and it took Melissa a while to convince her sister that she was not in danger of death. By the time she finally ended the call, she was exhausted and her head was aching. She went back to bed and fell asleep. It was the buzzing of the phone that woke her, and she stumbled through to the kitchen.

"Hello?" she said groggily.

"Melissa Hewitt? It's Sean Rosseau from Wildlife Services. I just wanted to let you know that we found your cougar."

"You did?"

"Yes. We ran some DNA tests, and it's definitely the cougar that attacked you. By the way, you did only see *one* cougar, didn't you?"

"Yes. Why?"

"Well, there was a second set of prints. And the cougar that attacked you was killed by another animal. A vicious attack too. Its throat had been ripped out and the body left in the open."

"Oh. That's – that's awful. But there was just the one cougar."

"Hmm." Rosseau was silent a moment. "Well, I thought you'd want to know that the creature was dead. We would have destroyed it too, if we had found it alive, but the job was taken out of our hands."

"Thank you."

"Yes, of course. I hope you recover quickly. Goodbye."

The line went dead before Melissa had a chance to respond and she dropped the phone to the table. The last time she'd seen the cougar it had been alive. Injured, but alive. Had the panther followed it and finished the job? If so, why? She thought again about the creature that had chased off her attacker – huge, as black as pitch, and with mesmerizing green eyes. Where had it come from? She shook her head. What did it matter? The cougar was dead and she was alive.

She was just returning to her bed when her phone buzzed again.

"Hello? Is this Melissa Hewitt?" a bright and cheery voice asked on the other end. "This is Brittany Moore from CTV calling. I understand you were attacked by a cougar. Do you mind if I ask you a few questions."

Melissa sighed. "Yes, go ahead," she said.

Melissa's story had run on TV on Sunday evening, so it was no surprise that she was a minor celebrity when she walked through Quigs's office doors on Monday morning to start her two week notice period. It took most of the morning to explain what had happened, and when she mentioned that Lee had taken her to the hospital, there were gasps of surprise.

"How did he know?" Caro demanded.

"He was with a friend at Wildlife Services when the call came through," she said, parroting Lee's answer.

"How convenient," Caro muttered. Privately, Melissa agreed. There was something off in Lee's explanation, but she couldn't pinpoint what it was. And when she thought about it, he hadn't seemed at all surprised that she was the one injured when they'd met in the parking lot. In fact, it was almost as if he had been waiting for her.

It was mid-morning by the time she had a chance to settle down to some work, and by the afternoon, her arm was throbbing. She made it to her bus, then collapsed into bed as soon as she arrived home, falling into a restless sleep. Sharp teeth wrapped around her arm in her dreams, and she awoke in the early hours with tears streaming down her cheeks and her arm pulsing with pain.

The throbbing became a dull ache as the week dragged on, but the nightmares returned night after night as she relived the horror of the attack, and she'd lie awake, gulping for air as her heart raced furiously. In her dreams, the panther was as terrifying as the cougar, often turning on her with a snarl after the cougar vanished in the trees, its bright green eyes flashing with savagery.

She stayed in her apartment that weekend, huddled on

the couch with a cup of coffee and a book. The weather was beautiful and warm, but the thought of venturing beyond the city left her shaking. She'd get there eventually – just not yet.

Melissa's last week at Quigs was no different from any other week. Lee had not returned from Toronto and was not expected back until the end of the week. She and Kasper met with AB Trucking to deliver their final report, and she handed her files to Kasper as the days went by. On Friday afternoon, Kasper and Caro came to her desk.

"We're going out for drinks," Kasper said. "You should come too, celebrate your new job."

"Maybe Lee will join us during the evening," Caro said. "It'll be a bit dull, otherwise."

"Nonsense," Kasper said. "Besides, Melissa and Lee don't get on, so she's probably glad he's not around." He glanced at her. "Right?"

She nodded. "Yes."

They left the office a short while later and headed to the same pub where Lee had taken Melissa after their meeting with Hong Industries. She pushed thoughts of him away as she ordered a cocktail and joined in the repartee until Caro flashed her phone around the table.

"I've just had a message from Lee," she said. "He's sorry he can't hang out with us, but he won't be back till tomorrow." She turned to Melissa. "Lee's quite the playboy – definitely not your type. He wouldn't be seen dead hiking in the mountains or spending time outdoors."

Melissa looked at her in surprise. "Lee was in the mountains when he took me to the hospital," she said cautiously.

"I know! Strange, isn't it? But you said he was visiting

a friend, and there's no explaining some friends."

Melissa took a sip of her drink as Tracy slid into a seat beside her. "Caro thinks she knows everything about Lee, but if you ask me, there's more to him than meets the eye." She smiled. "So are you excited for your new job?"

More people from Quigs joined the group as the evening wore on until Melissa finally excused herself amid protests. It was only when she said she needed to visit someone at the hospital that they finally let her go.

"Keep in touch now, Mel," Kasper called, holding up a drink in her direction.

"I will," she said. She gathered her purse and turned to leave, then paused. Lee was leaning against the door, his eyes trained on her. She glanced back to see if Caro had noticed him, but when she looked back, he was gone. She frowned and scanned the crowd, then gave her head a mental shake. Clearly she had imagined him, which was a very disturbing thought. But if he truly had been there, why wouldn't he have joined the group? She shook her head. On Monday she'd be starting her new life, and she could finally put Lee behind her once and for all.

Chapter 11

Melissa tapped the steering wheel in time to the music as she drove down the highway toward the mountains. It was September, and already the trees were turning, painting the landscape in reds and yellows.

Almost two months had passed since she'd started working at Mercer Engineering, and she had quickly settled into the new routine. She thought, a little grimly, about her first day in her new office. No sooner had she arrived than Annika called her into a meeting.

"It will take you a few days to get settled," she'd said, "but I just wanted to be clear about a few things from the start. I expect you to be here at eight every morning, as I am. If you're going to be in late, let me know in advance. The day ends at five, and unless there is urgent work, I do not expect you to stay beyond that time. In fact, even though I'm usually here a bit later, I discourage my staff from putting in unnecessary overtime. I expect all of you to be fully committed to your work. I got the sense that you're someone who will put in the hard work necessary to get a job done well, which is why I hired you. However, let me just say that I have no tolerance for poor performance, a slack attitude, or dishonesty of any kind. If you need time off for any legitimate reason, I'm prepared to be fair and understanding, but do not seek to take advantage of my good nature in any way." She smiled, and the stern expression vanished. "I'm quite confident that these warnings are unnecessary, however. I look forward to developing our professional relationship."

It had not been a very encouraging start, but Melissa soon learned that although Annika was meticulous and demanding, she was also generous and fair-minded. She placed a high value on personal time, and in fact left the office at three every Friday so she could watch her grandsons play hockey. She was patient with Melissa, taking the time to answer her questions as she learned her new role, and in just two months, Melissa felt as though she'd completely settled in. And leaving the office at five every day had meant she'd had more time to spend with Emma. She wasn't the girl's only visitor, though. Melissa received weekly updates from Emma about the time Lee spent with her.

"He visited me, hmm, three days ago," Emma had said, holding up two fingers, the first time Melissa visited after starting at Mercer Engineering.

"He did?"

"Yes. He read to me."

"Jungle Book?"

"Nope."

"Then what?"

"Beauty and the Beast," she said with a giggle.

"Oh."

"S'okay, Mel," she said seriously, "I'll tell you what happens."

Melissa smiled. "Thank you, Em," she said. "But how about you choose a book for just you and me to read."

Emma's forehead furrowed as she considered. "How 'bout *Cinderella*? I bet you do good mouse voices."

"Okay. *Cinderella* will be *our* story, okay?"

Emma nodded furiously. "'Kay."

Lee visited Emma every week, except when he was out of town, but thankfully, never on the same day as Melissa. She had neither seen nor heard from him since leaving Quigs, although when she'd run into Kasper once, he told her that Lee had been cranky ever since she'd left.

"I think he's annoyed with you for leaving just when he was starting to give you more project work. Either that, or he's going through some mid-life crisis," he added with a grin.

"He's thirty, Kasper."

"I know! Pretty sad, isn't it?"

Whatever was eating Lee, Melissa was pretty certain it had nothing to do with her, nor was she in the slightest bit interested in his personal issues. He'd made it clear what he thought of her, after all.

A signpost on the highway read "Turner Valley," and Melissa slowed to make the turn. It was her first time venturing into the mountains since the cougar attack, and her arm ached at the mere thought of being there again. But if she didn't conquer her fear now, she might never be able to. It was highly unlikely that she'd be targeted by a cougar for a second time. Even so, she wasn't quite ready to tackle the trail where she'd been attacked. Instead, she'd chosen a much shorter hike close by – a popular trail that was sure to be busy. She had also timed her arrival for late morning – the busiest time on the trails.

She pulled into a space at the trail parking lot a short while later and stared through the windshield. I can do this, she told herself. A map of routes was posted on the notice board, and she stopped to study them. Two trails followed the river for a short distance to the waterfall and a viewing platform, then veered into the forest, where they split, one route going west and circling back to the parking lot, the other continuing north until it eventually crossed the river and headed south on the opposite bank. The longer trail was over twenty kilometers, but the shorter was easily done in a few hours.

As she stepped onto the path, she examined the brush. A stick, three feet in length and two inches thick, lay on the ground a short distance away. She grabbed it and immediately felt safer. A crude weapon, but a weapon nonetheless.

It was a beautiful fall day, the sun warm and the sky clear. Midges buzzed as Melissa walked, and she swatted them with her free hand. As she had expected, the trail was busy, and ahead of her ran two young children, laughing in delight as they examined the flowers along the path. She followed the family to the waterfall, where the children stopped to hang over the railing and watch the tumbling river, but she continued without stopping into the deep shadows of the forest. Up ahead was a couple, and from the heavy hiking boots they wore and walking sticks they carried, Melissa guessed they would set a steady pace. They wore matching red shirts that served as a beacon through the trees. She matched their pace as the sound of the waterfall faded away. Sunlight filtered through the forest, making spiders' webs glisten, while moss hid in the shadows. The path climbed a little, over some large boulders, and she clambered over them, keeping up with the couple ahead.

The path curved to meet the river again farther upstream, and she passed a family with two boys, the younger chatting animatedly with his father while the older walked sullenly behind. The path became steeper, and as the sun rose higher, the air in the forest grew hot and humid. She glanced at her phone and saw it was already close to one. Pausing for a moment, she reached for her water and took a long chug, downing almost the entire bottle. Up ahead the path curved around a small mound of rock, blocking the couple she'd been following from view, and she hurried on. When she rounded the curve, they had disappeared from sight, but up ahead a streak of red appeared between the branches, and she quickened her pace to catch up. A group of young men passed her going in the other direction, and she nodded at them as they greeted her.

She reached the split in the path a few minutes later without catching up to the couple, but if they were taking the longer route, she had no desire to follow them anyway. There was no sign to indicate which way to go, but she took the left fork with little hesitation, certain of the direction. Another family passed her going the other way, their voices ringing loudly as they came nearer, and some of the tension she hadn't realized she'd been holding slipped away. She smiled to herself. This was what she loved – the intoxicating scent of the outdoors. She breathed in deeply, smelling the pine mingled with the earthy scent of mulch.

As she walked, the sound of other hikers faded into the

distance until she was alone with her thoughts, and some time passed before she realized it had been a while since she'd seen anyone. She gripped the stick she carried and continued walking, wiping her slick palms against her jeans as she hummed softly beneath her breath. A crashing sound in the forest near the trail had her spinning around. It was a deer, and she gave a shaky laugh as it bounded away. She pulled out her phone to check the time and was surprised to see that it was past two. Surely she should have reached the end of the trail by now. And where were the other hikers?

The trees thinned, and after a while she stepped out from beneath the forest canopy into full sunlight. To the west she could see ranges of mountains, but to the east the view was blocked by a low cliff. Before her the way lay open with long grasses and low, scrubby bushes, and she could see the path stretching onward. She checked the time again – mid-afternoon. There was no way the shorter trail would take this long, which meant she must have taken the wrong path. She gritted her teeth. At this point it was better to just keep going forward.

Melissa gripped the stick tighter as she continued walking. The map at the trailhead had shown a bridge crossing the river, so as soon as she reached the water, she should see it. She rounded the cliff, and breathed a sigh of relief when she saw the river glistening in the sunshine. She quickened her pace, eager to find the crossing, but when she reached the riverbank, all she could see was a few wooden pylons. The bridge had been washed away. She stared at it in disbelief, then slumped to the ground as tears of frustration filled her eyes. She blinked them away furiously. No wonder she hadn't seen anyone on the path!

After a few dejected moments, she rose and walked to

the edge of the bank. Reaching the water would take a scramble down the six-foot cliff. It was a treacherous place to cross, with rocks in the river creating swirling rapids. Lifting her gaze, she saw the path on the other side, and for a moment, she was awash with self-pity. If only she could swing over the river like Tarzan! She pushed the thought away and looked downstream. Too many rapids. Perhaps if she walked upstream for a while, she could find a point shallow and narrow enough to wade through. The idea of fording the glacial water, still frigid despite being the end of summer, made her shiver, but she pushed the thought away. One challenge at a time, and the first was finding a place suitable to cross.

Hefting her backpack, she turned upstream and continued walking. The path was blocked ahead by a large clump of bushes that grew alongside the bank, and she veered to the west to circumvent the growth, picking her way through the knee-high scrub. When the river came back in sight she froze. Between her and the river was a grizzly mother with two half-grown cubs, scavenging the bushes for berries. She dared not breathe as she stared at the creatures. They hadn't noticed her yet, but it was only a matter of seconds before they did. She scanned the area, taking in her surroundings. To the north was a forest, through which the river flowed. She looked back at the bears to see they were moving closer. Her heart pounded furiously, and she pulled back, sure that the grizzlies would hear her. She crouched in the grass and slowly moved in the direction of the forest. Glancing over her shoulder, she saw that the bears were still at the bushes, and she rose to her feet and ran toward the trees. As soon as she reached the first one, she spun around with her back against the trunk and searched the bushes, but the bears had disappeared.

Her heart was racing, and she gasped for breath as she slumped down against the trunk, her chest heaving. Tears spilled down her cheeks, and she scrubbed at them angrily. She needed to think. The bridges was gone, the water was too deep to ford and she could have three grizzlies stalking her. She pulled out her phone, but of course there was no reception, and she threw it back in her pack in frustration. Leaning her head against the tree for a moment, she considered her options, but when she saw that the bears were headed in her direction, she turned into the forest and ran, stumbling over roots and stones. The undergrowth was thick and branches slapped across her legs and scraped her arms as she fought her way through. Her backpack bounced against her back, and she wrested it from her shoulders and let it drop to the ground. She heard a crashing sound behind her, and pushed herself to go faster. Her lungs were screaming with pain and each breath burned through her chest, but she stumbled forward, clawing her way through the branches.

When she reached the edge of the forest, she fell onto her knees. Her jeans were ripped and blood trailed down her arms, but she scrambled back to her feet and continued running. Glancing up, she almost cried again – this time from relief – when she saw a structure ahead. If she could just reach it, she would be safe. She tripped again and cried in pain as her knee hit a stone, but she pushed herself up and ran toward the building. She could see now that it was a small cabin. Her heart felt as though it would explode, and her lungs were at bursting point as she covered the last few meters to the cabin and stumbled against the stairs. The door opened, and in a moment someone was crouching beside her.

CHAPTER 12

"Melissa!" A voice cut through her fear. "What are you doing here?"

"Lee?"

"This is my cabin," he said. "How did you get here?"

She looked around wildly. Her breath was unsteady, and her hands were trembling. "Bears."

"Bears?"

"Grizzlies. Tracking me."

Lee scanned the horizon. "I don't see any bears." His gaze returned to her and he held out a hand to help her to her feet. "We'd better get you inside." She grimaced as pain shot through her knee.

"Are you hurt?"

"I fell, but it's nothing."

Lee took her arm and led her into the cabin.

"How did you get here?" he asked as she sank onto a

couch.

"The bridge was washed away, so I couldn't cross the river. And then I saw the bears."

"Hmm. I should put up a sign about the bridge before any more unwanted hikers land at my door."

She looked down and examined her nails. They were caked in dirt. "I'm sorry," she whispered. He had mentioned to her once that his cabin was near the river, but she'd forgotten that fact as she'd raced from danger.

"You're probably hungry," he finally said. "I'll find you something to eat."

As he walked away, she looked around to see that she was in a sitting room. A wood-burning stove stood against the wooden wall, with a thick black pipe that went through the roof. Long windows graced either side, through which she could see the wide expanse of the mountains. Wooden rafters spanned the ceiling, and a ladder against the opposite wall led to a loft. Beside the couch were two large chairs, and a small bookshelf filled with books and games stood in the corner. She heard Lee returning and twisted around to see him step out of the kitchen, past a table with four chairs.

He handed her a glass of water and a plate with cold meats, cheese and a slice of bread. "Sorry," he said. "That's all I've got. I started a pot of coffee as well."

"It looks wonderful," Melissa said, taking the plate. She hadn't realized how ravenous she was until she saw the food, and she ate it hungrily.

"You'll have to stay the night," Lee said. "I'll take you to your car in the morning."

"Stay the night? Can't you take me now?" She drew a horrified breath. "Oh, no!"

"What is it?"

"My keys are in my backpack. I dropped it in the forest."

"We'll look for it in the morning. You can't leave tonight anyway since it'll be dark soon, and it's not easy to drive around these mountains at night. You can sleep in the bedroom and I'll take the loft."

"Thank you," she said. "I'm sorry to intrude." It came out more sarcastically than she intended, and she looked away with a blush. When she glanced back at Lee he was staring at her. His lips were pressed together, and the stubble around his mouth and down his cheeks made him look a little dangerous. She swallowed hard and glanced out the window. It was already dusk, and she could just make out the outline of the mountains against the darkening sky. Rising cautiously, she limped over to look out. Beyond the building was a sea of shadows, but around the cabin was a wide deck with a pair of Adirondack chairs. "I'll sit outside for a bit, if that's okay."

"Of course," he said.

She stepped onto the wooden deck, easing herself into a chair. The dropping sun had taken the heat with it, and she wrapped her arms around her chest to keep herself warm. A faint smudge of gray streaked the sky behind the mountains, while up above the clear night sky twinkled with millions of stars. She stared at them, marveling at how many she could see.

"It's a full moon tonight," Lee said behind her. He held out a blanket and a cup of coffee, and she took them gratefully. "You can see it clearly on the other side of the house."

"The moon was almost full when we went to Bow Valley," she said. She winced. How stupid to bring up a reminder of that day. He was silent and she took a sip of coffee. "Do you come here often?"

"Every weekend, if possible. I love it here. But I've told you that before – when we went to Bow Valley, in fact."

"Yes," she said.

He stood silent for a moment, then sat in the chair beside her. "I thought you might be put off hiking after the attack. I'm surprised you did such a long walk."

"It's the first time I've been out. I was planning something short, with lots of people on the trail."

"What happened?"

"I took the wrong fork." She spent the next few minutes telling him about her adventures of the day. When she got to the part about the bears, she paused. "I guess I overreacted a bit. I was spooked by the forest, and my imagination was going overtime."

"What happened in the forest?"

"Nothing. I saw creatures in the shadows." She laughed self-consciously. "I have an overactive imagination. I blame it on the attack, combined with the nightmares."

Lee frowned. "You've been having nightmares? About the cougar?"

"That too." She sighed. "But I've been having nightmares about a panther for years."

"About a panther?" He appeared startled. "For how long?"

"They started around the time I began working at Quigs. But they got worse when I joined your team. I think it was my mind trying to cope with the stress of impressing you."

He was silent a moment. "So after you ran from the bears, you found the cabin?"

"Yes. I knew if I could just reach it, I'd be safe. I didn't realize it was yours."

"And here I thought you were tracking me down."

She groaned. "Please tell me you didn't think that."

"Not really. After all, you told me quite clearly that I'm not welcome anymore." He said the last few words in a sing-song voice, and Melissa blushed, remembering the song she'd hummed in the taxi.

"You told me you wanted nothing to do with me. Besides, I wasn't really singing it to you. It was playing on the radio."

"But it suited what you wanted to say perfectly."

"Maybe. You're quite a jerk, you know." She laughed humorlessly.

"Yeah, sometimes." He paused. "So are we good?"

"You've helped me twice now, so yes. Anyway, I'm quite over you." The words came out with confidence, but seeing him now, she knew it wasn't true.

Lee walked over to the deck railing and stared into the darkness. "Are you seeing someone else?"

"Someone *else*? I thought you made it clear that we were never in a relationship. That I was throwing myself at you."

He turned to look at her. "You're right. I did say that."

His gaze met hers with an intensity that contradicted his words. Her mouth went dry, and when she finally pulled her eyes away, she realized she'd stopped breathing. "I, uh, I think I'll have a shower, if you don't mind, then try and get some sleep."

"I'll find you something to wear."

He disappeared into the house, and she limped in behind. He was back a moment later with a t-shirt and a pair of sweatpants. On top was a towel. "This is the best I can do," he said. "I'll show you the room."

The bedroom was across from the bathroom, below the loft. A queen-sized bed with a faded quilt stood in the middle of the room, with a small bedside table beside it. On the opposite wall was a chest of drawers with two half-melted candles on top. Lee placed the pile on the bed and pulled a lighter from the drawer, using it to light the candles.

"No electricity?"

"Not this deep in the mountains. I have a generator for essentials."

"How …" The first word that came to mind was romantic. "… rustic," she finished.

"The last bastion against civilization."

"I like it."

"I thought you would." He walked to the door and paused. "Sleep well, Mel," he said, and then he was gone, closing the door behind him.

A short while later, Melissa stood beneath the warm spray of water and thought about the moment on the deck. She'd seen something in his gaze that had made her stomach clench. This was exactly why she'd left Quigs. Merely seeing Lee did something to her. Leaning her head against the shower wall, she took a deep breath. She had to get over this obsession for him. But it didn't help that he just kept reappearing in her life. How was it even possible, that of all the places she could have ended up, it was here at his cabin? She grabbed Lee's body wash and squeezed some into her hands. Her knee was bruised and swollen from her fall, and her arms were covered in scratches and scrapes. She washed herself carefully, then let the hot water wash over her before reluctantly turning it off. Lee's t-shirt hung halfway to her knees, and she rolled his pants to her ankles before stepping out of the bathroom. He was nowhere to be seen, and she crossed over to the room and closed the door. Through the window, she could see the moon hanging full and fat above the jagged mountain peaks. As she lay down, a strong, masculine scent rose from the bed, immediately bringing Lee to mind. She turned the pillow over and buried her face in the cool fabric.

CHAPTER 13

The panther was chasing Melissa through the trees, bounding beside her as she ran. She needed to escape, but the forest was thick and the undergrowth snagged her shirt and jeans, slowing her progress. She saw a small rise to the left and, changing direction, ran up the short incline, hoping to find a way over and out of the trees. But as she reached the top, her heart sank. The mouth of a cave yawned before her, and she knew she was trapped. She spun around to see the panther stalking closer, its shining green eyes intent. She backed up to the cave entrance as the panther stopped its prowling and dropped to its haunches to watch her.

Melissa bolted upright, instantly awake, and stared at the unfamiliar surroundings. Through the window shone a multitude of stars, and she sighed in relief as she remembered where she was. She was about to lie down again when some sixth sense made her freeze. Her door was open, and something warned her she wasn't alone. She narrowed her eyes and peered into the darkness.

"Lee?" she whispered. She could see a shape near the door. There was a faint rustling as it shifted, and she froze. Whatever it was crouched on the floor, and when it moved, she saw it was the shape of a large animal. She scrambled backward in the bed, pulling the quilt to her chin as the creature looked at her, its green eyes brightly reflective. It watched her for a moment, then padded to the door and slipped through, its long tail disappearing into the darkness. Melissa stared at the door, frozen in shock. Her heart was pounding, and the quilt beneath her chin trembled from her shaking hands.

"Lee?" she whispered. All was silent. "Lee?" she said, a little louder. There was a creaking sound, then a heavy thud outside the cabin that made her jump. She glanced out the window. Stalking across the moonlit clearing was a huge black cat. A panther. Her heart hammered furiously as it disappeared into the shadows of the forest. She crept from the bed and headed to the door. She was still shaking, and her mouth was dry.

"Lee," she hissed. All was silent. She stepped out of the room and, placing her back to the wall, inched into the sitting room. Light from the moon spilled through the kitchen window and lit the cabin, but all was still and quiet. The front door stood ajar, and after a moment she dashed across the room and pushed it shut. She leaned against the door, panting, then twisted the key. She could see the ladder leading to the loft, and in a loud whisper, she called Lee's name again. There was no reply, and after a moment's hesitation, she crossed the room and quickly ascended the ladder. She paused at the top and peered into the low-ceilinged room. The bed was neatly made and there was no sign of Lee. She climbed back down and ran to the door, turning the key back in the lock. Lee must have gone for a walk in the dark, and she'd just locked him out of his own home! She wondered whether he knew about the panther, and if he was armed for protection, but after a moment she gave a mental shrug. He'd been coming to this cabin for so many years, he must be aware of the dangers that lurked outside; and besides, she thought wryly, he'd told her once he was the cat-whisperer.

Hurrying back to her room, she closed her door firmly behind her and lay on the bed. She couldn't quite dispel her concern for Lee, and she listened for a long time for sounds of his return before finally falling into a fitful sleep.

She woke to the sun shining brightly into her room, her back against the wall. She sat up with a groan, then froze as the memories from the night before came flooding back. It wasn't enough that she'd been attacked by a cougar and tracked by bears. Now she was entertaining panthers in her room. How had life become so bizarre?

Stripping off Lee's clothes, she pulled on her own, shivering as the cold air in the cabin touched her skin. The shirt was a little ripped, and mud clung to the knees of her jeans, but they would do. She wrinkled her nose as she pulled on her socks and shoes, but her feet were cold, so she endured the smell.

The tantalizing scent of bacon and coffee had her hobbling from the room. She paused when she saw her backpack on the table. Lee stepped out from the kitchen.

"I went for an early walk this morning and found this," he said. "Did you sleep well?"

"An early-morning walk? But what time did you get back last night?"

He frowned. "Last night? What are you talking about?"

"I was looking for you." He gave her a questioning look. "There was a panther in my room," she blurted out.

"A panther?" His tone was incredulous. "You must have been dreaming."

"No. It was real." Lee returned to the kitchen, and she followed him to the doorway. "It looked at me, then left. I saw it outside my window before it disappeared into the forest. I tried to find you, but you weren't here."

"Coffee?" he asked. He filled a mug with the steaming brew and handed it her. "You were dreaming, Melissa."

She frowned. "No, I wasn't. I know what I saw. After it left, I locked the front door, then climbed to the loft to tell you what had happened, but you weren't there."

"How do you think a panther got into the cabin?"

"I don't know – you tell me! Maybe you left the door open when you went out. But I know what I saw."

He dished up slices of bacon and scrambled eggs onto two plates and carried them to the table. "First of all, a panther is unlikely to enter a building of its own accord. Second, if it did come inside, why didn't it attack you?"

"Maybe it was the same panther that saved me before," Melissa said as they sat down. "Perhaps it recognized me."

Lee rolled his eyes. "Seriously?"

"Yes! Seriously! Do you have a better explanation?"

"Yes. You dreamed it. That overactive imagination you mentioned last night."

She leaned forward across the table, carefully enunciating each word. "I did not dream it. It was really there. I can't believe you've never seen it."

Lee was silent as he took a mouthful. "I didn't say I hadn't seen it," he said finally. He looked up to meet her gaze.

"So you have seen it! Does that mean you believe me?

That the panther was in my room?"

He sighed, then pushed his plate away. "Melissa, I—" He rose and began pacing the room.

"Just tell me that you believe me."

"Fine. There was a panther in the cabin."

"So did you leave the front door open? Is that how it got in?"

Lee stopped his pacing. "No," he said slowly. "The panther was already here."

Melissa frowned in confusion. "Already here?"

"Yes."

"But how's that possible?"

"It was here – in the room, and …" he sighed, "… it's here now."

Her eyes darted around the room in confusion. "Where?"

"Standing right in front of you."

What on earth was he talking about?

"It's me, Mel," he said. "You saw *me*."

Her eyes narrowed as she looked at him. "Great! Now you're mocking me."

"No." He ran his hand over his scalp, pulling on the knot at the back of his head. "I'm a Changer, Mel. I have the ability to change into a panther."

Melissa stared at him, then dropped her head into her hands. "Fine," she said. "Whatever."

"You don't believe me."

Melissa looked at him incredulously. "First you tell me I'm dreaming things, then you tell me you change into a panther. And you expect me to believe you?" She laughed dryly as she pushed herself from the table. "I think it's time for me to go. I'm sure I can find my own way back." She reached for her backpack.

"Melissa."

With a sigh of exasperation, she looked up and snorted when she saw him stripping off his shirt. "Seriously?" she said. She turned away when he pulled off his jeans. A frisson of energy stroked her arm and crackled through the room, and the air began to shimmer. She turned to see Lee become a blur of black, then disappear as a huge black cat took his place. She stumbled backward as a scream rose in her throat. It stalked toward her, and she spun and ran to the bedroom, but her way was blocked a moment later when the panther sprang past her and landed a foot away. She careened to a stop, then without another thought spun around again, grabbed her pack and sprinted for the door. A growl rose behind her as she yanked it open. She threw herself down the porch stairs and ran into the forest that lay behind the cabin, twisting around trees and between bushes that suddenly veered up before her. She dared not look back, but kept running, away from the danger behind her. She heard no sound of pursuit, and eventually she slowed to a fast walk, but she didn't dare stop, instead heading deeper into the mountains.

The sun was high when she heard the sound of voices ahead. She slowed as they grew closer, then stopped when she saw a tent between the trees. Three men were sitting at a camping table nearby, laughing. She hesitated a moment, but then one of them looked up and saw her.

"Well, well," he said, taking in her disheveled appearance. "Look what we have here."

"I need help," Melissa said.

"I'd say you do," he said, approaching her.

"Don't mind Tony," said one of the other men. "My name's Mark. How can we help you?"

"I got lost. I need to get to my car."

"I'm sure we can help," Mark said. "Where are you parked?"

"Sheep River Falls. Near Sandy McNabb," she added when she saw their looks of confusion.

Mark glanced at his friends. "I don't think that's around here."

"Past Turner Valley," she said. "About thirty kilometers."

"We're nowhere near Turner Valley!" Tony said.

"Where are we?" she asked in a whisper.

"Highway 66. Near Bragg Creek."

"Bragg Creek?" Bragg Creek was on the other side of the mountains.

"We'll drive you there," Mark said.

"It's over a hundred kilometers away!" Tony protested.

"How did you get here?" Mark asked.

"I was hiking and lost the trail. I, uh, spent the night in the woods."

Tony snorted. "What a pity you didn't find us last night. I could've warmed you up, baby."

Melissa stepped away as Mark shot his friend a dark look. "I just need a ride to Calgary," she said.

"I'm sure we can manage that," said Mark. "We're just about to pack up and then we'll be on our way." She glanced at the third man, who was now standing with his arms folded across his chest, glowering at her.

Melissa hesitated a moment. "Thank you," she said. "I'll – I'll just wait here." She sat down at the table, shifting uncomfortably as the third man continued to stare at her. After a long moment he disappeared into the tent.

"Don't mind Neil," Mark said. "He's not a morning person."

Tony laughed unpleasantly as he turned away.

Melissa stared at her ruined clothes as the men started dismantling their tent. For the first time since leaving the cabin, she allowed herself to think of Lee and what he'd shown her. She shook her head, still not sure she believed what she'd seen. Shapeshifters, werewolves and vampires – those were all fairy tales. How could someone who seemed so solidly *normal* be something like that! But she'd seen him change right in front of her. She leaned over as a wave of nausea washed over her.

"Ready?" said Mark. She looked up to see that the campsite had been packed up. She followed Mark to his truck and reluctantly slid into the back seat beside Tony.

She screamed when the panther shot out of the trees and landed on the hood.

"What the hell?" shouted Tony as Neil jumped in beside Mark and slammed the door.

The panther snarled, baring its teeth as it paced past the windshield while Mark fumbled with his cell phone. The big cat roared, and the phone fell from his trembling hands. The panther fixed Melissa with a stare, then leaped off the truck.

"Drive, dammit," Tony yelled.

Mark grabbed the gearshift and the vehicle lurched forward, then stalled. He cursed as the snarling face of the panther appeared at Melissa's window, and she scooted back as Tony swore.

"It's a cat, idiot!" Neil shouted. "It can't open doors." The panther dropped away, but a moment later the door swung open and the panther leaped inside, crashing past Melissa's face as it crammed into the small space between her and Tony. Its tail brushed against Tony's face as it butted Melissa with its head.

Tony laughed nervously as he fumbled with the handle

in desperation. "It looks like it wants you, sweetheart," he said. "Out you get." In an instant, the panther was snarling in Tony's face. The man paled and pressed himself against the door, narrowly missing the swiping claws. Turning back, the panther butted Melissa again, and she stumbled from the truck.

"Go!" she heard Tony scream. The wheels spun in the ground, showering leaves and dirt everywhere, then lurched away. Melissa didn't even pause to watch but climbed onto the picnic table, her backpack a shield before her.

"Stay away from me!" The panther stared at her for a moment, then turned and disappeared between the trees. She dropped the backpack and sank to the table, but a moment later she was on full alert as Lee strode through the trees, pulling on his shirt. He grabbed her by the arm and yanked her from the table.

"What are you doing?" she yelled.

"Do you have any idea who those men are?" he shouted. "You ran from me and threw yourself on the mercy of men you don't even know!"

"At least they wouldn't eat me," she said.

He stared down at her, his expression incredulous. "You're such an idiot! I can smell things, Melissa. That man next to you – he wanted you from the moment you set foot in their camp."

"How do you know?"

"I can *smell* things. I could smell his lust from a mile away!"

He grabbed her arm again and yanked her forward and she stumbled after him. "Where are you taking me?" she demanded.

"Back to your car," he said. "Although God knows how

you're going to make it home. But that's your problem, not mine."

"I can't walk all the way back," she said. "And you just lost me my ride."

"My truck's past the trees." He dragged her forward again, and after a few minutes she saw his black truck a short distance away. He opened the passenger door and pushed her in, then slammed it shut after her and climbed into the driver's side. The truck shot forward as he revved the engine, flattening grass and bushes as he drove haphazardly over the hills. His eyes were staring straight ahead and his jaw was clenched in fury. Both hands were on the steering wheel, the knuckles white with anger as he steered the truck unerringly through the brush, and forty-five minutes later they reached the parking lot where she'd left her car. Without a word, he skidded up beside it, and did not look at her when she stepped out. Her feet had just touched the ground when he flung the truck forward and she stumbled back as he roared away in a cloud of dust. Leaning against her car, she dropped her head into her hands, taking great gulps of air as he turned onto the road and roared into the distance.

CHAPTER 14

How Melissa made it home, she couldn't say. Her mind was a blank as she sped along the highway. When she finally arrived home, every muscle was screaming in pain. She stumbled through her doorway and collapsed on the couch, but after a few minutes she made her way to the bathroom and started a bath, adding a large glob of shower gel into the warm water. It swirled around her, at first stinging her wounds, but her tension ebbed as she pushed away all thoughts of the previous thirty-six hours. When the bath cooled, she added more hot water, holding her toes beneath the scalding stream. Slowly, despite her efforts to resist, one thought insisted on seeping through her consciousness.

Lee. Was he prowling around the mountains right now? she wondered. The image of a panther rose in her mind, black and sleek with glossy fur and eyes that shone in the moonlight. She imagined herself running her fingers over the fur, then pushed the image away when Lee's snarling face turned to her. She frowned. How was it even possible that a man could turn into a panther? Or that a panther could be a man? Panthers were dangerous, yet she'd felt more threatened by Tony than she ever had with Lee. Even in his moments of anger, Lee was always in control. She sighed, remembering his fury as he drove her back to her car. Would he have hurt her if she hadn't run off? Deep down she knew the answer, but acknowledging it would mean admitting how foolish her reaction had been. After all, she'd already been attacked by one wild cat. Only an idiot would risk being killed by another. But if Lee really was able to change into a panther – and she could hardly doubt it after seeing it with her own eyes – could he do so at will? And how much of his humanity did he retain while an animal? Was that the reason he kept pushing her away?

She pulled the plug and watched as the water swirled down the drain. She could not think about Lee any longer. Even believing the fairy tale that he could change into a panther did not change anything between them. She limped to her bedroom and pulled on her PJs, then swallowed three painkillers and collapsed into bed.

She managed to drag herself from her bed the next morning, despite a pounding headache and aching muscles. As she bounced with the bus on her way to work, she pulled out her phone and typed Lee a message. *We need to talk,* she wrote. Her finger hovered above the screen as she hesitated for a second, then pressed the SEND button. She stared as the screen went blank, then slowly replaced the phone in her purse.

Somehow she made it through the day, and by the time she dragged herself home, she felt as though Lee's truck had driven over her, repeatedly. She hadn't heard back from him, which didn't really surprise her, but he was never far from her thoughts. She'd done some Google searches during her lunch hour, and every site she read assured her that shapeshifters and other such creatures were nothing more than fantasy. She'd shaken her head. For a fantasy creature, Lee was far more real than he had any right to be. If she ever saw him again, she'd tell him exactly that!

She had just arrived at the office on Wednesday morning when she received a call from Annika.

"My grandchildren stayed with me last night, and one of them has woken with a fever. I'm going to work from home."

"Okay. Anything in particular you need me to do?"

"I'd signed up for a conference on benefit programs this morning. Pat Ramsbottom is presenting. You'll have to go in my place. All the information is on my desk." Melissa heard a cry in the background. "Call me if you need anything," Annika said before the phone went dead.

Melissa found a small folder on Annika's desk with the time and location of the conference printed on top. She glanced at her watch; she was already late. Ten minutes later, she arrived at the nearby venue and made her way to the conference room.

"They've only just started," said a woman at the sign-in desk, who handed Melissa some notes and pushed open the door. She stepped into the room, then stopped with an inward groan. In her haste to get there, she hadn't checked Annika's information about the presenters, but apparently Pat wasn't the only one scheduled to speak that morning, because standing at the front of the room, before an audience of around twenty people, stood Lee. She stood at the door, her hand on the handle, as Lee looked up; he seemed as startled to see her as she felt, but he quickly recovered and smiled sardonically before turning back to the audience.

"A grand entrance by Ms. Hewitt from Mercer Engineering," he said as a ripple of laughter ran through the crowd.

Melissa glared at Lee as she sank into a chair at the back of the room, but he paid her no further attention as he expertly delivered facts and figures. He had discarded his jacket, and wore a dark blue shirt with a tie and a pair of suit pants. He looked so normal – so ordinary – that for a moment Melissa doubted what she'd seen on the weekend. But he paced the room with a feline grace, and beneath his shirt she could see his well-built form, so out of place in a suit. She remembered the snarling panther tattooed on his arm – the beast that lay within him, he'd said, and a shiver crawled up her spine. Lee's green eyes flashed to her for an instant before returning to the crowd.

Melissa barely heard a word of the presentation. She felt like the prey caught in the hypnotizing gaze of the predator. She wanted to run but was frozen in place, and by the time the presentation was finished, it was as though she had been running the entire time. She rose and headed over to the coffee table.

"Ms. Hewitt, is it?" said a voice beside her. She turned to see a middle-aged man smiling at her. "Dan Dobson. I know Annika," he said, blushing slightly. Melissa smiled and shook his hand. "Good presentation, wasn't it? Ah, look, there's Leander now! Lee!" he called, waving him over. Melissa stared at the cup in her hand as Lee headed toward them.

"Dan," he said. "Ms. Hewitt."

Melissa took a sip of her coffee before looking up and meeting his cool gaze. "Annika had to stay with her grandchildren this morning and asked me to come in her place," she said. She cringed at the possibility that he thought she was stalking him.

"Your presentation was as informative as always," Dan cut in.

"Thank you, Dan. I think you'll find the next one even more so. Our partner, Pat Ramsbottom, will be presenting."

"I sent you a message," Melissa said.

"Yes." Lee's tone was icy.

"We need to talk."

Lee looked at Dan with a sigh. "Will you excuse us please, Dan. I just need a quick word with Ms. Hewitt."

"Of course," Dan said, his eyes darting between them before he moved away. Lee walked to the corner of the room as Melissa followed.

"Well?" He turned to face her, but his eyes were on the room behind.

"Why are you so angry with me?" she asked.

He looked at her incredulously. "Why? You ran from me and straight into the arms of danger. After all I've done to protect you."

"You turned into a *panther*. What did you expect me to do?"

"Actually, you reacted exactly as I expected. Which is why we can never be together. You bring out the beast in me." He began to move away but stopped when Melissa grabbed his arm.

"What do you mean?"

"My control slips when I'm with you."

"Is that why you keep pushing me away?"

He looked across the room. "I have to go," he said. "People are waiting to talk to me."

"Please! Don't just walk away. Meet me later. Downstairs at the coffee shop. You can leave when Pat starts presenting." He hesitated, then gave a tight nod before heading back to the other attendees.

Melissa went downstairs a short while later and ordered coffee. When she'd sat down at the back of the conference room, the last thing she had planned to do was corner Lee and demand answers. But seeing him afterward she knew she couldn't let the opportunity slip by. She needed to know exactly what he was. And whether changing into a panther – she still couldn't quite wrap her head around that – was the reason he kept pushing her away. Because for some reason, she had not been able to get Lee from her mind, despite changing employers in an effort to avoid him. She was on her third cup of coffee when Lee strode through the door and headed in her direction. He took a seat across from her.

"Well?"

"What are you, Lee?"

"I told you. I'm a Changer."

"A shapeshifter?"

"Yes. But Changers can only take one form."

"A panther."

"As you saw."

"Why did you show yourself to me?"

He sighed. "I could see you wouldn't let go of the idea that you'd seen a panther. It seemed like the best course of action at the time."

"Is that the only reason?"

He didn't answer at first. "A part of me wanted you to know," he finally said. "So you can understand why it would never work between us."

"Is that why you keep pushing me away?"

He toyed with a packet of sugar. "Yes."

"But only me."

"You're the only one who has an effect on me."

"What do you mean?"

"It doesn't matter. It would never work."

Melissa ran her finger around the edge of her coffee cup. Lee was right – it could never work between them. He was part beast. A vicious predator. Except, not once had she been in danger from him – in fact, he had saved her life a few times. And she'd seen the kind of man he truly was. A man who spent time with Emma, a child he barely knew; a man who could make her laugh, and with whom she could spend hours talking; a man who cared about the loss of her parents. How could she just accept things wouldn't work without even giving it a try?

"Why wouldn't it work?"

"Because of what I am."

"Do you forget who you are when you're an animal?"

"No."

"Then that's not a good enough reason. Unless you really aren't interested in me."

"You're terrified of me."

"I *was* terrified. And can you blame me? You turned into a wild predator without warning."

"You were warned. I told you what I was."

Melissa leaned back in her seat. "And I was supposed to believe you? Because people turn into animals all the time?"

"Okay, I can see it was a bit of a shock, but it still won't work."

"Why not?"

"As I mentioned before, you bring out the worst in me."

"You need to tell me what that means."

Lee sighed. "I've spent years learning to control myself, Melissa. The urge to change is driven by the moon. Just like the tides, the fuller the moon, the stronger the pull on the animal side of my nature. But I can control it. The desire to change is there, but I can resist it, and not change at all. But the more I'm with you, the harder it is to resist. I cannot fight both the moon and you. And when the moon is full – well, you've already seen what it does to me when I'm around you."

"Your eyes?"

"Yes. But that's not all. The night in the cabin, I went into your room to check on you. I wanted to make sure you were warm and comfortable. But you were so beautiful, lying there in my clothes. The moon was full that night, and as I watched you, I changed. I had no thought of doing it – it just happened. And then you woke and saw me. I could smell your fear, and I left."

"You had no control over it?"

"No. That's why I stayed away from you for so long. From the first time I met you, I felt attracted to you. At first I thought I could handle it, but as time went on, I realized that your effect on me was more than I could manage, so I pushed you away. But I let my guard slip when we went to the meeting together. I thought perhaps I had grown stronger, more resistant. I was wrong."

"Does this happen with other women?"

He snorted. "There are no other women, Melissa."

"You've had plenty of girlfriends!"

"Dates. One-night stands. You're the only one I've ever

felt something for, and I pushed you away."

"But why?"

"Are you not listening? I'm an animal. And *you* bring out the beast in me."

"So that's it? You're just going to walk away?"

His jaw clenched. "Yes."

"I see. So what I think doesn't matter. It's all about you?"

"You don't understand."

She leaned forward on the table. "What are you scared of?" she asked softly.

He stared at her for a long moment. "Only you."

"Give us a chance."

"I can't."

"You've never walked away from a challenge before."

He flashed her a bitterly amused grin. "You think you can manipulate me?"

"If you walk away now, you'll never know if it could have worked." She inched her hand forward on the table and touched his. He stared down at it, then slowly wrapped his little finger around hers. The breath caught in her throat as he lifted his gaze to hers.

"I don't know if I can do this," he said.

"You can."

"I – I have to get back to the conference."

"When will I see you?"

"I don't know. I need to think. Away from you." He stood. "Please—" He stopped, then turned and walked away.

Melissa's mind was spinning as she watched Lee stride out the door. What he'd revealed both thrilled and terrified her. He felt something for her, but those feelings brought out the animal in him. It all made sense now – the mood swings and volatility, the way he kept distancing himself from her. She stared at her empty coffee cup. She'd told Lee that she wanted to give their relationship a try, but could she accept both man and beast? It took only a moment to find the answer – of course she could, because the feelings she'd had for Lee had never gone away. She owed it to both of them to see if they could make things work. And because deep inside, she believed that their connection was strong enough to withstand the challenges. She only hoped that Lee believed it too.

Chapter 15

Children's laughter rang through the hospital corridors when Melissa headed through the passages on Friday evening. The kids were in the common room, playing a game that involved whacks, shouting "die" and a lot of noise. She paused at the door.

"Hey, guys!" she called out. She looked at the kids huddled in a group in the middle of the room, some in wheelchairs, some on crutches and some on their hands and knees, as they threw pillows and soft toys onto someone lying on the floor. He turned to look at her, and she caught her breath when she saw it was Lee. Fridays were her visiting nights and he'd avoided Fridays for months, but here he was, at the hospital, on her night. The moment of shock passed, and Melissa leaned against the door to watch in amusement. He peered at her between his arms, raised to cover his head.

"They're playing 'kill the panther,'" he said.

"Kill the panther?" she repeated faintly.

He yelled as one of the kids bonked him with a pillow. "Yep," he shouted. "Emma told them I was Bagheera."

"Huh. I thought Bagheera was the good guy."

"So did I. Imagine my surprise when I discovered they wanted to kill me."

"I'll bet." After a few more moments of watching, she headed to Emma's room. "Hi, Em," she said as she entered. "I heard you set the others on Lee."

"Bagheera," she corrected.

"Ah, yes. Bagheera. I thought he was good."

Emma shook her head solemnly. "I thought so too. But Daddy brought me a book yesterday, and it says panthers are dangerous."

"Hmm. Only those that don't have humans as friends."

"Like Mowgli and Bagheera."

"Yep."

"And you and Lee."

"Like me and – what do you mean?"

"You're Mowgli and Lee's Bagheera. You know, when you read the story."

"Yes, of course," Melissa said faintly. Behind her someone cleared their throat, and she turned to see Lee standing at the doorway, his expression inscrutable.

"Hey kid," he said. He staggered into the room, clutching his chest. "I'm dead."

Emma laughed. "No, you're not."

"I am! I stood no chance against all those kids beating me up."

"Then why are you still talking?"

He clutched his throat. "I'm not," he croaked. "It's just my last words." He fell onto the floor.

"Don't be silly," Emma said. "You're not dead!" She peered over the bed at Lee's fallen form, and Melissa smiled at the concern that grew as Lee remained still. When he finally rolled over to his back and winked at her, her expression cleared. "Told you!"

"You're just too smart for me," Lee said as he rose to his feet. He glanced at the book on her nightstand. "Want me to read to you?"

She shook her head. "Nah. That's Daddy's book. He was reading to me 'bout panthers."

"I heard you telling Mel. But your Dad's right – panthers are dangerous, especially when they're scared."

"Panthers get scared?"

"Yep. They're scared of people. But if you give them a chance to keep away, they will."

"How do you do that?"

"Just let them know you're coming." He glanced at Melissa. "They'll keep their distance."

"'Kay. Grandma's coming to visit tomorrow."

Melissa smiled. "That's wonderful, Em."

"She gets sad sometimes, and then she goes home. I hope she won't get sad this time."

"Me too," she said. "So what do you want to do?"

"Color!" She produced a coloring book from the pile on the table. "Daddy bringed me a new one."

"Okay." Melissa sat on the bed as Emma opened the book to a picture of a girl with a kite, while Lee sat down in the corner. By the time the picture was done, Emma was yawning.

"You must get some sleep so you're not tired when your Grandma comes," Melissa said.

Emma lay down. "'Kay. I'm going home soon."

"You are?"

"Uh-huh. Pamela told Daddy I could go home real soon. Do you think that's why Grandma gets sad?"

"No, Em. I think your Grandma loves you very much and will be very glad when you're home."

Emma wrapped her arms around Melissa's neck. "Love you, Mel."

"I love you too, Em."

"Goodnight, kiddo," Lee said. He glanced at Melissa, and together they left the room. They walked in silence down the corridor, but Lee stopped as they neared the cafeteria.

"Want to grab a coffee? There are some benches outside – we can sit and talk."

The hospital was built on a ridge overlooking the city with the mountains in the distance, and benches had been placed along the edge of the ridge. It was here that Melissa and Lee headed, coffees in hand.

"I've been thinking about what you said," Lee said as they walked.

"And?"

"I don't think I can stay away from you."

"Is that why you showed up tonight? Because you knew I'd be here?" She bit her lip, wondering if her words sounded flippant. "You stayed away before."

"I did," Lee said, "but that was before you knew what I was. But now you know, and that changes everything."

"Then why were you so hesitant on Wednesday?"

"I'm sorry about that. I was still annoyed with you for running to strangers for protection. And I needed time to think."

"So you're willing to give it a try?" Melissa said. They reached the bench and sat down.

"I think I am – with some caveats."

"Which are?"

"I cannot promise anything, Mel. This is—" He glanced at the mountains. "I've never done this before."

"Me either," she said. He glanced at her with a wry grin.

"I can't have you seeing me while I'm changing, or while I'm a panther."

"But—"

"No. Never." Lee held up a hand. "And I can't be around you when the moon's full."

"Why not?"

"I told you before. I can't stop myself from changing when I'm with you."

"What's wrong with that?"

Lee sighed. "You ran away, Mel. Remember? Straight to some strange men."

"It was a shock."

"I know. And you've had time to get used to the idea. But knowing something will happen and experiencing it are two different things."

"You're scared."

"Didn't you hear me tell Emma that panthers are scared of people?"

"I didn't think you were scared of anything."

"Just you," he whispered.

"Okay," she said. "No panthers. For now."

"One step at a time, Mel."

"Does the first step involve kissing me?"

He smiled. "Oh, yes."

"Anything else?" she asked hopefully.

"You're very greedy." He bent down, and she could feel his breath on her lips. "One step at a time." His lips descended to hers as he cupped her face, and she leaned into him as she kissed him back.

They spent every free moment together over the next few weeks. They went to the movies, and hiked in the mountains. She dragged him shopping with her, and when Lee took Melissa out for dinner, she shook her head in amazement at the amount of food he consumed – always meat, and always very, very rare. They visited Emma together, and when she saw Lee holding Melissa's hand, she clapped. Melissa learned from Pamela that Emma was due to be discharged in a few weeks.

"She's been making terrific progress, and it's hard on her dad that she's so far away. The local hospital will take over her care."

"Will she be all right?"

Pamela sighed. "She's young and resilient. I just hope her father can give her what she needs."

Melissa agreed.

They were leaving the hospital one evening when Lee turned to her. "How about a trip to the zoo?"

"I wouldn't have thought you'd like zoos much."

"I don't. Too many tasty things to eat!"

Melissa looked at him in shock, and he smiled. "I'm just teasing. Sort of." He smirked. "But you're right, I'm not all that fond of zoos. They make me claustrophobic."

"So why do you go?"

"I like to visit the big cats. I tell them what's happening in the outside world."

"Seriously?"

"No. They don't really care." Melissa poked him in the ribs. "Actually, it helps me put things in perspective. It can be confusing when you know you don't quite fit into the human world." He snorted softly. "So, you up for a trip to the zoo?"

"Sure."

They arrived shortly after opening the next morning, and Melissa followed Lee as he headed past the Canadian Wilds and dinosaurs. He veered to the right and led her to a large enclosure where a tiger could be seen lounging on the ground.

"I come here to remind myself of who I am," he said.

"And who are you?"

He stared at the tiger for a long moment. "I'm not like him. His concerns only extend to his immediate needs. He doesn't think about tomorrow, nor does he consider solutions to problems. He knows what he needs, and seeks to meet those needs." He turned to Melissa. "But I'm also not like you," he said. "I can change into a predator at will, and feel the way a cat feels. I know his primal mind."

"You can change at will?"

"Yes. And I can usually resist. The exception is when I'm with you and the moon is full. You have such a strong pull on me, I can't prevent the change. And the more I'm with you, the stronger your pull."

"You said that when you're a panther, you know what you are."

"Yes. I retain my human intellect, although my animal instincts become stronger. I know who people are, can name them in my mind, and can understand when they speak, even though I cannot reply."

Melissa thought about that for a moment. "So how did you come to be like this?"

"All I know are the legends and folk tales, handed down from generation to generation, which say that we belong to a tribe of people that existed over a thousand years ago." Lee leaned against the railing, facing her.

"They lived in a small area where France, Italy and Switzerland intersect, and their lands were constantly being invaded – first by Romans, and later by Vikings. The Roman invaders wanted power and control, and once they achieved those aims, they left the people to themselves. The Vikings were far more brutal. They wanted total dominance. You've heard about berserkers, right? They didn't just conquer their enemies – they set out to completely annihilate them. It was around this time that the first of my ancestors changed into a panther.

"Legends say that the first Changer was a man named Osman – the divine protector. He was the tribal chief, and it was his duty to protect the people. He was also deeply spiritual, and one morning he called his people together and told them he'd received a vision the night before, in which an angel promised him that he'd receive divine strength and protection at the next full moon. The night of the next full moon, Osman slept outside, surrounded by ten of his bravest men. When they awoke, their leader was gone and a panther lay in his place. They were terrified, of course, but he did nothing to harm them. Instead, he disappeared into the trees, and that night he attacked the enemy camp. Now fighting soldiers is one thing, but having a powerful animal slinking through your camp is quite another, and after a few nights of this, the remaining enemy warriors fled, certain they were being attacked by a dark force. The next morning Osman returned to the village as though nothing had happened."

"But he was still able to change?"

"He was in his bed beside his wife at the next full moon. He mated with her, and—"

"What? As a panther?"

"Yes."

"Wow. What happened next?"

"She got pregnant and they had a son. He carried the panther gene, and ever since, it has been passed through the male line."

"What about the daughters?"

"Osman sent his youngest daughter to a convent as thanks for divine protection."

Melissa scoffed. "Typical."

Lee smiled. "Daughters are a force to be feared."

"Did the enemy ever return?"

"The village was often under attack because of its strategic location. But Osman and his descendants were able to defend the villagers. And later, they joined William the Conqueror when he defeated the English."

"The Normans hardly needed protection," Melissa protested. "They should have joined the English."

Lee shrugged. "Maybe. We all choose our sides." Melissa frowned, and he leaned closer. "I'll always protect your side," he said, brushing his lips against hers. Melissa slipped her arms around his waist.

"Always?" she said.

"Mmm. Always." She returned the kiss, then drew away when she heard people approaching.

"Look at the tiger, Mommy," shouted a little boy.

Lee took Melissa's hand and drew her away.

"So your father and brother are also Changers?" Melissa asked as they walked between the pens.

"No. Not every male receives the gene. And sometimes it skips a generation. My grandfather was a Changer, but my father isn't. My grandfather's the one who taught me the legends. He had a cousin who was also a Changer, but he died without any children. Maybe there are others, but I don't know them."

They headed toward the African Savannah, where lions lay in the grass. "So can you speak to wild cats?" Melissa asked.

"They don't have much to say. Eat, defend, mate is the sum total of their interests."

"Hmm," Melissa said with a grin. "Sounds a lot like you."

"What do you mean?" Lee feigned offense. "I haven't mentioned mating once!"

"That's not my fault," she said. Lee had been very serious about "one step at a time."

He gave her a tug and she fell against his chest. "I think about a lot more than just 'mate,'" he whispered into her hair. "Like, I want to hold you, and feel you, and kiss you till you can't stand it anymore. I want to run my fingers through your hair, and breathe in your scent." He brought his mouth to hers, and Melissa forgot all else but the feel of his hands roaming her back and his lips against hers.

Chapter 16

"You know it's Thanksgiving next weekend?" Lee said to Melissa a few days later.

"Already?"

"It's almost October. Are you planning to celebrate American Thanksgiving instead of Canadian this year?"

She poked him in the side. "Of course not! I just can't believe how time has flown."

"My parents say that all the time," Lee said. "You must be getting old. Speaking of family, my brother is coming to visit."

Melissa raised her eyebrows. "How does getting old remind you of your brother?"

"It doesn't. But he'll be here for Thanksgiving. We'll do it at my place, and I'll cook."

"You'll cook Thanksgiving dinner? You do know we need more than just meat."

"Bring a salad."

"And pumpkin pie?"

"Yes. I do like pumpkin pie."

"You know it's made with pumpkin?"

"Add lots of spices," he said, "and maybe a little ground beef?"

"Ugh, no!"

"Okay, okay," he said, holding his hands out in surrender. "Just spices."

Lee's apartment was a penthouse suite, with floor-to-ceiling windows and views to both the east and west. The first time Melissa had seen it, she'd been amazed.

"This must have cost a fortune," she'd remarked.

"My grandfather left my brother and me some money. I used my share to invest in property."

"It's incredible. Do you sit and stare at the mountains?"

"Or the moon."

Her mind was on that conversation as she stepped out of the elevator into Lee's apartment on Thanksgiving Sunday. The elevator opened directly into the apartment, and both a key and a code were needed to access the penthouse suite. Lee had given her both when he'd first taken her there. He was waiting for her as the doors slid open, and he greeted her with a kiss before stepping back.

"Mel, this is my brother, Caleb." Melissa smiled at the young man standing a few paces behind Lee. Although he was younger than Lee by six years, it was clear they were brothers with their dark looks and similar height, but Caleb's eyes were dark brown and his hair hung messily around his neck.

"Nice to meet you, Melissa. It's great to finally meet one of Lee's girlfriends!"

"Caleb!" Lee said warningly. He shot his brother a meaningful glance, then turned to Melissa. "The turkey's on the barbecue and the meat's in the oven."

"Sounds delicious," Caleb said. "Are there any vegetables?"

Lee lifted his eyebrows in Melissa's direction. "I think Mel brought a salad."

"I brought salad, scalloped potatoes and pumpkin pie." She glanced at Caleb. "They're in my car. Want to help me bring them up?"

"Sure." He stepped into the elevator behind her. "So Lee's told you about his pantherism?" Caleb said as they rode down to the parking lot.

"Pantherism?"

The younger man grinned. "Changing tendencies? Feline qualities?"

Melissa laughed. "Yes."

"You know he's never told anyone else. Not even his friends growing up. Not that he was really close to anyone. But it's this big family secret. No one talks about it."

"But he must have talked to you when you were kids?"

Caleb shook his head. "Nope. I didn't know about it till I was eleven." They left the elevator and he followed her to her car. "I kinda suspected before then, though."

"How did you know?" She opened her trunk and handed him a basket.

He shrugged. "It was just a feeling. I used to tell my friends that I knew a panther. Even then, I knew better than to say it was my brother."

"Did they believe you?"

Caleb laughed. "No, of course not. But there was this one kid, Craig, who was always messing with me. So one day after school he was having a go at me and I told him

I'd set the panther on him. He laughed and threw my backpack over the wall, which made me really mad. I threw myself at him, but this kid was massive, and he flung me to the ground. Just then we both heard a growl, and we saw a huge black panther stalking towards us. Lee was picking me up from school that day, see? He'd just got his driver's license a few weeks before. Anyway, I just knew it was Lee, so I turned to Craig, probably with the smuggest expression ever!"

"What did he do?"

"He peed his pants, then ran away. He never bothered me again."

Melissa laughed. "I'll bet." They headed back to the elevator, and Melissa keyed in the code. "So that's how you found out about Lee?"

"Yep. He took me into the woods and showed me how he could change. And he made me promise not to tell anyone. Not even our parents."

"Why not?"

Caleb's brown eyes were intense. "You'll have to ask him that."

The elevator opened in Lees's apartment, and he stepped from the kitchen. He caught his brother's eye with a frown, but Caleb just shrugged. "You already told her," he said.

"I did."

Melissa glanced between them. "You heard us?" Her words came out with a gasp.

"Of course. Cats have the best hearing range of all animals."

"You could hear us in the parking garage?"

"I *was* listening," Lee admitted.

"Wow." She sat on the couch as Caleb headed into the

kitchen with the basket. Lee sat beside her and grazed his nose up her cheek, breathing her in.

"You're okay?" he whispered.

"Yes."

"Mel, I'd never—"

"Shhh," she said. "I know. It's a surprise, that's all. I haven't really thought about how different you are when you're human." She looked at him. "Are all your senses like that?"

"More acute? I guess so. Caleb and I did some experiments once, and my hearing and smell are infinitely better than humans', but my sight is pretty much the same, until I change. Same for touch. When I change, I can sense things a human can't, but I lose that in human form. As for taste, I don't think I taste quite as much as you. I can't tell the difference between peaches and plums, or spinach and lettuce."

"So when you smelled me just now?"

"I scented your emotions as soon as you realized I'd heard you, and I knew you were surprised, but not scared. I just wanted to smell your sweet fragrance."

"That's crazy," she said with a shaky laugh.

"Not really. Everyone has their own unique scent. Yours is sweet and spicy all at once." He pulled her onto his lap and kissed her. "I might not be able to taste much," he whispered a few moments later, "but I like the way you feel when I kiss you. Hot and sexy with the most gorgeous tongue." She felt herself blush, and he cupped her face in his hands and kissed her again. "Mmm, wonderful," he murmured.

A few more minutes passed before Melissa finally pulled away and, a little lightheaded, made her way to the kitchen. She heated the scalloped potatoes she'd prepared beforehand and tossed the salad as Lee finished preparing his dishes, and a short while later they were ready to eat. The smell of succulent roasted turkey, beef roast and ham drifted through the air. Caleb and Melissa shared amused glances as they sat down.

"You sure there's enough to eat, Leander?" Caleb said as he helped himself to some potatoes. He glanced at Melissa. "Do you know Leander means lion man?"

"And Caleb means bold, a synonym for brat," Lee quickly rejoined.

"Lion man?" Melissa said. "How appropriate. Did your parents know that when they named you?"

"Yes. It's been passed down through generations of Garretts. Now let's eat."

By the time the meal was done, the ham and beef were finished, and only a small amount of turkey remained. Melissa eyed the empty dishes. "You can't possible have space for anything else."

"I will in a few minutes," Lee said.

"Where do you fit it all?"

He patted his stomach. "I've told you before, I have a very fast metabolism," he said. "You can heat up the pie."

"Seriously," she said with a laugh. She headed to the kitchen and returned a few minutes later.

Lee tucked in with gusto. "It's delicious," he said between mouthfuls.

"Really?"

He glanced at Caleb, who nodded. "I think so," Lee said. "I can taste the spices."

Melissa rolled her eyes. "I can see my cooking skills will be completely wasted on you. I might as well just carve up a cow and feed you the pieces raw."

"You could. I won't mind."

Caleb laughed. "Don't worry – I enjoyed your pie, Mel."

"Thank you, Caleb," she said primly.

She rose and started clearing the dishes from the table, but Lee was quicker. "I'll do that," he said. "You just sit."

"But you did the meal," she protested.

"And now I'll do the cleaning. I'll bring you a glass of wine and you can enjoy the view."

Melissa accepted the glass of wine and walked to the massive glass wall. The moon hung over the horizon, half full. She was still at the window when Lee came up behind her and wrapped his arms around her waist. "I have to go to Toronto on Wednesday," he said.

She leaned against him. "Does this have anything to do with the full moon?"

"Maybe," he said, dropping his mouth to her neck. She shivered and turned in his arms. His green eyes held hers and she lifted her fingers to his brows.

"Your eyes are lighter again," she said.

"Only when I'm with you."

"Do you see differently when they lighten?"

"A little. Some colors are not as clear as others, but I see better than you in the dark."

"So when will you be back?"

He lifted his gaze to the window. "End of the week. I'll go to the cabin when I get back."

"I could come with you," she said.

His demeanor darkened. "No. We talked about this, Mel."

"I know," she said with a sigh. "I just don't want you to go."

"I must."

"For now." She wrapped her hands around his neck

and pulled his face to hers. He resisted for a moment, then with a sigh, leaned closer and returned her kiss.

Melissa was on her way to work on Tuesday morning when she received a text message from Cynthia: *Coffee sometime?*

Sure, she texted back. As Melissa bounced around on the bus, they arranged a time and place to meet later that morning. Melissa arrived at the coffee shop a few minutes after ten to find Cynthia was already waiting.

"Hey, Mel," she said. "How's the new job going?"

"Great! I have to thank you again. I owe you big time."

"Quigley Ramsbottom must have been upset to lose you."

Melissa shrugged. "They'll get over it. How's married life?"

"Good. For the most part, that is," she added with a sigh. "Richard wants me to go hunting with him next weekend."

"Hunting. That's kind of a … man thing."

"He doesn't want me to *hunt*, just go with him for the weekend. His friend Mike has a new girlfriend, and he's insisting she comes along. So now Richard wants me to go too."

"So are you going?"

Cynthia moaned and dropped her head in her hands. "I don't think I have a choice. And I'll have to hang out with this Lesley woman." She lifted her head. "I can't imagine why she'd want to go out with them – she really isn't the outdoors type. Actually, I think she's just jealous of Mike spending time with anyone other than her."

"Sounds like you'll have a great time," Melissa said, grinning when Cynthia grimaced.

"Ugh! If it was anyone else … you! You've got to come with me."

"No way. You know me. I'm really not a fan of hunting."

"*We* won't be hunting! Come on, Mel. It'll be fun. You love hiking and being outdoors. It will be far more fun with you there. What else are you doing next weekend?"

"I'll be …" Melissa stopped. Lee had made it clear he didn't want to see her. And Cynthia wasn't suggesting that *they* actually go hunting. "You know what?" Maybe I will come. It'll be fun hanging out with you."

"Really? That's fantastic! Richard's already booked a cabin up near Sundre. It's got four bedrooms, so there'll be plenty of space. You can drive with us – we'll leave after work on Friday."

"You've got to be kidding me," Lee said when Melissa told him her plans. They were spending the evening in his penthouse before he flew to Toronto the next day. "You're going out with a hunting party? What, exactly, do they plan to hunt?"

"Deer, mainly. Not," she quickly added, "trophy hunting. No cougars, or, uh, anything like that."

He smirked. "Tell them elk has the best flavor."

"Elk, hmm? And will you be hunting?"

Lee wrapped his arm around her and pulled her close. "I'm always on the hunt," he whispered into her ear. She shivered slightly.

"What's it like?"

"Hunting?" He gave a slight shrug. "Primal."

"Do you enjoy it?"

"I don't know that *enjoy* is quite the right word. I have a goal in mind, and I pursue that goal single-mindedly."

"And when you catch your prey?"

"What about it?"

"How does it make you feel?"

He left the couch and paced the room. "Why are you asking me this?"

"I want to know."

He turned his gaze on her, and she was taken aback at the bitterness in his expression. "You want to know what it feels like to kill? Whether the taste of blood excites me?" He continued his pacing. "Fine! It does." He stopped behind the couch, and she jumped when his nose skimmed her ear. "I follow the scent of my prey," he said, his voice low. "At first they're unaware of the predator stalking them, but then I can smell their fear." His lips slid down her neck. "It's exciting, knowing I have the power over life and death. As soon as I'm close enough, I go for the kill. The animal always tries to run, but I'm faster." He grazed his teeth over her shoulder. "I go for the neck. One blow will break the spinal column. Death is swift." She shivered as he stepped away and moved to the front of the couch. He leaned down, placing his hands on either side of her head. His pupils were growing, swallowing the whites of his eyes in a sea of green. His lips curled sardonically. "I use my teeth to rip apart the flesh. It's still warm and tastes – wonderful." He brought his lips to her ear again. "Is that what you want to hear, Melissa? What an animal I am?"

A slice of fear flashed through her, he pulled away with a sardonic laugh. He turned to the window and crossed his arms over his chest as he stared out into the night. Melissa watched him for a moment, then slipped from the couch and approached him. Placing her head against his back, she slid her arms around his waist. His body was taut, his muscles straining against his shirt as he remained motionless. Keeping her hands on his body, she moved around to face him. He was staring out the window, but when she lifted her hand to his face, he dropped his bright green gaze to hers. Her hands slid around his neck, and she brought her lips to his. He stood frozen for a moment, and then his arms wrapped around her and he pushed her against the glass wall. Pressing himself against her, he returned the kiss. It wasn't gentle, but filled with savage intensity and she pressed her fingers into his skull as she drew him closer, her fingers burying in the knot of hair on his crown. He broke the kiss a moment later and stood with his forehead against hers.

"Mel – I'm sorry."

"There's nothing to be sorry for," she whispered. "Don't hide yourself from me."

"You were scared."

"Only for a moment. I was also" – she dropped her eyes with a blush – "a little turned on."

He pulled away, and she sneaked a quick peek at his face. He was smiling curiously. "You were?" he said.

She pushed him away and headed back to the couch. He caught her by the arm and, turning her to face him, brought his lips to hers for another kiss.

Lee left first thing Wednesday morning, and that evening Melissa went to the hospital to visit Emma since she wouldn't make her usual Friday date. She walked into her room to see a man she didn't know standing at the child's bedside.

"Mel," Emma cried out.

"Melissa?" the man said. "I'm John. Emma's dad."

Melissa shook the outstretched hand. It was worn and calloused – the hand of a farmer. "I'm so sorry for your loss," she said. John's eyes clouded for a moment.

"Thank you. And thank you for all you've done for Emma. I'm taking her home at the end of the week, so I'm glad I got the chance to thank you in person."

"Where's Lee?" Emma demanded.

"He had to go to Toronto. I know he'll be sad he couldn't say goodbye."

"You didn't fighted?"

"No, we didn't fight," she said with an embarrassed glance at John.

"If you're ever down Lethbridge way, you must stop by for a visit." John glanced at his daughter. "I'm sure Emma would love to see you."

"Yes! Yes," Emma shouted, clapping her hands. "Say you'll visit."

"Of course I will."

"I'll leave you two while I go find some coffee downstairs," John said. "Can I get you anything, Melissa?"

"I'm fine, thank you," she said as John exited the room. Melissa climbed onto the bed with Emma. "So what we doing this evening?"

"Daddy brought me a puzzle. Wanna do it with me?"

"Sure." Melissa brought the rolling table forward and cleared the books from the surface. The puzzle had a picture of two kittens playing with a ball of string, and Melissa nudged the correct pieces Emma's way as the girl screwed her eyes in concentration. John was back before they were done and he settled himself on the chair in the corner with his coffee and phone. Emma grinned triumphantly as she placed the last piece.

"Look, I finished it," she crowed.

"You sure did." Melissa wrapped her arm around the girl's shoulder. "I'm going to miss you, Em, but I'm really glad you're going home."

"Me too. Promise you'll visit?"

"I promise," Melissa said, kissing her on the forehead before climbing off the bed. "I'll see you soon."

"'Kay." Emma leaned back against her pillow. "Love you, Mel."

"I love you too," Melissa said.

CHAPTER 17

Cynthia and Richard picked Melissa up at her apartment after work on Friday.

"There's been a change of plans," Cynthia said as Melissa slid into the back seat of Richard's truck. "Richard heard that the hunting's been good in the Sheep River Valley. We're heading there instead."

"I thought everything was booked for Sundre?"

"I was able to cancel and found a place in Turner Valley where we can all stay," Richard said.

"I hope you don't mind sleeping on a sleeper couch," Cynthia said. "He could only find something with two rooms."

Melissa sighed inwardly. "That's fine," she said brightly.

"Mike and Lesley will meet us there."

The cabins lay beyond the town of Turner Valley,

deeper into the mountains, and an hour and a half later Richard stopped outside a red-roofed structure. A thin layer of snow lay on the ground and hung on the branches of the spruces that stood outside.

"This is it," Richard said, glancing over at Cynthia. "Mike hasn't arrived yet."

"Ha! Lesley's probably still packing."

"Be nice," Richard said. "Mike's really into her."

"I know, I know." Cynthia turned to Melissa. "Let's go check it out."

The cabin was built from logs, much like Lee's, with a large front room that led to a kitchen. A narrow staircase led upstairs to the two bedrooms.

"Not bad," Cynthia said.

She and Melissa carried their cases inside, then returned for the crates of food that Cynthia had brought, while Richard carefully unloaded his hunting equipment. Once assured that his guns were safe, he started a fire in the wood stove that stood in the corner of the living room. It was roaring by the time they heard another vehicle pulling up outside.

"Must be Mike," Richard said, going outside to meet his friend.

A moment later a woman's voice drifted through the open door. "This place looks so primitive."

"I don't know, Lesley," a male voice replied. "Not bad compared to some of the places Richard and I have stayed in."

Lesley entered the cabin a moment later and swept an appraising glance around the room before coming to rest on Cynthia.

"Cynthia! Why didn't you tell Richard to find someplace nicer?"

"Lesley, this is my friend, Melissa," Cynthia said, waving a hand in Melissa's direction. Lesley gave Melissa a cursory glance then looked into the kitchen.

"Good God," she said, "we have to cook?" She turned to the man who'd had just entered behind her. "You didn't tell me we'd have to work, Mike. I thought this was a holiday!"

"Come on, Les," he said, "it'll be fun." He looked at Cynthia. "Hi Cynth. Is this your friend?"

Cynthia introduced them and said, "Why don't you check out the bedrooms? Yours is the second one. And please take off your boots."

Lesley glared at Cynthia, but after a moment sat on the stairs and tugged off her three-inch heeled boots, which she threw onto the floor. "Happy?" she said.

"I'm so glad you're here," Cynthia whispered to Melissa as Lesley made her way up the stairs.

Melissa was up early the next morning, along with Cynthia, Richard and Mike.

"What's your sister up to these days?" Mike asked as he poured some cereal into a bowl.

"Which one? Rheagan? Last I heard she was protesting a pipeline in British Columbia. And back in the summer, she was doing demonstrations with PETA."

"What about her studies?"

Richard grimaced. "She's dropped out to focus on 'more important work.'" He did an air quote. "Mom and Dad are furious."

Mike grinned. "I'll bet. She must love that you go hunting."

"Don't even get me started on that! She keeps sending me emails with videos of animal cruelty. What does she think I do? Torture the animal to death?"

Mike laughed. "You've got to say this for Rheagan – she keeps life interesting."

"But she does have a point," Melissa said. "Hunting does seem pretty cruel."

"Depends on the hunter," Richard replied. "I'm very careful, and only hunt animals we can use for meat. Besides, I like getting into nature – there's nothing more natural than man providing for himself."

Melissa was silent. Before Lee, she'd had a vague idea that she didn't agree with hunting, but beyond that hadn't given it much thought. Lee, of course, hunted, although he could survive on human food. Did that make him cruel? Or was he following his instinct? Was it kinder to raise cattle in sheds only to slaughter them? She was pulled from her thoughts as the men rose from the table.

"We're on our way," Richard said. He dropped a kiss on Cynthia's forehead. "Have fun." They were out the door a moment later, guns over their shoulders.

It was late morning when Lesley finally made an appearance.

"That's the worst bed I've ever slept on," she said as she made her way down the stairs. She glanced around the room. "Where are the boys?"

"They left hours ago," Cynthia said.

"Oh." She frowned.

"We've been waiting for you to get up," Melissa said. "We thought we could go into Turner Valley for lunch, then browse a little."

"Shopping in Turner Valley. Wow, what fun."

"You can stay here if you want," Cynthia said. "Melissa and I will go."

Lesley shuddered. "Stay here alone? No, thank you. I'd rather hang out with you in Turner Valley than stay here."

She made a sweeping gesture with her hand. "This place doesn't even have a proper Internet connection."

"I've heard there's free wifi at some of the restaurants," Melissa said.

"Then what are we waiting for?"

The three women piled into Richard's pickup a half-hour later. The snowfall had created a thin layer of sludgy mud on the road that sprayed onto the truck as they drove. They reached the single main road a short while later and pulled into a parking space outside a restaurant.

After a homey lunch, during which Lesley caught up on her texting, they spent the next hour browsing the stores. Lesley lifted items gingerly, before quickly replacing them with distaste. After a few minutes in the art gallery, which Lesley declared to be dull and provincial, they drove to the next town, browsing for another few hours. Melissa and Cynthia left Lesley sitting at a coffee shop checking her emails while they strolled through the town. It was almost dark when they arrived back at the cabin to see that the men had beaten them back.

"How was the hunting?" Cynthia asked as they entered the cabin. The two men were in the kitchen, scrubbing down their arms.

"Great!" Richard said. "We bagged a mule deer and already have it packed on ice. We want to go out again in the morning before we head back to Calgary."

"Seriously?" said Lesley, coming up behind them. "Please tell me I don't have to stay in this place another day."

"Come on, baby," Mike said, his voice cajoling. "It's great out here in the fresh mountain air. Didn't you have fun today?"

"Fun? Have you seen the towns around here? You

didn't tell me we were staying two whole days."

"We'll leave by lunchtime, I promise."

"Fine." She put her hands on his chest. "You'll have to make it up to me," she simpered.

"You know I will, baby." He bent to kiss her. She turned her face away sulkily, but when he wrapped his arms around her, she allowed herself to be kissed.

Melissa went to the kitchen. "Coffee anyone?" she called.

There was no TV in the cabin, and Cynthia, Richard and Melissa spent the evening playing games while Mike and Lesley disappeared upstairs. The cabin had been solidly built, but even so, they could hear the bed creaking above them. Two bottles of wine later, Richard and Cynthia went upstairs, giggling as they climbed the stairs, while Melissa pulled out the sleeper couch. She checked her phone, but there was nothing from Lee. His cabin was just a few miles away – did he realize how close she was? She closed her eyes and imagined the huge panther lying beside her, his fur brushing her skin.

She woke the next morning to the smell of coffee, and went to the kitchen to find Cynthia already up and dressed.

"Morning, sleepyhead," she said.

Melissa glanced at the clock. "It's only seven o'clock."

"Coffee?" Cynthia asked with a grin.

"Absolutely."

Mike and Richard had already left to go hunting, apparently creeping past Melissa as she slept. "I made sure you were properly covered," Cynthia said with a smirk.

Melissa retrieved her clothes and went to the bathroom to change, where she looked at her clothes with a frown. She hadn't paid attention to what she was grabbing when she packed on Friday, and everything she'd brought was either black or brown – even her jacket hanging at the front door. She got dressed and examined herself in the mirror. A bit dull, but passable she thought, as she pulled her hair into a messy ponytail. When she came out, she was surprised to see that Lesley was already up.

"It's all Mike's fault," she complained. "He woke me up when he got out of bed, and I couldn't go back to sleep."

"Oh well," Cynthia said. "We thought we'd do some hiking, so at least we can make an early start."

"Hiking?" Lesley said, her face aghast.

"It'll be fun. I brought my DSLR camera, and I'm hoping I can get some good shots. But you could stay here, if you want."

"And do what?"

Cynthia shrugged. "Read?"

"A puzzle?" Melissa said.

"God, you two are so boring." Lesley looked disgusted. "Fine. I'll come with you, but only because there's nothing better to do."

"I hope you have some proper hiking boots," Melissa said.

"There's nothing wrong with my boots," Lesley said before turning on her heel and disappearing back upstairs.

"I don't think you need to worry about her wanting to go hunting with Mike again," Melissa said.

"No. I think this trip's cured her of that."

They left a little after nine, and Melissa smiled in amusement at Lesley's three inch heels as she climbed awkwardly into the truck.

The first trailhead they passed was closed for the winter, but the second was open, and Cynthia guided the truck into a parking spot. Theirs was the only vehicle in the lot.

"This *is* just a short walk?" Lesley asked as they got out of the truck.

"About eight kilometers round trip," Melissa said. "Will take about a couple of hours."

"Couple of hours? You can't be serious!"

"You could wait in the truck," Cynthia said.

She glared at the two women. "Fine! I'll come," she grumbled.

"Lesley, seriously, what did you expect when you came to the mountains?" Melissa asked as they started on the trail.

"I thought we'd stay in a hotel. You know, like Banff Park Lodge."

Cynthia laughed. "It's a *hunting* trip."

"Yeah. Thanks. Got that," Lesley snapped.

The first hundred meters of the trail were muddy, and they skirted the edges of the path, but the ground soon became firmer as they went deeper between the trees.

"Are you sure we won't run into bears?" Lesley asked as she checked her shoulder nervously.

"If we stay together, we'll be fine," Melissa assured her. "I'm more worried about cougars."

Lesley stopped. "Cougars? I'm not going anywhere if there are cougars around."

"They won't attack a group of us," Cynthia said. She looked at Melissa. "Will they?"

"I don't think so. Still, it's a good idea to have a weapon, just in case."

"Weapon?" Lesley said.

"Yes. Like a stick. But don't worry, we'll be fine."

"Well, you're the cougar expert," Cynthia said.

"Why's that?" Lesley asked.

"She was attacked by a cougar in the summer."

"Really, it was nothing," Melissa said.

"Nothing!" Cynthia scoffed. "How many stitches did you need?"

"A few."

"What happened?" Lesley asked.

"It attacked me unawares, and chewed on my arm a bit. It's all good now."

"How awful! And I'm not supposed to be scared? Shit!"

No one responded.

The trail was a well-worn path that led through the trees, switchbacking up a steep slope until it rose above the tree line. In the distance was the river, glittering as it wound through the valley below. The path followed along the ridge on the other side before once more descending into woods and looping back to the parking lot. The air was quiet as they walked, except for the occasional chirping of chickadees and sparrows that flitted between the branches. More than once Melissa had the feeling they were being watched, and she peered through the trees, searching for green eyes and a large black cat, but she saw nothing. They stopped after an hour beside the bank of a small stream, and Lesley collapsed onto a rock.

"My legs are aching," she complained.

"You're building your calves," Cynthia said, dropping down beside her. "Besides, isn't it worth it to be out here in nature?"

"I can think of a few other things I'd rather be doing."

Leaving the path, Cynthia approached the stream and knelt to take a photo of ice clinging to the bank. "Why don't you continue on," she said to Melissa. "I don't think Lesley can go any farther. I'll stay with her and take some photos."

"You sure?"

"Yes, go." Cynthia dropped to her stomach and adjusted her lens.

"Okay. I won't go far."

"Take all the time you want," Lesley said, closing her eyes and lifting her face to the weak rays of sun filtering through the trees.

Melissa continued along the path, leaving the others behind. She couldn't shake the feeling that Lee was close by, maybe even watching her now. She peered between the trees, and in the distance saw a movement of black shadow. Leaving the path, she headed into the forest, but when she reached the place she thought she'd seen him, she realized it was just the blackened trunk of a fallen tree. This deep in the woods, all was silent and still, and she continued forward, enticed by the calm and serenity. Little snow was on the ground, and in a few places some plants were still clinging tenaciously to life before the onslaught of winter. A large web, strung between some trees, caught her eye, and she twisted between huge, gnarled trunks to get a better view. A few rays of sunshine filtered between the branches, making the web sparkle like spun glass. She drew a little closer, searching for a spider, just as the air was ripped by an explosion of sound. The blast of a gun, the roar of a panther, her own terrified scream as powerful legs covered in black fur wrapped around her and sent her flying. She landed on the ground with a heavy thud, the huge black form draped heavily over her. Awkwardly, the panther rolled off her and dropped to her side.

She lay stunned for a moment, her hand buried in his fur, until she felt the stickiness between her fingers. She rose to her knees and gasped when she saw the open wound in his side.

"Lee!" she cried. "Lee, you've been shot!"

"Get away, Melissa," someone shouted behind her. "You could get hurt!"

Melissa ignored the voice as she looked at the wounded animal. "Lee," she said again, her voice growing more frantic, "please, Lee, look at me."

Behind her came another shout. "Get away, Mel. It's dangerous!" She spun to see Richard and Mike running toward her, hunting rifles in their hands. Jumping to her feet, she ran to them.

"You shot him!" she shouted.

"Melissa, please," Richard said, and she could hear the note of pleading in his tone. "It was an accident."

"You must help him!"

"The creature's been badly injured. We've got to put it down."

"No!" she shouted as a loud snarl sounded behind her. She turned to see Mike raising his gun and pointing it at the injured cat.

"No," she screamed again, hurtling herself at Mike. She knocked into him as the gun went off, its bullet ricocheting off a tree. She wrenched the weapon from his hands as Cynthia and Lesley ran into the clearing.

"You idiot," Mike shouted. "I could have hit someone!"

Cynthia ran up to Richard. "What happened?"

"Give me my rifle," Mike said. "We have to kill it."

"No," she said, clutching the rifle to her chest and running back to Lee. She dropped to her knees beside him. "We have to get him help. Call 9-1-1!"

"Are you crazy? Get away from it," Richard insisted. "It could hurt you." He grabbed Melissa by the arm, but she twisted from his grip as the panther bared his teeth and snarled. He backed away. "Look at it," he said. "It's a wild animal. It's been injured. And look at the size of it! There's no knowing what it will do."

"I'm not leaving. He won't hurt me."

"What happened?" Cynthia said again, bewilderment etching her features.

"I saw movement between the trees," Richard said, "and thought it was a deer. I was …" He paused and turned back to Melissa. "It was you. I was aiming at you by mistake. I'm sorry."

Melissa stared at him, then at Lee. "You took a bullet for me," she whispered. "Why did you do that?" His green eyes met hers, and in that moment she knew what it meant to truly be loved.

She whipped around to face the two men. "This is your fault – both of you. And now you have to make it right. We're going to get him to a doctor."

"Melissa, please—"

"This is not a discussion! We have to help him now!"

Richard held up his hands in surrender. "Fine! Okay! There's probably a vet at the Wildlife Station. But get away from it."

"I'm not moving. Now phone 9-1-1 and get some help."

"There's no signal here," Lesley said. She had pulled out her phone and was tapping the screen.

"Okay, okay," Richard ran his hands through his hair. "We'll go back the way we came and see if we can get a signal. Cynthia, you go back to the truck." He glanced at Melissa. "Keep the rifle. And if the panther comes for you, shoot!" He quickly demonstrated how to release the safety catch.

"Got it. Now go! And take Lesley with you," Melissa said.

"You can't stay here alone!"

"I don't think she'll be much help. Now hurry! There's not much time."

"Come on, let's go," Mike said, grabbing Richard by the shoulder. "She's got the rifle if she needs it."

"You sure you're okay?" Cynthia said.

"Yes! Go!"

"Promise me you won't get too close."

"I'll stay safe, I promise." Cynthia nodded, then headed back out of the trees to the path, Lesley on her heels.

Once she was sure they were out of sight, Melissa dropped the rifle to the ground and allowed herself to look at the wound at Lee's side. A ragged hole showed where the bullet had entered. It was sticky with blood that matted the fur. She pulled off her jacket, then her shirt and, wadding the fabric into a ball, pressed it against Lee's wound. He opened his eyes again, and the tip of his tail flicked against the ground.

"Why did you do it?" she said gently. She stroked his face as she spoke, and he rasped his tongue over her fingers.

"Can you change?" she asked.

He looked at the wound.

"Not when you're injured?"

Next, he looked at the sky.

"The moon? Not when it's full?"

He blinked and she buried her head into the fur in his neck. "You can't die," she said between tears. "I won't let you die." She pulled back and shook her head. "What kind of idiot panther goes and takes a bullet for someone?"

He growled softly again.

"I can't lose you," she said. "You have to live."

Nearly an hour had passed by the time Richard and Mike

came crashing through the trees. Lee had closed his eyes, and although she could feel his heart beating, his pulse was slow and uneven. Melissa rose and headed towards them.

"Wildlife Services is sending someone out," Richard said. "They should be here soon. Is it still alive?"

"Yes. He's lost a lot of blood, though."

"You didn't get too close, did you?"

"I kept a safe distance." Even a few inches was safe in Melissa's mind.

They fell silent as Mike retrieved his rifle, and a few minutes later a man wearing a brown uniform stepped through the trees, Cynthia a step behind.

"Lesley decided to wait at the truck," she said.

The man stopped when he saw Melissa crouching beside the injured cat and gave a low whistle.

"A black cougar! And the biggest I've ever seen! You're the one who called it in?" he said, looking at Richard. "Never seen a black cougar before." He crouched beside Melissa. "Wonder where it came from." He observed him for a minute, then turned back to Richard.

"You said it was an accident?"

"That's right."

"Why haven't you killed it?"

Mike snorted. "I was quite ready to put it out of its misery, but she" – he pointed at Melissa – "wouldn't let us do it."

The man turned to her. "Why's that?"

"He saved my life," she said simply, "and now I'm saving him."

"As beautiful as this animal is, you really aren't doing it any favors by saving it. It's extremely difficult to rehabilitate cougars. We need to destroy it."

"No!" Melissa placed herself between Lee and the man.

"Look, miss, I don't think you understand. This is a wild animal, not a cat you can take home and keep. If it's released into the wild again after recovering, it will look for easy targets for food – dogs, cats, even babies. The only option we'll have is to send it to a zoo. Surely you don't want this creature caged and on display?"

"I'm not letting you kill it," she said firmly.

"Besides," he continued, "Wildlife Services doesn't have unlimited funds to cover the expense of medical care for a cougar."

"I'll pay."

"The cost could be in the thousands."

"Whatever it takes."

The man stared at her for a moment, then shrugged. "Fine. Find someone willing to help you, and I'll let you take the animal. But Wildlife Services won't have any involvement in this. Do you have a way of transporting the animal?"

"I have a truck," Richard said in resignation.

"Good. I have a stretcher and tranquilizer gun in mine. I'll help you get the cat loaded, and then you're on your own. I'll be back in twenty minutes." He disappeared into the trees.

"Why are you doing this?" Cynthia demanded as the man walked away.

Melissa gazed down at Lee as she answered. "I know it doesn't make sense, but I have to protect him. He's more than just a cougar."

"Because he's a rare black one? He's still a dangerous animal. You heard what the officer said – that cougars don't rehabilitate well. It's far kinder to just let him die."

"I have to do this. I will do anything – *anything* – to

make sure he recovers."

Cynthia stared at her for a long moment. "Okay. I don't get it, but if that's what you want, I'll help you."

"Thank you."

The man returned a short while later, lugging a canvas stretcher with looped rope holds and a rifle with two long barrels. "I'll tranquilize it first, in case it wakes up."

"He doesn't need—" Melissa stopped when the man faced her.

"You seem to forget we're dealing with a wild animal here, miss. If it wakes up, it could be extremely dangerous. Despite your insistence that the animal should be saved, I refuse to risk your life and the lives of your friends. Besides which," he added as he knelt down on the ground and pulled out a small vial, "it will be more comfortable for the cougar during transport."

He filled and loaded the dart, then, stepping back, waved everyone out of the way. The dart sank into Lee's hide and after a moment, the man retrieved it and laid the stretcher beside the unconscious animal. Richard and Mike helped maneuver the limp body onto the canvas, and they all took a rope handle and slowly made their way through the trees.

"I can't believe I'm having to do this," Mike muttered beneath his breath.

From the corner of her eye, Melissa saw Richard grit his teeth, but he remained silent. With each step they took, Lee seemed to grow heavier.

"So where are we going to take it?" Richard asked as he ducked beneath the branch of a tree.

"You can try the Wildlife Society in Calgary," the wildlife officer said. "Don't think they'll take such a big mammal, and this one's really huge, but maybe they can tell you who will."

"I'll call when we're at the truck," Melissa said.

They reached Richard's truck an hour later, where Lesley sat with her phone, and heaved Lee over the tailgate and onto the truck bed. Richard slammed it shut as Melissa pulled out her phone. She found the number for the Wildlife Society, but when she tried calling, the office was closed. Further searches were fruitless, and in desperation she looked for vets in Turner Valley. She found two numbers, but when she called the first, she reached a message. The second number, however, was more successful.

"Turner Valley Veterinarian Clinic," answered a woman cheerily.

"I have an emergency," Melissa said.

"An ill pet is always distressing," the woman said kindly. "What seems to be the problem?"

"Well, actually he's a cougar, and he's been shot."

"Oh, my dear – a cougar? I'm not sure we can help you."

"Please," Melissa said, "I'm begging you. They want to kill him."

"Kill him? No, we don't want that. Let me speak to the doctor. Just hold a moment, please, dear."

The phone went silent, and Melissa drew patterns on the ground with her boot while she waited. A few minutes passed before a new voice sounded over the phone.

"Hello? I'm Dr. Marshall. Nancy said something about a cougar?"

"Yes, I know it sounds strange, but I have a cougar that's been shot and I can't let him die. I can explain later, but can you help him?"

"Where are you?"

"Sheep River."

"And where's the cougar?"

"In my friend's truck."

"Oh! How did you manage that?"

"Wildlife Services helped. He's been tranquilized."

"And what do Wildlife Services think?"

"They said he should be destroyed. But I absolutely cannot let them do that."

"I can understand your distress, but it really is the best thing in this situation. And I'm not really equipped to deal with such large mammals."

"Please! I'll pay whatever it costs – anything. You have to help him. There's no one else."

Dr. Marshall was silent for a moment, then let out a long sigh. "Bring him in," he said.

CHAPTER 18

Mike and Lesley left with the wildlife officer, who offered to drive them back to Mike's car, while the others climbed into Richard's truck. The truck bumped and swerved as Richard wound along the road, and Melissa watched anxiously through the window as Lee slid across the truck bed. When they finally reached the vet clinic, a short, motherly-looking woman stepped out.

"Are you the one who called?" she said as she hurried to the truck. She leaned in, then pulled away. "Oh my. I'll just tell the doctor you've arrived."

Richard let down the tailgate as the woman bustled back inside, returning a moment later followed by a tall, balding man. "I'm Dr. Marshall," he said, holding out a hand as Melissa stepped forward and introduced herself.

"And here's my patient," he said, turning to the truck. He stopped and his eyes widened slightly. "Incredible."

He glanced at Melissa. "Melanistic, or black, cougars are very rare; many people think they're a myth. Hmm, most interesting." He pulled a pair of gloves from his pocket and snapped them over his hands before leaning forward and gently fingering the wound in Lee's side.

"Looks fairly clean. We won't know the extent of the damage until I've had a closer look. You understand that there's a chance he won't survive the surgery."

Melissa felt the blood drain from her face. "I know," she said hoarsely. "Please, you have to do whatever it takes to save him. Anything!"

The doctor nodded. "Let's get him inside." He called to the woman who was standing at the door. "Nancy, bring me a stretcher, please."

"Yes, doctor," she said, hurrying back inside. She returned a moment later with a stretcher with two wooden poles protruding from either end.

"Good," he said. Together, Richard, Melissa, Cynthia and the doctor maneuvered Lee onto the stretcher and lifted him from the truck. Nancy walked ahead of them and opened the door into the surgery. "On the table," Dr. Marshall said. They laid down the stretcher and carefully pulled it from beneath Lee, leaving him on the cold metal surface.

"Before I do anything for this animal," the doctor said, "we need a plan for his recovery. I obviously don't have the facilities here to house a cougar, and we can't let him go free."

"I'll take him," Melissa said.

"Where? Your home?"

"No. I have a friend with a cabin. We can build an enclosure and keep him there."

"For how long? No, that's a temporary solution, but

won't do long term." The doctor tapped his chin. "Let me make a few phone calls and see what I can arrange." He turned to Nancy. "Start prepping for surgery. I'll just be a moment."

"I'm afraid you'll have to wait outside," Nancy said as she opened cupboards and took out various instruments and tools.

Cynthia and Richard headed out, but Melissa approached the table, and buried her hand in the thick fur at Lee's neck. "It's going to be okay," she whispered. "You're going to be fine." She blinked away tears as she left the room. In the passage, Richard glared at her.

"You're being an idiot," he said. "You haven't thought this through at all. There's nowhere for it to go!"

"I'll figure something out," Melissa said. "I know you don't agree with me, but if you hadn't tried to shoot me, none of this would've happened."

"Oh, come on. I wasn't *trying* to shoot you – it was an accident! You're still blaming me?"

"Yes! No – I don't know. Look, I really appreciate all you've done. I know it doesn't make sense, but I really have to do this."

"Okay," Cynthia said, frowning in Richard's direction.

A door farther down the passage opened and Dr. Marshall emerged. "All right," he said. "I've spoken to a colleague at the Calgary Zoo. He's sending someone to fetch our friend, who'll take him once the surgery's done."

"The zoo! No, he can't go to the zoo!" Melissa was horrified.

"Melissa," the doctor said, "Are you a specialist in wild animal care? You can't just build a pen for an injured cougar and think you can keep it for a pet. And as I've already explained, I don't have the facilities to care for him. There are specialists at the zoo who can oversee his recovery. This is a temporary solution until we figure out the best course of action." Melissa frowned. "He'll be given the best care, I assure you. Despite supposed sightings, the scientific community has always considered melanistic cougars to be a myth. Our friend here will generate a lot of interest among scientists."

"Great. So you want to turn him into a lab rat."

"I want to give him the best possible chance of recovery, and right at the moment the zoo is the best option for him."

"Okay, fine." Melissa sighed. "But this *is* just a temporary solution. I won't have him caged once he's recovered."

Dr. Marshall shrugged. "I'm sure you'll have plenty of opportunity to discuss his situation with zoo officials. But right now I need to start surgery. Leave your number on the front desk, and Nancy will call you when we're done."

"No! I'm not leaving," Melissa said.

"Look, there's no point in you sticking around. We could be in surgery for a while, and he'll be sedated after that."

"He's right," Cynthia said, placing her hand on her friend's arm. "You can't do anything by waiting. Go home, get your car, and if you want to come back, you can."

Melissa turned to the doctor. "You cannot let him die," she said adamantly. "Whatever it takes, you must save him."

"I'll do my best."

"I'll be back in a couple of hours. Don't let the zoo take him before I've returned."

"I won't," he said. He opened the door to the surgery and shut it firmly behind him.

Lee's blood stained the underside of Melissa's nails, and she stared at them as she sat in the back of Richard's truck. They drove in silence, and after what seemed like forever, he pulled up outside her apartment, then sped off as soon as she climbed out. She took the back stairs, too impatient to wait for an elevator, and was out the door again five minutes later. It was by now late in the afternoon, and the sun glared through her windshield as she headed west out of the city and made her way through the foothills, back to Turner Valley. Usually when she drove this road, she took time to appreciate the beautiful surroundings, but today she barely even noticed them.

She raced through the little towns, and skidded to a halt outside the vet clinic. Only one other car was in the lot, and the clinic looked dark. The door wasn't locked, however, and as Melissa rushed inside, she found Dr. Marshall leaning over the front desk.

"How did it go? Where is he? Can I see him?"

"It all went fine," he said. "The bullet was lodged pretty deep in his flank and was a bit tricky to get out, but it missed all the internal organs, so he should recover just fine."

"Wonderful!" Melissa breathed in relief. "Is he still in the operating room?"

"Actually" – the doctor glanced down at the desk – "he's already been taken."

"What? But I thought—"

"The driver was in a hurry to get back. They didn't want your cougar coming around before getting him to a safe place."

"But you knew I was coming straight back."

"Look, I'll give you the name and number of my contact

at the zoo. If you go there tomorrow, you can ask for him. I'm sure he'd be happy to show you your friend."

"Tomorrow?" Melissa gaped at him. "I can't see him until tomorrow?" She shook her head. "No! I have to see him tonight."

"I'm afraid that's impossible. There's no public access after closing."

"Then phone your friend. Tell him I'm coming."

"Look, Melissa, it's getting late and I need to get home. You said you'd settle the medical bill – I have it here." He rummaged through some papers on the desk. "Here we go."

He held out the sheet, and Melissa stared at it blankly for a moment before handing him her credit card.

"I know you're upset about the panther being gone," he said as he processed the payment, "but the zoo really is the best place for him now. You'll see him soon."

"Yes, of course. And I do appreciate all you've done to help him – thank you."

"Don't forget this," Dr. Marshall held out a piece of paper. "David Pettigrew's name and number. You can try calling him now, but I doubt he'd answer."

Melissa headed out and climbed into her car, where she sat for a long time, her thoughts spinning as she tried to process what had happened. Lee was gone. She glanced down at the contact details Dr. Marshall had given her, then pulling out her phone, dialed the number. It rang for a moment before going to voice mail. "Hi, you've reached Dr. Dave Pettigrew, Manager of Animal Health and Research at the Calgary Zoo. I'm afraid I'm—"

Melissa hit the END button and started her car. Perhaps if she hurried, she could reach the zoo before the transport truck arrived. She passed through the town and headed down the open country road, her foot flat on the gas. The light from her headlamps skittered over rocks and grass as she flew along the road as fast as she dared, while the city lights shone in the distance. Skirting the city limits, she headed in the direction of the zoo, then took a small slip road that led to the back entrance. Parking outside the fence, she climbed from her car and peered through the gates. Apart from a few lamps, the grounds were in darkness. A uniformed man appeared, strolling along the pathway, and she rattled the gates.

"Hey," she shouted.

The man approached. "Zoo's closed, miss," he said.

"I know. But there's a panther being brought here. It was injured. Has it arrived?"

"I wouldn't know, miss."

"I need to see him."

"I'm sorry, miss, but you'll have to come back tomorrow."

"Please," she begged, "I just need to know he's okay."

"Who?"

"The panther. Look." She fumbled in her jacket and pulled out the paper with the name and number. "Look, this is the man who brought him here. If I could just speak to him."

"Look, miss, I'm just a security guard. I don't know the higher-ups. You'll just have to come back tomorrow."

"Please," she said again, but he was already walking away. "Damn," she muttered, turning back to her car. She found her phone and dialed a number. It rang twice before being answered.

"Hello?"

"Caleb! It's Melissa."

"Melissa? What's wrong?"

"It's Lee." His name caught in her throat.

"What's happened?"

"He's been" – she hesitated – "shot."

"Shot? How?"

"Near Sheep River. I was there with friends. He didn't want me around – you know, full moon. And Richard shot him."

"He shot him?"

"It was an accident. He thought he saw a deer, but it was me, and Lee was trying to protect me ... oh my God, it's all my fault."

"Tell me he's okay."

"He's ... I don't know. I got him to a vet, who stitched him up, but now he's at the zoo. And I can't get in."

"At the zoo? What's going on?" Caleb took a breath. "Okay, just start at the beginning. He was shot. Then what?"

Slowly, between tears, Melissa told Caleb what had happened. "And now he's at the zoo and it's Sunday night and I can't get in to see him," she finished. "What am I supposed to do?"

Caleb was silent for a moment. "There's nothing more you can do now. Go home, get some rest, and go back in the morning."

"What if I can't get him out?"

"As soon as he can change, he can escape. And he'll be pretty desperate to get out."

"I know. But what if he can't change? He's injured. If they keep him tranquilized, he might not be able to."

"Okay. You're right." He drew in a deep breath. "Look, I'll fly out tomorrow."

"Can you do that? What about your classes?"

"It'll be fine. I'll call you in the morning and let you

know what's happening."

"Okay," she said. He was right. There was little more she could do, so she needed to calm herself and get some sleep. The next day was sure to be difficult.

CHAPTER 19

After a fitful night, Melissa was awake long before the first hint of sunrise. She lay in bed for a few minutes, going through the events of the previous day, wondering what she could have done differently. If only Lee had let her stay with him, she'd never have gone away with Cynthia and this never would have happened. She cursed under her breath. Why hadn't she just stayed on the path instead of chasing shadows!

She headed to the kitchen and made a pot of coffee, her mind on Lee lying alone in a concrete cage. What had he thought when he woke from the surgery to find himself caged at the zoo? Would he be able to change?

She sent Annika a message: *Family emergency. Need a few days off.* She spent a few minutes thinking how she would explain the situation. Her boss would ask questions, and she'd need a very solid story.

She arrived at the zoo at 8:35 and sat on a bench to wait for it to open at nine. Her phone beeped, and she pulled it out to see a message from Caleb. *Flight booked. Arriving at 2. Will call from airport.*

Annika called a few minutes later. "I got your message," she said. "Is everything all right?"

"My brother-in-law in Vancouver is in hospital," she said, hoping she sounded convincing. Annika asked Melissa a few questions, and thankfully seemed satisfied with her replies.

"Take all the time you need," she said as she ended the call.

She waited a few minutes, then dialed Dr. Pettigrew's number and was rewarded once more with a voice-mail message. She sighed as she shoved the phone back into her purse.

At nine o'clock, Melissa was the first visitor in line. "Do you know where I can find Dr. Pettigrew?" she asked the woman behind the window.

"Who?"

"Dr. David Pettigrew? Animal Research?"

The woman shrugged. "You can try the health building. Past the tigers."

Melissa took her change. "Thank you."

The grounds of the zoo spread along the banks of the river and spilled over to the island in the middle. Without taking any notice of the surrounding exhibits, Melissa hurried over the footbridge and along the paths to the far side of the island, past the snow leopard and tigers. Seeing the tigers made her think of her visit to the zoo with Lee. He found zoos claustrophobic, he'd said, and now he was locked in one! She rushed past and headed to the buildings at the far end. They were squat and gray, clearly not intended for visitors. A small sign indicated that she had reached Animal Health and Research. She skirted the building until she found a door, but when she tried the handle, it was locked. She pounded with her fist, but it remained firmly closed. With a growl of frustration, she pulled out her phone once more and dialed Pettigrew's number. This time it was answered right away. She gave her name.

"I'm calling about the black cougar," she said.

"Who told you about that? I have no statement to make at this time."

Statement? "Please, wait," she said, hearing his tone of dismissal. "I'm the one who took him to the vet, Dr. Marshall. He gave me your number."

There was a pause. "Oh. I see. Well, he's in good hands now, and he'll be well looked after."

"That's great. But I want to see him."

"I'm afraid that's impossible … Ms. Hewitt, is it? He doesn't need the public peering at him while he's recovering."

"I'm not the public!" Melissa said indignantly. "I rescued him and paid his medical bills. And I need to see him!"

There was a long sigh on the other end of the phone. "Very well. I suppose a few minutes won't hurt. Let me know when you arrive, and I'll send someone to fetch you."

"I'm already here," Melissa said. "Outside the Animal Health Building."

"Oh! Well then, I'll just come out."

Melissa had only just put her phone away when the door to the building opened and a man dressed in corduroys and a knitted cable sweater stepped out. He introduced himself, and she followed him through the door into a brightly lit corridor. "You understand that Guen needs to recover, and any excitement may upset him."

"Guen?"

"It's what we named him. It's short for Guenhwyvar." He glanced back at her. "You know, the black panther in the *Forgotten Realms* novels."

Melissa frowned. "You gave him a name?"

"We name all the animals that come through our doors. It's easier than calling him 'the black cougar.'"

"But his name is Lee."

He gave her a strange look. "Well, here at the zoo his name is Guen."

Opening a door, he led her through, then stopped outside a room. The lower half of the wall was concrete brick, but the top half was tempered glass. Through it she saw a large black cat spread out over the concrete floor. His side had been shaved, revealing smooth black skin, and she could see the stitches that pulled the flesh together.

"Guen is quite a remarkable creature," Dr. Pettigrew said. "I don't know if you're aware, Ms. Hewitt, but black cougars, or panthers, are thought to be the stuff of legend. In fact, there isn't a scientist in North America who believes they exist. And yet here we have one, from our own backyard." His delight was evident in his tone. "You may think his injury unfortunate, but we think it was quite a stroke of luck. Once he's recovered, we'll run some tests and discover more about this mythical beast. Already, researchers from across the continent are planning to come and see him."

Melissa looked at him in horror. "Tests? What kind of

tests?"

"DNA, cell analysis – whatever we deem necessary."

A movement came from within the cage as Lee lifted his head and looked at her. His eyes were dull and his head swayed slightly. He bared his teeth with a small snarl, then looked away as he lay back on the floor. She turned to the doctor. "What's wrong with him?"

"We've given him some drugs to keep him comfortable."

"But they'll wear off?"

"Eventually. But in cases like these, it's better to keep administering them until the animal is completely healed."

"How long?"

He shrugged. "A week? Perhaps ten days."

Melissa looked at him, aghast. "Ten days? You can't keep him drugged for ten days!"

"Are you questioning my judgment, Ms. Hewitt? I am an expert in my field, I assure you."

Melissa swallowed her retort. It would be foolish to antagonize this man. "Of course," she said. "I'm sorry. It's just a bit of a shock, seeing him lying there like that."

His expression softened slightly. "I understand. Now that you've seen him, I'll show you out," he said.

She gave him what she hoped was a warm smile. "I know I'm being a nuisance," she said, "but if I could just have a few more minutes, I would so much appreciate it. He's such a beautiful animal, and I can't help admiring him."

"I know what you mean," he said. He glanced at his watch. "I need to speak to one of our researchers before I head over to a meeting in the administration building. It will just take a few minutes, but you can wait here for me to show you out."

"Thank you." She watched as he walked away, then turned back to the window.

"Lee? Please, look at me," she said. He lay still for a moment, then slowly lifted his head. "Can you change?" He dropped his head back to the floor. "I'll take that as a no. Is it the drugs?" Lee didn't move. "Okay, we'll figure it out. Caleb's flying in this afternoon. Between us we'll find a way to get you out of here." She stared at him for a moment. "I'm so sorry. I wish …" She swallowed a sob. "I'd take your place if I could." Footsteps approached. "I'll be back as soon as I can."

Melissa followed Dr. Pettigrew out of the building and they walked together along the path.

"Thank you so much for letting me see him. Do you think – I'd really like to see him again, just to know he's doing okay."

"I think that can be arranged, Ms. Hewitt. Call me in a few days, and we'll see how he's doing."

She beamed. "Thank you!"

They separated at the botanical gardens, with Dr. Pettigrew hurrying away to his meeting. Melissa drove home to sit and wait for Caleb.

"I don't know what to do," Melissa said to Caleb as they walked out of the airport to her car. "I can't even see him for more than a few minutes at a time. And the doctor in charge wants to run tests. That would be a disaster."

"What kind of tests?"

"He wasn't specific. DNA, that kind of thing."

"Not good. But we'll figure this out."

"If only he could change! But they're pumping him full of drugs, and I'm guessing that's the reason he can't."

"Can we see him now?"

"We can try. The doctor told me to call him in a few days, but I can try to convince him otherwise."

"Then let's get to the zoo."

The distance from the airport to the zoo wasn't too far, and they made it there in good time. On the way, Melissa told Caleb about her visit that morning, and he smiled in amusement over Lee's new name.

The zoo was busier than it had been that morning, with groups of school children shouting and laughing as they ran between the enclosures. They had just crossed the river when Melissa spied the doctor hurrying along another path with a woman at his side.

"Dr. Pettigrew," she shouted, running toward him. He turned in surprise. "Ms. Hewitt. I didn't expect to see you again so soon."

"Doctor, this is a friend," she said, indicating Caleb. "Please can you let us see, uh, Guen again?"

"Ms. Hewitt, I think I explained that Guen is not here for the public's viewing pleasure."

"I completely understand. It's just that Caleb—" She looked at him helplessly.

"Melissa has been quite distressed about the whole situation," Caleb said, "and as I'm a very close friend, she called me for support."

"I see. And how many more supportive friends are you planning to bring here, Ms. Hewitt?"

"Only Caleb. I promise."

"Perhaps I should mention that I'm helping with the not inconsiderable medical costs Melissa has already incurred," Caleb added.

"Hmm. I'm not very happy about this, Ms. Hewitt." He looked at the woman beside him. "What do you think, Ruth?"

"Guen's quite stable, doctor," she said. "I think it'll be fine."

"Very well. I'll let you see him, but only for a few minutes."

"Thank you," Melissa said.

They followed the pair to the building, where Dr. Pettigrew waved a card over the card reader at the door before leading them to Lee's cage.

"Ruth and I have to get to a meeting," the doctor said, "but I'll have someone show you the way out in a few minutes."

"Thank you," Melissa said again. They watched as the two walked away, then peered through the window. Lee was lying on the floor in the same place Melissa had seen him earlier.

Caleb gave a low whistle. "Certainly not the best I've seen you, bro."

Lee lifted his head and looked at Caleb with a low growl.

"No need to be grumpy. We'll figure out a way to get you out of here. Rather nice to be the one helping you, instead of the other way around. What was that song Mom used to sing? 'Lean on me, when you need a hand.' Although, in this case, maybe it's paw." He chuckled, and Lee bared his teeth in a snarl.

"Tetchy, aren't you?"

Lee looked at Melissa, and she almost laughed – his expression so clearly questioned why she'd brought Caleb. She shrugged. "He's your brother."

Approaching footsteps had them looking down the passage as a young woman drew near. "Isn't Guen the most incredible creature you've ever seen?" she said. "I can't believe I actually got to see a black cougar! Dr.

Pettigrew's beside himself with excitement. It won't be long before word leaks out, but for now, Dr. Pettigrew is only sharing the news with the scientific community."

"Well, I'm not sure what the excitement's about," Caleb said, turning away from the window and grinning at the girl. "You're far prettier."

Within the cage, Lee growled and placed his head back on the floor while Melissa hid a smile.

"I think he's splendid. I'm Melissa, by the way."

"Oh! I'm sorry – Abigail. I work here. I'm supposed to show you out."

Caleb pushed himself from the window and introduced himself. "It must be pretty sweet, working with all these animals."

She blushed. "It's very cool. And Dr. Pettigrew is absolutely amazing. He's already arranging for the world's most renowned researchers to come check out Guen, so I'll get to meet them."

"You must be pretty amazing yourself," Caleb said, "to work at a place like this. So why do all these scientists want to see our panther?"

"Are you kidding me? Just look at him! There's never been a verified sighting of a melanistic cougar before, and now we have one right here."

"Melanistic?"

"Dark colored. The opposite of albino."

"Ah. So what will these scientists be doing when they come?"

"Study him. Run his DNA. Figure out where he comes from and his range. Once we've had a chance to study him better, they'll decide what to do with him."

Caleb frowned. "Why don't they just release him back into the wild?"

"For one thing, we might never have an opportunity to study such a unique specimen again. Besides, he'll become a target once word of this leaks out; also, cougars that are released after rehabilitation in captivity never do well." A door banged, and Abigail glanced over her shoulder. "I'll show you out," she said.

"Actually, do you mind giving us a couple more minutes?" Caleb said. "Melissa is completely in love with – what did you call him? Guen? Anyway, she'd spend all day watching him if she could."

"Just a few more minutes?" Melissa pleaded.

"Hey, I'd love to see what other animals you have here," Caleb said.

"Well …"

"You know," he added, "*you'll* probably be running a place like this one of these days."

She laughed. "You think flattery's going to work? I bet you're one of those people who always gets his way." He flashed her a grin. "Okay, fine, I'll show you around, but we have to be quick. Dr. Pettigrew hates it when people wander his corridors."

"Got it," Caleb said.

He glanced back at Lee with a wink, then followed Abigail along the corridor. Melissa placed her hands against the glass and leaned her forehead on the cool surface. "Your brother's quite the flirt," she said. Lee rose and walked awkwardly toward her, then licked the glass where her fingers rested. Tears filled her eyes and spilled down her cheeks as she watched him. "I'm sorry, Lee. I didn't know what else to do." He pulled back, his green eyes holding hers, telling her that he understood. She brushed away her tears. If Lee could bear to be locked in a cage, she was determined to find a way to release him.

"We'll figure this out. We'll have a daring raid to rescue the endangered panther. And next time you won't send me away when the moon is full."

Lee made a little rumbling sound. She heard approaching voices and glanced up the corridor to see Caleb and Abigail returning. "I'll be back, I promise," she said. "We'll find a way to get you out."

"Time to go, Mel," Caleb said. "I'm staying at my brother's place. Think you can give me a ride?"

"Of course." Melissa stroked her hand against the glass, wishing she could touch him, then pulled away.

Lee stared at her another moment, then at Caleb. Their gazes met. "We've got this, bro." Lee turned away and lay down again.

"Let's go, Melissa," Caleb said. He turned to Abigail. "Thanks for the tour. Maybe next time you can show me a bit more."

She smiled. "Sure. And don't lose that number."

"I won't."

"What was that about?" Melissa asked as they walked from the building.

"Abigail gave me her number and said that the next time we want to see Lee, we should just call her and she'll let us in."

Melissa looked at him in surprise. "Seriously? That's great! Will she stop them running DNA tests for you as well?"

He smiled. "I'm charming, but it might be a bit too soon to ask that."

"So have you told your parents what's happened?" she asked as they headed to her car.

"No! Lee would never forgive me if I did."

"Why? Shouldn't they know their son's been hurt?"

Caleb glanced at her as they walked. "Lee hasn't told you much about our parents, has he?"

"He's spoken a bit about your mom, but not really about your dad. Why? What is there to tell? Has he been hiding something?"

"It's … complicated."

"How?"

"You'll have to ask Lee."

She sighed. "You're being cryptic."

"I know. But it's really not my place to tell you."

"Okay. So do you have a plan to get Lee out of there?"

"Not yet. But I do have an inside source."

"You're such a player!"

"I told you I'm charming," he said with a grin.

"Don't hurt her feelings along the way."

He looked aggrieved. "What do you take me for? I wouldn't do that. But if she's interested in a little flirtation, then we may as well use it to our advantage."

"Fine. Whatever it takes."

They drove in silence until they neared Lee's apartment.

"Look," Caleb said, "why don't you stay here until this is sorted out?" Melissa was surprised at the offer, but he shrugged. "I'd rather have company."

"Actually, I think I would too. I'll just need to get a few things from my place."

"Good. I'll get supper started. Do you think Lee has anything besides meat?"

She laughed. "Perhaps I'll go past the grocery store on my way back."

She had just arrived back at Lee's apartment when her phone buzzed. It was from Cynthia: *Just wondering how UR doing?*

She leaned her head back for a moment in the car as she contemplated her reply. How was she doing?

Fine, she wrote. *The cougar was taken to the zoo.*

I'm sure that's the best place for him, Cynthia responded.

Yeah, not so much, Melissa thought. She sent a happy face and put the phone away before stepping out of the car and heading up to Lee's apartment.

Chapter 20

"I found a few things to throw together," Caleb said when Melissa stepped through the door. "Ham, garlic and cheese sauce." The smell of fresh garlic and cheese met her nose, and she breathed in with pleasure. Apart from a hot dog from a vendor at the zoo, she hadn't eaten all day.

"Sounds wonderful," Melissa said. She lifted the bags in her hands. "I picked up a few things from the grocery store – some fruit and veggies." Caleb had opened a bottle of wine, and she poured herself a glass before taking a seat on the couch. "What do you think Lee's doing right now?"

"Maybe they're feeding him. Nice raw steak."

"Mmm, sounds delicious!"

Caleb laughed, then turned serious. "Lee'll be okay. It's a good thing you found that vet to do the surgery, or he might not have survived. And we *will* find a way to get him out of there."

"What do you think they'll find if they run tests on him?"

"No idea. But whatever it is, it's bound to lead to more questions."

"We have to get him out of there before they start running tests. As long as they're drugging him, though, he can't change."

"I know. And with this wound, he really needs to."

"What do you mean?"

"When Lee changes, his physical form shifts and rearranges, so any injuries are gone with his new form."

"Wow! He just heals? That's incredible."

"Yep. So if he can't change–"

"It will take him much longer to recover."

"Yes." Caleb poured a pot of cooked pasta into the sauce and mixed them together. "What did your friends think about you saving him?"

Melissa grimaced. "They thought I was crazy, of course. Mike, Richard's friend, tried shooting him straight away."

"What happened?"

"I grabbed for the gun and knocked him, and the bullet hit a tree." She laughed ruefully. "He wasn't very happy. He only just missed hitting his girlfriend."

Caleb laughed. "Wow! That's quite a story."

Taking two plates from the cupboard, he spooned some pasta onto each, then handed one to Melissa. "We'll do some brainstorming as we eat."

But by the end of the meal they still had no ideas. Caleb leaned back in his chair and rubbed his forehead. "There must be something we can do to stop a wild animal from being prodded and poked, then kept in captivity."

"The animal-rights activists would have a field day,"

Melissa said, lifting her glass to take a sip of wine. She stopped midway. "That's it!"

"That's what?"

"Animal rights!" She placed the glass back on the table. "The guy who shot Lee – his sister's into that stuff. She's even done protests with PETA."

Caleb laughed. "Lee's shooter has a sister who hates hunting? You should give her a call – maybe she has some connections."

Melissa frowned. "But we don't want a protest. Attracting attention is the last thing we want."

"True, but she might have some ideas. I mean, do you have some legal rights because you saved him and paid his bills?"

"Hmm, good point." She reached for her phone and sent Cynthia a text: *Please send me Rheagan's number.*

The answer was immediate. *Is this about the cougar?*

Yes.

You're crazy. Let it go.

Please?

It took a few minutes before she replied. *It's really not a good idea to involve her, but I'll speak to Richard.*

Melissa put the phone aside. "So what's the plan for tomorrow?" she asked Caleb.

"We'll go to the zoo in the morning, and hopefully I can chat with Abigail a bit more. We need to know when these scientists are arriving. Maybe I can convince her to reduce Lee's pain meds. In the meantime, try and get hold of the sister."

"I will."

Melissa fell asleep with the scent of Lee on his sheets. When she woke the next morning, there was a message from Cynthia with Rheagan's number. She waited until after breakfast before making the call. A raspy voice answered, inviting her to leave a message after the tone. She gave her name and asked Rheagan to call her back.

"Is Abigail expecting us?" she asked Caleb as she ended the call.

"She'll be waiting for us."

"Then let's go."

They reached the zoo as the gates opened and hurried to the research building. Abigail was waiting at the door as they strode up, and she waved them inside. "Dr. Pettigrew will be here at ten," she said, "so you have a little time. Ruth checked him out this morning; there's no sign of infection, and the wound is healing nicely. She gave him some pain meds, so he might be a bit groggy." They reached the room where Lee lay on a bed of straw. "Everyone else has gone to a meeting," Abigail said, "so you can visit him without interruption for a little while."

"Why are you here?" Caleb asked.

"One of our warthogs is expecting, so I'm keeping an eye on her."

"Can I see?"

"Only if you're very quiet – we don't want to startle her."

"I'll be as quiet as a mouse," Caleb promised. He followed Abigail down the passage.

Melissa watched as they turned the corner, then quickly slid aside the bolt to Lee's cage and stepped into the room. The panther lifted his head as his tail swished over the floor, then, rising unsteadily to his feet, he prowled toward her. A wave of instinctive fear rose in Melissa as the predator stalked closer and his whiskers twitched as he sniffed the air. He froze, then dropped to his haunches, cocking his head as she took a step forward and sank to her knees in front of him.

"I'm not scared," she whispered. "It was an automatic reaction." She wrapped her arms around him and buried her face into his fur. He was still for a moment, then rubbed his snout over her neck. His whiskers tickled her ears, and she pulled back with a smile. "How are you feeling?" she said. He slipped from her grasp and lay on his flank. His wounded side was facing her, and she stared down at the stitches holding his black skin together. "Abigail said they gave you more pain meds. Does that mean you still can't change?" He laid his head on the floor, and after a moment, she lay down beside him. He lifted his paws and wrapped them around her, and she snuggled against his furry skin, careful to avoid the wound. She stroked her hand down his side as she looked into his green eyes. His tail swished over her legs.

"The guy who shot you," she said, "Richard – his sister's an animal-rights activist. I'm going to speak to her and see if she can give us some advice. Since I'm the one who paid your medical bill, we wondered if we could get a judge to say I'm responsible for you."

Lee pulled his paw away with a growl.

"I know you don't like it, but we don't have many options," she said. "Time's not on our side. What do you think those scientists will see when they start running DNA tests on you? And then they really won't want to let you go."

Lee snarled.

"Exactly," she said. "If only you could change!" He leaned forward and licked her cheek. She ran her hand over his ear, and he twitched beneath her fingers as he purred. "You like that, do you?" she whispered with a grin. He pulled back slightly to glare at her, but the purring grew louder, rumbling through his chest like an engine, and he ran his tongue around her fingers, then gently rasped his teeth against her skin. She shivered as a sudden wave of desire flooded through her, catching her off guard. His nostrils flared slightly and his jaws closed over her hand. His tongue was hot and rough, and his eyes burned into hers. She leaned forward, but he suddenly froze. Her hand fell from his mouth as he lurched up, his gaze on the door. Turning back to her, he butted her legs with his head. She jumped to her feet in understanding and flung open the door. Caleb's voice rang out in the passage, louder than necessary, and she quickly slid the bolt back into place as they rounded the corner. Caleb's eyes widened as he looked at her, and she glanced down to see a piece of straw clinging to her jacket. She brushed it away as Abigail looked up.

"Are you okay?" she asked. "You look a little flushed."

"Fine," said Melissa. "But I really need the bathroom. Is there somewhere here I can go?"

"Of course," Abigail said. She looked through the window at Lee, who was lying on the floor in the same spot as before, then pointed down the corridor. "Washroom's that way. You'll see the sign."

Melissa made her way down the passage. She locked the door and leaned against the sink, lifting her trembling hands to her face. She could still feel where Lee's tongue had rasped her skin and where his pointed teeth had scraped. She'd never look at him in the same way again, she thought. He wasn't just a panther, but a seductive predator.

Rheagan called as Melissa and Caleb walked back to the

car. "You said you were a friend of Cynthia's?" she said. Melissa could hear the suspicion in her voice.

"Yes. Cynthia said you were into animal rights – that sort of thing. I need some advice." Melissa glanced around before ducking into a quiet corner, pulling Caleb along with her.

"About what?"

"A cougar being held at the zoo."

Rheagan gave a dry laugh. "Cynthia gave you my number to help a cougar? The woman who works for a company that exploits the environment, pumps gases into the air, destroys the natural habitats of animals and kills ducks at its tailings ponds? Are you kidding me?"

"No. Look, the cougar was shot – by your brother, actually. I got him to a vet and paid for his medical bills, but the vet contacted a friend at the zoo, which is where they brought him. I want to know my legal rights about the animal, since I paid the bills. Can you recommend a lawyer who can advise me?"

"Let me get this straight. This cougar is at the zoo where it's recovering?"

"Yes."

"And you want to, what? Set it free?"

"The zoo's bringing some scientists to study him and do tests. I want to get him out and back in the wild."

"What's so special about this cougar that they want to run tests on him?"

"He's black. A panther."

There was a low whistle. "A black panther right here at the Calgary Zoo! And he was shot by my brother?"

"Yes. It was an accident. Look, I really don't want any publicity or anything. Just the name of someone who can give me some advice."

There was a moment of silence. "Okay," she finally said, "let me check around, make some calls and see what I can find out for you."

"Thank you," Melissa said. "And remember, no publicity."

"Got it. No publicity."

They returned to Lee's apartment where they waited for Rheagan's call, but the hours passed without hearing back from her.

"I can't sit around doing nothing," Melissa said as the afternoon wore on. "I'm going back to the zoo. Coming?"

"No, you go. I'm going to do some research of my own in case Rheagan doesn't come through. But I'll let Abigail know you're on your way."

"Okay, great. I hope you find something that'll help us."

She was nearly at the zoo when Caleb called. "We have a problem."

"What kind of problem?"

"I've just spoken to Abigail."

"And?"

"She said something about a protest and hung up on me."

"What protest?"

"I have no idea. But you might want to be prepared."

"Rheagan!"

"Who else?" When Melissa was silent, he said, "Look, Mel, I don't know what's happening. I just wanted to warn you."

She took a steadying breath. "Okay," she said. "I'm almost there. I'll let you know."

She arrived a few minutes later and hurried across the parking lot to the entrance gates. As they came into view she came to an abrupt stop – a group of about fifteen people were milling outside the zoo with signs. FREE THE PANTHER read one. Another read STOP IMPRISONING ANIMALS. To the side was a woman with a microphone and a cameraman beside her, interviewing a woman with short pink hair. Melissa watched for a moment then edged around the group and headed into the zoo. As soon as she was beyond the gates, she took off in a run toward the Animal Health building. She slowed as she reached it and, drawing in a breath, banged on the door.

"Lee," she shouted. There was a sound behind her, and she spun around to see a security guard approaching her. "Excuse me, miss," he said, "I've been instructed to escort you off zoo property."

"Why?"

He shrugged. "I'm just following orders."

"Wait," she said. She pulled out her phone and dialed Dr. Pettigrew's number.

He answered immediately. "Ms. Hewitt. How can I help you?"

"I have a security guard standing over me, telling me I have to leave. Why?"

"Trying to discredit us and the work we do here only works against you, Ms. Hewitt."

"I haven't done that."

"So you have nothing to do with the animal-rights activists outside our gate demanding we release Guen?"

"I asked them for advice, nothing more. In fact, I told them I didn't want any publicity."

"These people aren't interested in what you want. They aren't even interested in what's best for the animals. They want publicity, and you've given them the perfect reason to come here. You've opened a Pandora's Box, Ms. Hewitt.

And people who attempt to disrupt our work are not welcome here."

"Please! I'll go quietly, but just let me see him."

"I'm afraid that's out of the question." The line went silent.

"This way, miss," the guard said, his hand closing around her arm.

"I can find my own way out," she snapped, shaking herself free.

Her face was set as she strode back the way she'd come, the guard on her heels. Outside the gates, the pink-haired woman was leading the crowd in a chant, and Melissa marched over to her. "Are you Rheagan?" she asked.

"Melissa, I presume?"

"What is this? I said no publicity!"

"This isn't your story to hide. A panther in our backyard is a story everyone's interested in, especially since the zoo refuses to release him. You can try to gain legal access over the animal, but that will take time. Zoos are terrible places that imprison animals for human enjoyment. We'll use whatever methods we can to get the message across that zoos are places of torture and cruelty."

"Don't you see? You've just made him a target," Melissa said angrily. "When he's released, people like your brother will track him down and kill him."

"Your interest clearly only extends to this one animal, but we're interested in the inhumane treatment of *all* animals," Rheagan said. "And if your panther can help us get the message out, so much the better. There's nothing like a mystical creature to get people's attention."

"No wonder Cynthia doesn't like you." Melissa glanced up to see the camera focused on her, and quickly turned away. "I asked for your help, and you've just made things a thousand times worse."

She was shaking by the time she reached her car, and she sat in the driver's seat for a few minutes in an effort to calm down. It took a while before she felt steady enough to drive, and she slowly pulled into the traffic.

"What are we going to do?" Melissa said after she had apprised Caleb of the events at the zoo. "I can't even get in to see him anymore." She was on the verge of tears.

"I don't know," he said, running his hand through his hair.

"Have you tried calling Abigail again?"

"She's not answering."

"Just when I thought things couldn't get worse." She sank onto the couch and dropped her head in her hands. Her phone buzzed and she winced when she saw Annika's name on the screen.

"Hello?" she answered as Caleb disappeared into the kitchen.

"Melissa? I was just wondering how your family member is doing?"

"He's—"

"Because I was watching the five-thirty news. They were covering a protest at the zoo, and there you were."

"Well, you see—"

"You lied to me. I expect to see you at your desk at eight o'clock tomorrow morning."

"I'm not—"

"You know my policies. If you're not there, I'll be forced to let you go."

She pressed her hand against her eyes. "Then I resign."

There was a moment of silence. "I see," Annika finally said. "I won't hide that I'm incredibly disappointed,

Melissa. I had great hopes for you."

"I'm sorry, Annika. I don't want to do this. But other things are happening that take priority over work. It's – it's complicated. I can't explain right now."

"I see. Well, that's your decision to make, of course. I expect your resignation in writing before the end of tomorrow."

The line went dead, and Melissa threw the phone onto the couch.

"What was that?" Caleb asked as he came back into the room. He handed her a glass of wine.

"What's the time?"

"Almost six."

"Put on the news," she said.

He switched on the TV and found the local news station. After a few minutes, the screen filled with an image of protesters marching with their signs. To the side of the screen, Melissa could see herself remonstrating with Rheagan. The camera moved to a reporter.

"We are at the Calgary Zoo, where animal-rights activists are protesting the capture of a black cougar. We interviewed Rheagan Kelly, who is leading the protest, earlier today."

Rheagan's face appeared on the screen. "Zoos deprive animals of their right to live freely as they were meant to do," she shouted. "They're kept in cages, people! They're taken from their homes, deprived of their freedom and put on display for human entertainment. And what better way to entertain than with a black panther? They've taken his freedom, and now plan to prod and poke him, run tests on him and submit him to cruel and unusual punishment, all in the name of science. Well, we say *enough!* Let him go back home! Let him be the animal he was meant to be!"

Her face was replaced by the reporter's. "We have Dr. Pettigrew of the Calgary Zoo here to answer some questions." The camera swung to the scientist. "Dr. Pettigrew, is it true you have a black panther in captivity?"

"Yes, that's true. However, here at the Calgary Zoo we are committed to the conservation and preservation of wildlife. The cougar, whom we've named Guen, was seriously injured when he was shot by a hunter. He was taken to Dr. Marshall of Turner Valley, who performed surgery on him, saving his life. A cougar with these kinds of injuries cannot be released back into the wild, so Dr. Marshall contacted us and we gladly took over Guen's recuperation."

"The protesters want Guen released back into the wild. Is that possible?"

"I'm afraid not. Cougars do not readapt well after interaction with humans. The choice was either to save him, but keep him out of the wild for his own protection and the protection of humans, or leave him to die. We chose life."

"And the fact that he's a panther?"

"At this point we're not entirely sure what he is. Melanistic cougars were thought to be a myth. Only after we've run some tests will we know for sure what he is and where he comes from."

"I'm sure the public would love to see Guen. Will that be possible?"

"I'm afraid not. He has been through a traumatic event and we want to reduce his stress as much as possible."

"Thank you, Dr. Pettigrew."

Caleb switched off the TV.

"Annika saw me with the protesters," Melissa said dully. "She was going to fire me, so I resigned."

"I'm sure if you'd explained—"

"Explain what? That it's not a cougar stuck in a cage at the zoo, but my boyfriend? What did you expect me to say, Caleb?"

He rubbed his fingers over his brow. "I don't know."

Melissa rose from the couch and went to stand at the window. "Did you find out anything in your research?" she asked.

"I found a law firm that specializes in animal rights. I left a message but haven't heard back."

"Did you say that we need help urgently?"

"Of course I did," he snapped. "Lee might be your boyfriend, but it's *my brother* who's stuck in a cage at the zoo!" He turned and disappeared back into the kitchen as Melissa leaned against the window. Her head was pounding, and the cool glass helped to relieve some of the pain. She took a sip of wine and went to the kitchen, where Caleb was searching through the cupboards.

"I'm sorry," she said.

"We're both a bit uptight at the moment."

She smiled wryly. "Just a bit. I'm sure the lawyer will call back."

"I'll keep trying Abigail."

"Lee knows we're doing everything we can, doesn't he?"

Caleb nodded. "Of course he does."

CHAPTER 21

Melissa stood in the kitchen the following morning, toying with a bowl of cereal as Caleb dialed Abigail's number.

"Hello?" he said. He gave Melissa a thumbs-up, but a moment later he was frowning. "What do you mean?" The frown deepened as he listened. "Where?" he demanded, clenching his hands. "Please, Abigail, this is really important. I need to know where he is." Melissa felt the color drain from her cheeks as she listened, and she rose from her chair.

Caleb gave a harsh laugh. "You wouldn't believe me if I told you." There was another silence. "He's my brother," he said. Abigail's exclamation of derision could be heard before the line went dead. Caleb dropped the phone and covered his head with his hands.

"What happened?"

"They've sent him somewhere else."

"Where?"

"I don't know," he shouted. Grabbing a mug from the table, he hurled it across the kitchen, where it smashed against the wall. He stormed out of the room.

A wave of dizziness washed over Melissa, and she sat down heavily as the blood pounded in her ears. She waited for the dizziness to subside, then headed out the door. The air outside was crisp and cold, and she breathed deeply as she walked along the road. In the distance she could see the river winding along the edge of downtown, flowing from the mountains in the distance. The mountains where Lee had saved her – from the cougar, from the men at the campground, from Richard and his gun. It had been in the mountains that she'd first learned what he was – about the beast that lingered just below his human surface. And now he was trapped. Held prisoner by well-meaning guards. What would happen when they ran his DNA? When they discovered he was nothing like the creature they supposed him to be. Being scientists, they'd want to know and understand this new animal – where he came from and what made him different. They'd find a way to keep him captive forever, and she could not allow that.

When she'd first learned Lee's secret she'd been terrified, and if she was completely honest with herself, a part of her had been relieved when he insisted that she stay away from him when he took his animal form. But seeing him in his cage, running her fingers through his hair, feeling his paws around her waist and his tongue on her skin, her fear had been transformed into wonder at the creature he was. And she understood now why she had never been able to get over him. She loved him, and had done so for a long time. And even if he couldn't admit it yet, he loved her too. After all, he had risked his life for her.

She crossed the road and headed back to the apartment. She had no idea how they would find and free Lee, but even if it took months, she'd track him down and release him. There was nothing more important than that, and that knowledge was all she needed to strengthen her resolve. They *would* find him, and they *would* set him free.

Caleb was in the bedroom when she returned, and she could hear the muted sound of his voice as he talked on the phone. She pulled off her jacket as he came into the room.

"You might want to pack a bag," he said.

"Why?"

"Abigail just called me back. She wanted to know what I meant when I said Lee was my brother."

Melissa frowned. "Why the renewed interest in you?"

"Before they moved Lee, they took a sample of his blood. They just ran the test, and found some irregularities."

"Of course they did."

"Dr. Pettigrew is blaming Abigail for contaminating the sample, but she said that she followed all the procedures and is convinced it's not contaminated. Which made her think about what I said about Lee."

"Does she believe you?"

He snorted. "Of course not! She's a scientist. But she wanted to know why we're so interested in him. She thinks we're hiding something. And she did let something drop."

"What?"

"Lee's in Cranbrook."

"Cranbrook?" Cranbrook was a small town in British Columbia near the U.S. border, a four-hour drive away. "For how long?"

"Until they get permission from the Americans to take an exotic animal across the border. Apparently that can take a few days."

"That's excellent! It gives us some time. Did Abigail say where in Cranbrook?"

"Nope. All I could gather is that he's in a trailer."

"A trailer … hmm. Cranbrook's not very big. We'll find him."

She went to Lee's room and pulled out the case she had brought with her a few days before. Half her clothes were still packed, and she flung a few toiletries into a bag and dropped it in the case.

"Ready when you are," she called as she left the bedroom. Caleb was already at the front door with a bag over his shoulder.

"Let's go," he said, holding the door open for her.

"Did Abigail mention anything else useful?" Melissa asked as they rode the elevator to the parking lot.

"Not really. Only that they took a blood sample before Lee was tranquilized—"

"Lee's tranquilized? There's no way he'll be able to change in that condition."

"We need to get Lee's truck. I'm guessing it's at the cabin, since it's not in the parking lot."

"We were near the cabin when he was shot, so I'm certain that's where it is. It's not a long detour, and I'll leave my car there."

The morning rush-hour traffic had still not completely abated, and it was slow getting out of the city. "Why do you think Abigail told you about Lee?" Melissa asked as they waited at yet another light. "Is she helping us now?"

"No, I don't think so. She just wants to understand why the results were so strange. She mentioned Cranbrook because they're hoping the animal handler can get another sample from Lee while they're waiting."

"His blood will be full of tranquilizers."

"I guess they'll allow them to wear off first." He sighed. "I only know what she told me, Mel."

"I know, I know," she said with an impatient wave of her hand. "It's just so—"

"We're both frustrated."

"Yes."

They drove in silence for the next hour until they reached Turner Valley. The road took them through the center of the small town, past the vet clinic where Lee had been treated, then into the foothills beyond. It was another twenty minutes before they turned onto a nondescript dirt road and endured another half hour of bumping over a rutted path. Melissa winced with each bump and scrape of her car. She was glad Caleb was with her – she doubted she could have found the cabin on her own.

"Lee said you don't often come here," she said.

"We used to visit my grandparents when they were still alive. I haven't been back much since they died."

"Your grandfather was also a Changer?"

"Yes. He and Lee used to go out for days at a time, leaving me with Grandma." His eyes narrowed as he concentrated on the road. "It was before Lee had shown me what he was, so I didn't understand why I was always left behind. All Grandpa said was that I was too young. The place doesn't really hold fond memories for me."

"I'm sorry."

He shrugged. "I get it now. It's the secrets that I hate."

A particularly deep rut wrenched the steering wheel from Melissa's grasp, and she clenched it more tightly. The road had petered out to nothing, but she could see the cabin in the distance, and she kept her eyes on it as she carefully maneuvered between bushes and trees.

She breathed a sigh of relief as she pulled up outside the cabin. To the left stood Lee's truck, covered in a thin layer of snow.

"I'll just grab a few things," Caleb said. He returned a few minutes later with a tog bag, blankets and the keys. He slid into the driver's seat of the truck and started the engine as Melissa climbed in beside him.

Four hours later, they cruised into Cranbrook, dropping their speed as they reached the first low buildings that lined the highway.

"We're looking for any hotels or motels," Caleb said. "Any place where they might have stopped."

"There," said Melissa, pointing at a Super 8 motel just within the town's limits.

Caleb swung into the parking lot and drove slowly around the building, but no trailers could be seen. They pulled back into the street and continued along the main road. A few hundred meters farther was another motel, and they slowly circled the building but once again found nothing. They checked a dozen more establishments, but in none of them did they spot anything resembling a trailer. At the south edge of the town Caleb pulled onto the shoulder and looked at Melissa. "Any ideas?" he said.

"You're sure Abigail said Cranbrook?"

"Of course I'm sure."

"Do you think she sent us on a wild goose chase?"

Caleb leaned back as he considered, but after a moment said, "It's possible, but that seems very calculating, and she didn't strike me as someone like that."

"Okay. Maybe they stopped somewhere to eat. Let's

drive back up and check out all the restaurants."

Caleb put the truck back in drive and swung around in the road. He pulled into each restaurant, but again they saw no sign of an animal trailer.

"Maybe we're looking for the wrong kind of trailer," Melissa said.

"How many kinds of trailers do you think there are?"

"Okay, you're right. Maybe we just got here before they did. They'd have to stop quite often to check that Lee's okay, surely?"

Caleb shrugged. "Makes sense. Let's go get some coffee and find a place where we can watch the highway." They found a coffee shop with a window overlooking the road, and sat down to wait.

Melissa was finishing her third coffee when she grabbed Caleb's arm. "There. Look," she said. A white pick-up truck was driving slowly down the single-lane highway, pulling a long black trailer with narrow windows along the top. Melissa raced to the door with Caleb one step behind.

As Caleb steered Lee's truck onto the road, the truck and trailer were waiting at a red light a few blocks farther on. When they turned into the parking lot of a small motel a little farther down the road, Caleb followed them in, coming to a stop at the opposite end of the lot. A man and woman emerged from the truck.

"Look! It's the other woman from the zoo," Melissa said. "What was her name? Ruth? She must be the animal handler."

"And the man?"

"Never seen him before."

They watched as the two exchanged a few words, then the man turned to the motel lobby while Ruth walked to the back of the trailer. A large padlock held the bolt in place, and she unlocked it using a key she pulled from her jacket pocket. She slid back the bolt and pulled the door open a few inches before stepping inside and closing the door behind her.

"Now what?" Caleb said.

"We need to make sure it's actually Lee in there."

"And then?"

"Let's see what she does."

Ruth emerged from the trailer a few minutes later. She clicked the lock back in place, and after a scan of the parking lot, strode to the lobby. They waited until she had gone inside before climbing out and making their way to the trailer. Caleb shook the lock as Melissa stepped on the fender and balanced precariously as she peered through one of the windows. Lee was lying in a cage on a bed of straw, his eyes closed and his head on the floor. She dropped back to the ground.

"It's him," she said. "Now we just have to figure out how to get him out. How are your lock-picking skills?"

"Not so great. But I'm pretty good with a bolt cutter."

"Think Lee has a bolt cutter in the truck?"

"Doubt it."

"If Lee's tranquilized, how will we get him out?"

"We'll need a tarp." Caleb grabbed her arm. "They're coming back," he whispered. "Quick – hide!"

Melissa saw the driver and Ruth heading their way and ducked. The trailer was parked near the sidewalk, where a scraggly tree struggled against the onslaught of fumes, and she sprinted toward it, Caleb on her heels. She peeked around the trunk as the pair collected their belongings and headed back to the motel.

"Looks like they're planning to stay the night," Caleb

said. "I saw a hardware store when we were driving through the town. I'm going to go back and get some bolt cutters and a tarp. You wait here and keep an eye on the trailer."

"Okay. But be quick."

"I will."

Chapter 22

Melissa sat in the truck and watched the trailer. Ruth checked on Lee once before Caleb finally returned, carrying a large bag and two coffee cups in a tray, burgers and fries balanced between them. "Hope you like ketchup," he said, handing Melissa the food and coffee as he slid into the truck.

"Did you get what we need?" she asked, wrapping her hands around the warm cup.

"I did."

"Think someone will notice us carrying a panther?"

"Maybe. We'll have to wait for the town to go to sleep before attempting our rescue."

"So what are we going to do in the meantime?"

Caleb sank down into the seat. "We're on a stakeout. We're going to stay here and watch that they don't move him, and when it's dark and quiet, we'll spring the hostage from his prison. Maybe you can go get us some donuts to go with the coffee."

"Seriously? Maybe I'll just go book a room and sleep for a few hours."

"Really? You'd do that?"

"You're such an idiot. Of course not."

He leaned back and closed his eyes. "Just checking."

"Tell me what Lee was like when he was growing up," she said after a few minutes had passed.

He looked over at her. "There isn't much to tell. He was a pretty regular kid. A protective older brother. A bit of a loner."

"Was he popular with the girls?"

"He kept to himself. It wasn't until he was older that he began hanging out with girls. None of them were serious, though. You're the only one he's ever talked about. He told me when he first met you, you know."

"When we started dating, you mean?"

"No, when you first started working at Quigs as an intern."

Melissa's eyes widened in surprise. "What did he say?"

"Just that he'd met the woman he was meant to be with. When I asked him what he was going to do about it, he said he was going to stay away." He paused. "There's only one thing Lee's afraid of, Mel," he said softly. "Himself."

Melissa closed her eyes. "I know," she whispered.

The air in the truck grew colder and outside snow began to fall softly. She pulled a blanket around her shoulders as Caleb cleared the windshield. Ruth came to check on Lee again, a flashlight in her hand, and Melissa and Caleb both slid down in their seats as they watched her unlock the door and disappear inside. She stepped out a few minutes later and carefully locked it once more before heading back to the motel, leaving a trail of tracks in the snow.

"I'm going to get something else to eat," Melissa said. "Want anything?"

"Sure." Caleb gave her his order, and she stepped out into the cold air. It was quickly growing dark as she headed down the road and stepped into the first fast food restaurant she saw. It was warm and bright inside, and families laughed as they ate their meals. After the last few days, it seemed so normal. She placed her order and trudged back to the truck. They ate in silence, then took turns sneaking into the motel lobby to use the restroom.

The hours passed by slowly, and Melissa dozed on and off as she sat in the darkened truck. It continued to get colder, and Caleb cleared the snow off the windshield again. Every hour Ruth came out and checked on Lee, and at some point in the evening both she and the driver headed down the road. They returned half an hour later, coffees in hand, and disappeared back into the motel.

Every so often a car would turn into the motel parking lot and people would unload and disappear inside, and a few times they saw a police car cruising along the main strip, but the policeman paid them no attention. As the night wore on, the road became quieter, and except for the occasional truck passing through, eventually fell silent. At half past twelve, Ruth came out to check Lee once more. Once she'd gone back inside, Caleb turned to Melissa. "Think she's going to bed?"

"Yes. Let's rescue Lee."

He turned on the engine and slowly moved their truck toward the trailer, reversing so the two vehicles were back to back. "You open the tailgate while I cut the lock," he said.

Melissa did as instructed, then grabbed the tarp from the back as a loud snap rang through the air as the lock was cut apart. Caleb slid the bolt aside, wincing as metal screeched on metal. They both froze for a moment, but all was silent. Cautiously, they inched open the doors of the trailer to reveal the large metal cage. Lee lay on his side, and as they approached, he opened his eyes for a brief moment. There was a catch on the cage, and Melissa pulled it back and swung the door open.

"Lee?" Melissa whispered. "Lee, it's us." The huge cat lay still and she looked at Caleb. "He's out of it," she said. "How on earth are we going to do this?"

"Pass me the tarp. First we'll need to get it under him, then pull him out."

Melissa handed Caleb the heavy canvas sheet. Stooping, he climbed into the cage and crouched beside Lee. Carefully, he lifted Lee's haunches and pushed the tarp beneath him, but got no more than a few inches.

"I need your help," he said. "Do you think you can squeeze in?"

"I'll try." Melissa eased gingerly into the cage and stood across from Caleb.

"I'll lift him in stages, and you pull the tarp under him little by little." Caleb lifted Lee's back legs and Melissa eased the tarp up as far it would go, then tugged again as Caleb eased his hand under Lee's middle. They repeated the moves several times until Lee was almost fully lying on the tarp. He opened his eyes and pulled back his lips, but otherwise did not move.

"Okay, his head," Caleb said. He edged his way around in the small space, then, taking Lee by the shoulders, heaved him up. A snarl broke from Lee, growing as Melissa yanked on the tarp for all she was worth. The sheet resisted for a moment, then slid beneath Lee as Caleb laid his head back down.

"I'll hold this end," Caleb said. "You pull him out from that end."

Melissa grabbed the two corners in her fists and stepped out of the cage, straining to move Lee's deadweight. The lip of the trailer meant they had to lift Lee a few inches as they moved him over, and Melissa's muscles were trembling as they reached the tailgate of Lee's truck and eased him onto the bed.

"We did it!" she said after they jumped down. Sweat poured down her forehead, and her breath came in short gasps.

Caleb quietly closed the tailgate. "Close the back of the trailer while I move the truck," he said. He was heading to the driver's side when a voice rang through the air.

"Stop! What are you doing?" They turned to see Ruth racing toward them over the snowy parking lot.

"Let's go," Caleb shouted. "Get in the truck."

Melissa jumped in as Caleb flung the vehicle into drive and put his foot on the pedal. There was a bump as the truck mounted the curb. Melissa could see Ruth yelling and waving her hands in the air. "Stop!" she screamed. The wheels of the truck hit the road and it started to spin, but then straightened as Caleb yanked the steering wheel and hit the gas. The tires squealed as the engine revved and they raced down the road.

"Quickly," Melissa yelled, "she's calling the police." They reached the end of the town and Melissa saw a road veering to the right. "That way," she yelled. They turned down a dirt track and raced into a wooded area. The snow was falling heavily now, glistening in the light of the headlamps, and Caleb sat forward, peering through the windshield. The track petered to an end after a few miles, and they stopped the truck.

"Now what?" said Caleb.

"We'll have to wait here until Lee can change, then head back onto the road."

"What if he can't change for a while?" There was a scratching sound and they turned to see Lee slowly rising.

"The tranquilizers are wearing off already," she said. She opened the truck door and went to the back, where she unlatched the tailgate and swung it open. "You're free," she said to Lee with a smile. She leaned into the truck and stretched out her hand to stroke his fur. He stared at her for a moment, then his lips pulled back in a vicious snarl as he swiped his paw at her face. She stumbled backward as Caleb ran around the truck.

"Lee," he shouted, "Lee, stop!"

Lee leaped from the truck with a roar and launched himself at Melissa with claws outstretched. Grabbing her by the arm, Caleb yanked her away as Lee landed on the ground where she'd just been standing. He teetered slightly, then gained his footing and rounded on them with a snarl. He stalked forward, his teeth bared, as Melissa backed away, her heart pounding. The panther growled as Caleb pushed her aside.

"Get in the truck. Now," he said.

She backed toward the truck as Lee continued to snarl and hiss, and when she reached the still open door, she jumped inside and slammed it closed. She watched through the back window as Lee snarled at Caleb, then turned and disappeared into the darkness. Caleb climbed into the truck.

"He tr-tried to attack us," she stammered. Her hands were shaking.

"It must be the after-effects of the drugs," Caleb said. His face was ashen in the moonlight. "Let's get out of here. At least if they stop us, we won't have a panther as evidence."

"What if he returns here, looking for us?"

"I have no doubt he'll find us."

Melissa shook her head. "No. I'm not leaving. We've got to wait here for him."

Caleb leaned his head on the seat and closed his eyes in silent acquiescence. "Maybe we reached him too late," he said.

"You can't think like that," Melissa said, horrified. "As you said, it's the after-effects of the drugs."

"You're right." Caleb sighed. "As soon as they wear off, he'll be fine."

"Exactly!"

CHAPTER 23

Melissa scanned the darkness outside the truck, wondering if Lee was nearby. Her heart had resumed its normal rhythm and the shaking had stopped, but she could not forget the savagery in Lee's expression, nor her own fear. He had tried to attack her! He'd said that even in his animal form he retained his thoughts, but when he'd leaped from the truck, she had seen only a wild animal. The image of his snarling face stayed in her mind, and she could not forget the sharp claws that had been outstretched towards her. Was he lost to her forever? It was the effect of the drugs running through his system that had made him vicious – she was sure of that. But he'd been tranquilized, sedated and drugged ever since they had taken him from the mountain – could the drugs have driven his humanity so deep he could no longer reach it? She gave her head a mental shake. No – she didn't believe that. As soon as the drugs were out of his system, he'd be back. The thought that he might not was too awful to contemplate.

Beside her, Caleb dozed, mumbling as he pulled the blanket closer against the penetrating cold. It was still dark when he woke with a start and rubbed his eyes blearily. "What time is it?" he asked.

"Six."

He sat up and looked around. "He's not back?"

"No."

"He's probably long gone from here, Mel. And I daresay the police are looking for us, and if they find us here – well, we wouldn't seem very innocent. Let's drive back to Fernie and find somewhere to stay there. If Lee's looking for us, he'll find us."

"How?"

"He's a cat. He can see the truck from a mile away, and smell us from even farther. And he knows we wouldn't stay around the scene of the crime."

"Okay," Melissa said after a few moments.

The snow was still falling as they bumped back along the snow-covered track, then turned onto the highway, heading to Fernie, an hour's drive in the direction of Calgary – and far enough from Cranbrook it wouldn't be the first place police would look. The road wound around the mountains, but Melissa barely noticed as she stared unseeing out of the window.

The sun had still not risen when Caleb pulled up outside a motel with a bright neon sign.

"Wait here," he said. "I'll see if they have a room." She nodded mutely as he left the truck and disappeared into a brightly lit lobby.

A few minutes later, he returned with a key. "We're at

the back." Easing the truck around the building, he parked in a darkened corner. He grabbed his bag from behind the seat and headed to the first door, and after a moment, Melissa followed.

The room was typical of motel rooms – pokey with faded linen and a musty smell. A small desk with a bar fridge occupied one wall and a queen-sized bed the other. In the corner stood a chair.

"I'll sleep here," Caleb said, dropping onto the chair.

"We can share the bed," Melissa said. "It's no big deal. I trust you." She pulled off her boots and lay on one side with her jacket still on, facing the wall. After a moment, Caleb lay down stiffly beside her. She closed her eyes, and after what seemed like a long time fell into a restless sleep.

When she awoke she was alone on the bed, but the shower was running in the bathroom. She sat up and took in her surroundings. In the light of day, the room looked even worse than it had before. A small coffee machine sat on the desk, releasing the aroma of freshly made coffee. She poured herself a cup, then pulled out her phone as she waited for Caleb to finish his shower. There were three missed calls from a number she didn't recognize. She frowned, then put the phone aside as Caleb emerged from the bathroom.

"Good morning," he said. "Sleep well?"

"Well enough. Any sign of Lee?"

"No." He sat down on the bed beside her. "He'll find us, Mel. I'm one hundred percent sure of that."

"But what if he doesn't? What if he doesn't want to?" She truly hoped Caleb was right, but she couldn't shake off the nagging doubts. Lee had attacked her, something she'd never have expected. What if she was wrong about him coming back?

"I know my brother. He was confused last night. He's been tranquilized and pumped full of medications for days, not to mention recovering from a gunshot wound."

"You weren't so sure last night. What if he's too lost in himself to find his way out again?"

Caleb sighed. "You have to have faith, Mel."

"Faith," she scoffed. "My boyfriend, who's a wild animal, tried to attack me last night." She stared at her hands. "If he doesn't come back … I don't know what I'll do." She looked up to meet Caleb's gaze. "I love him so much," she whispered.

Caleb wrapped his arm around her shoulder and pulled her closer. "He loves you, too," he said. "Have faith in that. Now let's go find something to eat."

They walked to a place just off the main road that buzzed with conversation. In the corner was a TV, tuned into the local station. A ski report gave way to local news as they ate.

"Last night, in a startling heist, a cougar was stolen from a trailer in Cranbrook," the news announcer said.

Caleb and Melissa both stared at the screen.

"Ruth McAlister, an animal handler from the Calgary Zoo, saw a man and a woman loading the cougar onto the back of a truck. The lock on the trailer had been broken. The cougar was recently the center of attention at the Calgary Zoo when protesters demanded that the animal, being treated for a gunshot wound, be released. The animal was being moved to a more secure facility for its own protection."

"Right!" Melissa snickered.

"The man and woman are said to be in their twenties," the news reporter continued, "driving a dark truck with an Alberta number plate. Anyone with information can call 9-

1-1."

Across the room a man laughed. "Hear that, Tom?" he said. "A dark truck with Alberta plates. Describes half the vehicles here."

Melissa glanced at Caleb, who shrugged with a half grin. "Hide in plain sight," he said softly.

She was about to respond when her phone buzzed. She grabbed it from her bag, then frowned when she saw the number. "It's Dr. Pettigrew," she said. She looked at Caleb as she answered the call.

"Hello?"

"Ms. Hewitt? I'm glad to have reached you. Where are you?"

Melissa thought furiously. "Why do you want to know?"

"Do you know that Guen was stolen last night?"

"Stolen? That's terrible. By who?"

Dr. Pettigrew laughed. "Not very convincing, I'm afraid. I've already given your name and number to the police, so I'm sure you'll be hearing from them soon."

"I've got nothing to hide, Dr. Pettigrew. But thank you for the heads-up."

"I have no doubt you were involved, and you can be sure that the police will not let this matter go without a thorough investigation. Your cell will be even smaller than Guen's was."

Her fingers were shaking as she ended the call. "He's given my name to the police." She scrolled through the list of missed calls. "Someone tried to call me while we were sleeping – maybe it was them."

"He's trying to frighten you. All they can do is ask questions. No one saw you. And they won't be looking for Lee's truck."

"No, but if—" Her mouth hung open for a moment as she looked at Caleb. "Security cameras! We both passed though the motel lobby to use the restrooms." She glanced around. "Do you think they have cameras here?"

"Oh, God. I hadn't thought of that. And they can track your phone."

She stared at the phone on the table, then hurriedly powered it off as she gathered her thoughts. "Okay. I'm not leaving without Lee, but you've got to get out of here. Back to Calgary, then home. Or go home straight from here. Take the bus."

"I'm not leaving you here!"

"You have to. There's no point both of us being caught."

"They already have plenty of evidence that I'm here, Mel. We're in this together and I'm staying."

She slumped back in her seat. "I'm such an idiot," she said. "I should have known they'd come after me as soon as we took Lee. But all I could think of was getting Lee out of there."

Caleb laughed humorlessly. "You and me both," he said. "Just goes to show we're not cut out to be criminals. Still, I'd do it all again to know my brother's free."

"Me too," she said softly. "I just hope he really is free."

They returned to the motel after their meal and stayed in the room the rest of the day. They checked the news from time to time, but there was no new information. Caleb plugged earbuds into his ears and slumped down in the chair while Melissa tried to read. She couldn't concentrate, and after a while she lay on the bed and stared at the stains on the ceiling. As the sky grew dark she turned on the TV to watch old reruns. Later, Caleb went out to get pizza, and they ate it on the bed while watching

Mission Impossible. At midnight Caleb switched off the light and they both lay down.

"What if he doesn't come, Caleb?" Melissa said as she stared at the dark.

Caleb was silent for a moment. "He'll come," he finally said. "But it may take a little longer than we thought." He turned to look at her in the dark. "I think we need to go home. He's a smart boy and can find his way back if he wants to."

"One more day. Let's give him one more day."

Caleb was silent for a moment. "Okay," he finally said. "One more day."

Melissa woke as the light was starting to filter through the thin curtains. Caleb was no longer on the bed, but she wasn't alone. Sitting on the chair at the chipped plywood desk, his body stiff with tension, was Lee, wearing the clothes Caleb had brought from the cabin.

"You're here," she cried. "Are you alright? I've been so worried." He didn't appear hurt, but then Caleb had said he'd heal as soon as he changed. She leaped up and ran to him, but he immediately jumped from the chair and stepped back, his hands held out as a barrier.

"Stop," he whispered hoarsely.

"Lee? What is it?"

"I tried to hurt you."

"Yes, but you weren't thinking straight."

He made an angry noise. "I know very well what I did. I could have killed you."

"But you didn't," she said softly.

"This is why we can't be together, Melissa." His voice was harsh. "You had to rescue me. You had to free the panther. Then at the first chance, I attack you! I could smell your fear, and I can't blame you. You deserve better than a wild animal."

"No! I love you!"

He made a dismissive noise. "You love a wild animal? Maybe it's pity that you feel. Or perhaps the strangeness factor appeals to you. But you cannot love something you fear. I should have listened to my instincts – it would have saved us both a lot of trouble."

"Lee, please—"

"We're done, Melissa. This is an experiment gone wrong. A big mistake."

She stared at him in disbelief. She must be hearing wrong – after everything they'd been through, he couldn't possibly be saying what she thought he was saying. "Done? No! You don't mean that! We both know you feel something for me!"

Lee laughed sardonically. "Oh, I feel something, all right." He took a step closer and bared his teeth. "I feel you'd make a tasty snack."

Melissa stared at him angrily. "You think that's going to scare me? The only one scared here is you. You're scared of admitting that you love me. You're scared that you'll lose that tight control you keep over yourself." She poked a finger in his chest. "You're scared of feeling *anything*, so you push me away. But I will not be pushed away!"

Lee stepped back. "You don't have a choice," he said. "Once we're back home, I don't ever want to see you again. You can go back to your life, your job, your friends, and forget all about me."

"What job, Lee? I lost my job because I was at the zoo, trying to rescue you."

"You lost your job?" His expression softened slightly. "I'm very sorry about that, but it doesn't change anything."

"You're sorry?" she shouted. "You're sorry? Well, kiss my ass!" She flung the door open and stormed out, slamming it behind her as furious tears streamed down her cheeks. She heard footsteps behind her, then Caleb's voice.

"Melissa! Where are you going?"

She spun to face him. "Go ask Lee! He wants nothing more to do with me."

"What? Why?"

"All because he took that swipe at me. But he growled at you too. Does that mean you're no longer his brother?"

"He's feeling guilty, Mel."

"I know that! He doesn't trust himself to be in control around me. So whenever he feels like he's losing control, he pushes me away. What about what *I* want?"

"Give him time."

"I've given him plenty of time!" She began walking back to the room. "If he wants to get rid of me, then fine. Let's get home, and he can have his wish."

"Mel—"

"Caleb, stop. There's no more to say."

He sighed. "Fine! But when you've calmed down, think about how much you love him. And don't give up on him. He needs you."

Melissa's eyes filled with tears. "I need him too," she said softly.

They stepped into the room. It was empty, and on the bed was a note: *Go home*, it read. *I'll find my own way back.*

Melissa stared at it for a moment, then tossed it to Caleb. "Let's go," she said.

They arrived back at Lee's cabin four hours later. Melissa's car was covered in a layer of snow and she brushed it off angrily before climbing in and driving home.

She'd been home only a short while when she was startled by a knock at the door. She opened it to find a uniformed officer standing outside, his blue eyes looking at her questioningly.

"Ms. Hewitt? I'm Detective Hindley." He pulled out a badge and flashed it at her. "May I come in? I need to ask you a few questions."

Melissa moved aside as he entered. "I've been trying to get a hold of you for the last few days, Ms. Hewitt. Have you been away?"

"I was with my boyfriend," she said.

"And where's your boyfriend now?"

She shrugged. "No idea. We broke up."

"I see. You've had a busy few days, haven't you? Rescue a cougar, launch a protest, break up with your boyfriend."

Melissa raised her eyebrows but remained silent.

"You're aware by now that the cougar you rescued was stolen."

Melissa sat down on the couch. "I am."

"Did you steal it?"

Could a person be stolen? "No," she said, "I did not steal him."

"What about your friend? What was his name? Caleb?"

"I don't believe he stole the cougar, either."

"Ms. Hewitt, can you tell me where you were the last few days?"

"Fernie."

Detective Hindley sat down across from her. "And what were you doing in Fernie?"

"I've already told you. I was with my boyfriend."

"Ah, yes. Caleb, is it?"

"No. Leander Garrett."

"I see." He pulled out a notepad and made a note. "And where can I find Mr. Garrett?"

"I have no idea. He was going to find his own way home. He has an apartment in Crescent Heights."

Hindley leaned back in the seat. "I'm going to be honest with you, Ms. Hewitt. Things aren't looking good for you. Although you deny stealing the cougar, you admit to being in the area where the crime was committed."

"What would I do with a cougar, Detective Hindley?"

"You wanted it released, didn't you? My guess is that's exactly what you've done."

"Wouldn't that be a good thing, Detective? Free a wild animal from imprisonment and release it back in the wild? What makes it the property of the zoo?"

"The zoo had taken on the cost of the creature's recovery, and staff were acting with public interest in mind."

"Are you aware that I paid the initial medical bills for the cougar? The only reason he ended up at the zoo is because I rescued him, got him to a vet and paid the bill. He should never have been locked up."

The detective frowned slightly. "My information is that the zoo has covered all the creature's costs."

"You can contact Dr. Marshall at Turner Valley. He'll confirm I paid the bill."

"We've already spoken to him. He made no mention of that."

"What? But …" She paused. "Wait. I paid with my credit card. I can show you the payment."

She fetched her laptop and powered it on, then opened her bank account. "Look. There," she said, pointing at the entry.

"I see." He frowned some more and wrote a few more lines in his notepad. "Hmm. Well ... I'll be in touch, Ms. Hewitt. Good day."

He let himself out as Melissa slumped back on the couch.

Her first thoughts the next morning were of Lee. Had he made it home? Was he lost in the mountains? Maybe he'd been shot again. She shook her head, pushing the thoughts away. She walked through to the kitchen to start a pot of coffee and picked up her phone to see a message from Caleb: *Lee's home*.

She allowed herself a small smile of relief. Now she wondered, had Detective Hindley tried contacting Lee yet? Had he spoken to Caleb? She stared at the phone for a moment before typing in a new message. *Detective probably coming to your place to ask questions about theft of cougar*, she wrote to Lee. *I told him we were in Fernie for a few days and that we broke up.*

She put the phone away and made some coffee. Detective Hindley was only one of her problems. She'd lost her job, and worst of all, Lee had broken up with her. But what else had she expected – if he couldn't love himself, how could she expect him to love her?

She was on her second cup of coffee when her phone rang. It was Lauren.

"Where have you been?" Lauren demanded as soon as Melissa answered the call. "I've been trying to get hold of you."

"It's a long story."

"Well, you'd better get started." Melissa took in a deep breath, swallowing the sob that suddenly came out of nowhere. "Mel? Are you all right, sweetie?" Lauren's tone softened.

Melissa gulped back the tears. "Oh, Lar, I've lost my job, the police are asking questions about a missing cougar, and Lee's dumped me!"

"What? Wait! What are you talking about? You've lost your job? The police are talking to you? And who's Lee?" She paused, then said, "What's going on, Mel?"

"I can't explain it all. There was a cougar that was shot, and I helped it, and—"

"What cougar?"

Melissa closed her eyes and drew a deep breath, gathering her thoughts. Slowly, she related the events of the past week, starting with the hunting trip, and explaining what she'd done to save the cougar, omitting, of course, that the cougar was actually Lee. "When the zoo took him away, I had to get him free," she said.

"That's, er, admirable, but Mel, surely the zoo was the best place for him?"

"No! He's a wild animal. He shouldn't be locked in a cage!"

"So you risked everything for a cougar?" Lauren said incredulously. "Is that why you lost your job?"

"I told Annika I was in Vancouver with a sick family member, but she saw me on TV at the protest."

"Protest? What protest?" Lauren said in confusion. Melissa took a sip of her coffee, grimacing when the now cool liquid hit her tongue, then recounted the events that followed Lee been taken to the zoo. She explained how she'd contacted Rheagan, and how her protest had led to the cougar being taken away.

"Caleb and I tracked him to Cranbrook, where we released him from his cage."

"Who's Caleb?"

"Lee's brother."

"I'm confused. What's his brother got to do with all of this?"

"We wanted to free the cougar, but Lee was away, so Caleb helped me instead."

"And now this Lee's broken up with you?"

"Yes. He's an idiot," she said dully.

"They all are. What did he do?"

"He says he can't be with me anymore!" Melissa wailed. "He doesn't think he's lovable."

"Why not?"

Melissa sighed. "He's … different."

"Different, how?"

"Just … different. He's not like other men."

Lauren was silent for a moment. "Do you love him?"

"I do! Very much."

"And does he love you?"

"I think so."

"So what are you going to do?"

"I don't know. He did something he thinks is unforgivable."

"He isn't hurting you, is he?"

"No. But he thinks he could."

"Could he?"

"No more than Nick could hurt you."

"So give him a day or two, then go after him."

"You think so?"

"If you don't, you'll always wonder if you should have."

Melissa sighed. "You're right. I can't just let him walk away."

"But don't do anything stupid, sweetie. And if he hurts

you, get the hell away from him." Melissa wasn't surprised at the vehemence in Lauren's voice.

"I will."

"Okay. Love you. I'm glad you're alright – I was worried when I couldn't get a hold of you. And let me know what happens."

"Love you, too," Melissa said.

CHAPTER 24

Detective Hindley knocked on Melissa's door early on Monday morning.

"Ms. Hewitt," he said as he settled himself on the couch, "we've been in touch with Leander Garrett. He confirms you were together in Fernie until Friday morning when you split up." Melissa felt some of her tension ease. "Although I have no doubt that you were somehow involved in the cougar's disappearance," Hindley continued, "we've decided not to pursue charges against you."

Melissa clenched her hands in her lap to stop them trembling and lifted her chin. "I should think not," she said.

Hindley watched her for a moment. "I'm sure you can guess that zoo officials are not too happy about this decision, but since it was your actions that placed the cougar in their care, they can't claim ownership of the animal. There is the matter of you endangering public safety by releasing a dangerous animal back into the wild; however, at this stage, the extent of the danger is purely speculation, and it doesn't appear you released it in the center of town."

Detective Hindley rose to leave, then added, "If we find you involved in such activities again, we will not hesitate to come after you with the full weight of the law." He yanked the door open and strode from the apartment.

Melissa stared at the door as a wave of relief washed over her. One less thing to worry about. Now she just had to sort out the lack of employment issue. Having no income was definitely a problem. She spent the rest of the day trawling through websites, reading job listings, and making notes before finally slamming her laptop closed in frustration. Only a few positions were suitable for her, and none were particularly interesting. She had considered contacting Cynthia to see if she had any leads, but after all that had happened, it seemed wrong to ask her. She poured herself a glass of wine, then headed for the shower.

Despite her concern about her lack of employment, Melissa slept through the night for the first time since Lee had been shot. It had helped speaking to Lauren about him, even if she couldn't share everything, and the fact that she wasn't headed for a prison cell was also a relief.

The next morning, she took her time eating her cereal, then checked a few job sites before heading into the park for a jog. By the time she returned, it was already past noon, and she headed to the bathroom for a quick shower. There was a message flashing on her phone when she emerged from the bathroom a few minutes later. She didn't recognize the number and turned her attention to her dripping hair after pressing the PLAY button, only giving the message half her attention. She stopped what she was doing when she heard Pamela's voice.

Melissa! She sounded frantic. *Emma wandered off last night and they haven't been able to find her. It's all over the news!*

"No," Melissa whispered. She powered on her laptop and opened a local news feed, searching for the story. The article about Emma was halfway down the page, with a photo of the little girl. She read it with mounting horror.

'In the Lethbridge area, the search continues for a young girl. Emma Bell was last seen on Monday evening playing outside the family home. Police spent the night combing the area and are calling on citizens to help in searching for the little girl.

'Emma was badly injured in a car accident that took the lives of her mother and baby brother earlier this year, and was only recently released from Children's Hospital in Calgary. With temperatures dropping below zero, police are concerned about her chances of survival.'

Melissa sank down on the bed and stared blankly at the screen. How could they not find her? She was still recovering from her injuries – she couldn't possibly get very far. Melissa turned to the window and stared out as she thought of the little girl in the hospital bed. She had to help! She had to get to Lethbridge.

She was about to leave the apartment when she thought of Lee. Had he heard the news? she wondered. Would he have texted her if he had? She grabbed her phone and fumbled with the letters as she typed a message. *Did you hear about Emma?* She pressed SEND, and only a few seconds had passed when the phone rang.

"Did I hear what about Emma?" Lee demanded before

she could say anything. "What's happened?"

"She wandered from home last night and they can't find her," she said. "It's been on the news." Her voice was breaking, and she fought for control.

He was silent for a moment. "Are you at home?" he finally asked.

She swallowed a sob. "Yes."

"I'll be there in twenty minutes," he said. "We'll drive to Lethbridge together."

The line went dead before she could respond, and she headed downstairs. When Lee pulled up in front of her building fifteen minutes later, she was waiting at the curb.

"What else can you tell me?" he asked as they sped off.

She filled him in on what she'd learned.

"We'll find her," he said. "One way or another," he added darkly.

They lapsed into silence as Lee drove along the southbound highway, Melissa lost in her thoughts. He didn't even reduce his speed when they hit the small towns along the way, but flew through them as though the devil were on his tail. Melissa barely noticed at first, but when another small town blurred past, she looked over at him. His jaw was clenched and he tapped a monotonous rhythm with his fingers against the steering wheel. His body was aligned away from her, and every once in a while he opened his window slightly and breathed in the outside air.

"What are you doing?" she finally said when a small blast of cold air hit her for the fifth time.

"I need air," he muttered.

"What's wrong with the air in the truck?"

"It smells of you," he grumbled.

She looked at him incredulously for a moment, then

burst out laughing. "You don't want to smell me?" she sputtered between hysterical giggles.

"It's not funny," he said with a frown.

She gulped in some air and hiccupped. "I thought you liked my smell," she said, trying to keep her face straight.

"That's the problem!" he snapped. "After your little joyride with Caleb, your smell was all over everything. I thought I could handle it, but now that you're here, it's a hundred times worse."

"That little joyride was to save your butt," she snapped back. "And I'm glad you can smell me – it's a reminder of what you so callously threw away." He glowered at her for a moment, then turned back to the road. She stared out of the window, then grabbed the blanket from the back seat when Lee cracked the window open once more.

They did not speak again, and when they arrived at the Lethbridge Police Station, Melissa jumped from the truck without a glance in Lee's direction. She was already explaining to the police officer behind the desk why they were there when Lee came in behind her.

"I'll give you directions to the Bell place," the officer said. "The search isn't going well, so we appreciate all the help we can get. We just hope we can reach her in time."

"She's not dead," Melissa said firmly.

The officer looked at her questioningly, but remained silent as she wrote on a slip of paper. "Here you go," she said, handing the sheet to Lee. He took it without a word and headed back outside, Melissa behind him. They followed the directions out of town to the Bell farm.

It took another twenty minutes, bouncing over country roads, before they pulled up outside a small farmhouse with police cars and other vehicles parked outside. Lee grabbed a backpack from the back of the truck and stomped his way into the house, Melissa on his tail. On a couch in the front room sat Emma's father, John. He looked smaller than the last time Melissa had seen him, his expression dazed. A half dozen police officers stood around the room, and in one corner a desk had been cleared and a command center set up with phones, walkie-talkies, and maps spread across the surface. A police officer was scribbling on a pad of paper.

"We're here to help with the search," Lee said.

The police office looked up. "Good. We've set up a grid so that each area is covered." He stabbed a finger at the map. "You can head out here."

"What about the dogs?"

"It snowed overnight, and they haven't been able to pick up a scent."

As Lee talked to the officer, Melissa walked over to John.

"John?" When he looked up, his eyes were rimmed with red. "Remember me? From the hospital?"

"Oh, yes. Melissa, is it? Emma talks about you a lot." His eyes filled with tears as he mentioned his daughter's name. He wiped them away with the back of his hand. "I've lost my wife and son, and now my precious Emma. If she's gone ... I'll have nothing to live for anymore."

"Please don't say that. We'll find her, I know it."

"Melissa, let's go," Lee said. He didn't wait for her as he headed out the door.

Melissa caught up with him as he crossed the front yard. "Which way?"

"I'll know in a minute."

Their boots crunched through the thin layer of snow as they made their way into a field away from the house. They had been walking for a while when Lee stopped and sniffed the air. He turned and walked another few steps, then sniffed again. He did it a few more times, then pointed at a distant stand of trees. "She went this way," he said. "You wait here."

"What are you going to do?"

"I'll reach her much faster if I change." He handed her the backpack. "When I'm done, put my clothes in here and strap it to me."

She took the backpack as he stripped off the thin jacket he wore, followed by his shirt. He handed them to her, then pushed off his boots. Out of modesty, she turned when he started unbuckling his jeans, and a moment later she felt a surge of energy swell through the air. It lifted the hair on her neck, and she shivered slightly as she turned to look at the magnificent panther standing before her. She stared at him until he nudged her, his eyes on the backpack. She stuffed in his clothes, then looped the pack over his legs and clipped the waist belt around his middle. He turned and took off flying over the fields, and she watched as he disappeared from view.

The sun was already low on the horizon, taking away the little warmth it had offered, and she shivered. How could Emma have survived such temperatures? she wondered, rubbing her hands over her arms. Standing still, the cold seeped through the fabric of her jacket. She began to pace as her toes grew numb. In the fading light she could see the distant beams of flashlights of other searchers, and the occasional shout of "Emma!" drifted through the air.

It was almost dark when she finally saw someone coming toward her. She ran forward when she recognized Lee's human form, a small bundle held tight against his chest, covered with his jacket.

"Is she okay?" She reached Lee and gently pulled away the jacket. "Emma? Sweetie?" Tears streamed unheeded down her cheeks, and she sobbed even harder when Emma opened her eyes and slowly turned a pale, mud streaked face to her.

"Mel? What are you doing here?"

"Looking for you, baby!" she said, her voice ragged.

"I saw Bagheera, Mel. He showed Lee where to find me."

"You're safe now, baby girl. Bagheera made sure of that."

"Is Daddy mad? He said I'm not allowed to go outside." She started crying. "I wanted to go to the jungle, but nobody would take me!"

Melissa glanced at Lee. "I think she means the forest," he said.

"It's okay," Melissa said. "Your daddy's not mad. Just worried. Lee's going to carry you home so Daddy can see you're safe."

"Will you be there too?"

"I'll be there."

Emma closed her eyes. "'Kay."

Lee pulled her closer to his chest as they started a quick walk back to the farmhouse. "She'd wriggled her way under some bushes," he said. "That protection saved her life."

John saw them first as they stepped into the house, and within a moment was rushing forward.

"Emma!" he cried.

"Daddy?" Lee pushed Emma into John's outstretched arms as the room suddenly swarmed into motion.

"Quick! Get the paramedics," shouted an officer.

"Where did you find her?" demanded another.

Lee answered the questions as Melissa watched John hold his daughter against his chest and cry. "I'm sorry, Daddy," she whispered, making the tears flow faster.

"It's okay, baby," he said gently. "You've got nothing to be sorry for. I'm just glad you're safe." He dropped to the couch as the tears streamed down his face. "I thought I'd lost you, too."

It was late by the time Lee had finished answering the officers' questions, and he and Melissa were finally able to head back home.

"The police must have been surprised at how quickly you found Emma," Melissa said as they made their way back to the highway.

"They were," he replied. "That's why they took so long questioning me. They thought I might have been involved in her disappearance."

"Huh," Melissa grunted, offended.

Lee gave her grin. "It's not unreasonable," he said. "My answers weren't very satisfactory."

"What did you tell them?"

"That Emma and I read *The Jungle Book* while she was in hospital, and because of her fascination with Bagheera, I thought she might head for the forest."

"I suppose that does sound rather vague," Melissa conceded. "What did Emma do when she saw you? Was she scared?"

"Not at all!" Lee sounded as if he couldn't quite believe it. "I knew where to find her as soon as I picked up her scent. My plan was to change before she saw me, but I wasn't quick enough. She called me Bagheera and said she knew I'd find her. And after I changed, she kept asking where Bagheera was."

"What did you tell her?"

"That his job had been to lead me to her, and once he'd done that, he knew he could go."

She smiled. "You saved Emma tonight."

"Someone else might have found her."

"Not as quickly as you. Your ability to change means Emma is alive."

His jaw tightened. "It's not a gift."

She touched his hand lightly with her fingers. "Yes," she said. "It is."

He was silent as she gently caressed his hand.

CHAPTER 25

Melissa dozed as Lee flew along the highway, and she was startled when he shook her awake.

"You're home, Mel," he said softly. She looked around blearily to see they were outside her apartment block. He stepped out of the truck and opened her door. "Let's get you to bed," he said, taking her by the hand and helping her out. The cold night air hit her face, chasing away all traces of sleep as she followed Lee into the building. He dropped her hand when they reached the elevator, and they rode to her floor in silence.

When she opened the door he started backing away. "Goodnight, Mel."

"Don't go," she said.

"I can't stay."

"Please? Just for a few minutes."

He looked down the passage for a moment, then turned

back to her. "Think you can make some coffee? It's been a pretty long day."

"I think I can manage that." He followed her into the kitchen. "How's the wound?" she asked as she filled the coffee pot.

"Fine. Changing forms heals all wounds." He smiled grimly. "The problem was I couldn't change."

"Caleb said you'd be healed when you changed. I couldn't quite imagine it, though."

He lifted his shirt to show his smooth skin. "Look."

Melissa stared at his side. "You should never have taken that bullet for me, Lee," she said.

He snorted softly beneath his breath. "I said I'd always protect you, didn't I?" He sighed. "The only thing I can't protect you from is me."

Melissa shook her head, but it was no use arguing. "I was so scared seeing you wounded like that. I was sure Richard or Mike were going to kill you."

"They would have if you hadn't fought so hard for me. Thank you."

"What was it like? Being stuck in that cage?"

He leaned against the wall as the smell of brewing coffee filled the room. "When I woke up after the surgery, I was already at the zoo. The fact that I couldn't change made me pretty mad, groggy as I was. But you came by the next morning, and then later again with Caleb, and I knew then that it would be okay."

"You mean you weren't sure I'd come back for you?" she said in surprise.

"I was in pain and full of drugs. I wasn't thinking clearly."

"I would've stayed longer if I could."

"You were scared of me."

"Just for a moment. It was an instinctive reaction. A flight response."

"That's exactly as it should be. You should be scared when you see a wild panther."

Melissa shook her head. "You're not wild. And I'm not scared of you."

He smiled wryly. "Your instinctive reaction is one of fear. And you should always follow your instincts."

"No." She leaned against the counter. "Sometimes instincts are wrong. Just like your instinct to attack after your release was wrong. You'd been in a cage for days, unable to change, pumped full of drugs, then tranquilized. I'm not surprised you acted as you did."

"The wildness was growing in me," he admitted. "Each day that passed and I was unable to change, I felt like I was becoming more and more the wild cat and leaving my humanity behind. And after you released me – when you opened the truck – your scent overwhelmed me, and it was more than I could bear. All rational thought was gone – I was purely following instinct. I just wanted to taste you."

Melissa swallowed as she stared at him. "The drugs made you crazy," she said. "They do that to regular people, too. But I think you still want me. You want to breathe in my scent, and taste my kisses." She took a step towards him and lifted her hand to his cheek. "Tell me I'm wrong," she whispered.

"Stop," he said hoarsely. "I can't do this, Mel. Me being with you – it puts you in danger."

"I don't believe that," she said. "You won't harm me. You want to be with me."

"It doesn't matter what I want," he said angrily. "Don't you see that I'm doing this for you?"

"No," she said, "you're doing this because you have

some misguided belief that you're dangerous, and you can't let go of your control." His jaw clenched. "I love you, Lee," she said.

He groaned. "Don't!"

"Tell me you don't love me."

"I don't love you."

She swallowed the lump in her throat. "I don't believe you."

"I mean it," he snarled, "I don't love you. I don't know how to love."

"You do. Just let your heart go."

She leaned closer, and then his lips were on hers, hot and demanding as his fingers wound into her hair. He pushed her against the wall, pressing himself into her as she wrapped her hands around his neck and pulled him closer. She slipped her hands under his shirt and he groaned, but a moment later he was gone as he tore himself away with a savage growl.

"Are you happy now?" he spat. "I want you as my mate, Mel, but it's never going to happen, because I'm nothing but an animal."

"No," she said. "You're not. You're the man I love. And I'm prepared to take whatever risk you think I'm taking to be with you. But I know I have nothing to fear, because you're a good man, Lee."

"You don't know that."

"I do. I feel it in my bones." When he remained silent, she wrapped her arms around his waist. "I love you, Lee. Love me in return."

She felt the moment his resistance started to weaken. The tension in his back loosened, and his hands slipped loosely around her. "I do love you, Mel," he whispered hoarsely. "I wish I could stay with you forever."

"You can."

"I'm a Changer. We can't be together."

"Is there a Changer law that says you cannot be with a human?"

He gave a cynical smile. "Not exactly."

"Then explain it for me, and don't tell me it's because you're a danger to me."

"You're the first – and only – person I've ever loved," he said. "The animal inside me knows that, and recognizes you as my mate."

"I'm your mate?" she said with a grin.

"Only if we join together."

"So what's the problem?"

"The first time we make love, it will start the mating cycle."

"Mating cycle?"

"When that happens, the pull of the next full moon will be stronger than anything before. You already know how I struggle to resist the pull of the moon when I'm with you." Melissa nodded. "The pull will be even stronger. I'll …" He drew in a deep breath. "I'll start changing a little at a time. By the time the moon is full, I'll have changed completely."

"When you say a little at a time—"

"I'll be half human, half animal."

"How long does it last?"

"Until the moon starts waning. But if the mating cycle isn't completed, it will happen each time the moon is full."

"How do you complete the mating cycle?"

He stared down at her for a moment before replying. "We'd have to consummate the joining while I'm in panther form." Melissa's eyes opened wide, and he gave a soft snort. "Now do you see why we can't be together?"

"You'd have to make love to me as an animal?"

"Yes."

"And if we don't?"

"Then the next time the moon starts waxing, I'll start changing again. With each lunar cycle, the pull will be stronger and I'll start changing earlier in the cycle. If the union is never consummated, I'd eventually be unable to take the human form at all."

"You'd be a panther forever?"

"Yes."

"But you've been with other woman. Why hasn't it happened before?"

"The mating cycle only begins when I'm with the one I choose as my mate – the one the animal within me recognizes as its mate. And that's you."

"How do you know all this? Has it happened before?"

"My grandfather had a cousin whose mating cycle was never completed. His wife was too terrified to let her panther husband near her. Grandfather said by the end there was nothing human left in him."

"What happened to him?"

"He killed his wife and ate her."

"Oh. I … I see." She pulled away and grabbed some mugs from the cupboard.

"Still think I'm not a danger?" he said dryly. He went into the sitting room, dropping to the couch with his head between his hands.

Melissa poured coffee into the mugs. What Lee had described was animalistic. Bestial. Except Lee wouldn't truly be an animal. Even when he was in animal form, he retained his humanity – except for when he was pumped full of drugs. But his humanity was evident in how he looked at her and the way he touched her. She closed her eyes and thought of him as she'd seen him at the zoo. He was incredibly beautiful – sleek and feline. And when his tongue had rasped over her skin – she shivered again, but not from repulsion. She carried the coffee into the living room.

"You're not a danger. I want you, Lee, and you want me."

He looked at her incredulously. "Did you not just hear me tell you what would happen?"

"I heard you say you wanted me for a mate. And I want to be your mate."

"You want to be my mate?" He laughed, but without humor. "Were you listening when I said what would happen when we don't complete the cycle? Do you want to force me into becoming a full-time animal?"

"I want you in any form I can have you."

"No," he said, "you wouldn't be able to do it. You'd be scared and would leave me high and dry."

"You know, your lack of faith in me is insulting."

"It's not a lack of faith," he said. "But I've smelled your fear."

"Sure, when you were about to attack me. And you smelled a whiff of fear when I entered the cage with you. What about all the other times I wasn't afraid?"

He looked away.

"If you're worried, then give me a chance to get used to you in panther form." Sitting beside him, she said, "In the cage you licked my hand … it was very sexy." She met his surprised look. "Show me how incredible the panther can be." She saw him swallow, and she smiled.

"I don't know, Mel."

"I do. *I want you.*"

He met her gaze, then bent down and covered her

mouth with his own. His kiss was slow and leisurely as he stroked her with his tongue. "I love you," he said when he pulled away.

"Are you sure?" she teased. "I seem to remember you telling me most emphatically that you don't." She pulled back, but he caught her by her shirt and yanked her closer. "Maybe you're right," he said. "I definitely don't love you."

"Me neither," she said with a laugh as he kissed her once more.

"Did you mean it when you said you wanted me in any form you can have me? That you want to be my mate?"

"I've never been as certain of anything in my life."

"Then marry me first." The smile fell from her face as he slipped off the couch and dropped to his knee. "Melissa Hewitt," he said, "will you do me the honor of becoming my wife?"

"Lee … I … just a few minutes ago you weren't even sure you could be with me, and now you want to marry me?"

"A few minutes ago you said you wanted to be my mate. Have you changed your mind?"

"No. It's just—"

He rose from the floor and sat down beside her. "Mating is far more permanent than marriage. And I've always wanted you. I just never thought I could have you."

"But … marriage? We've only been together for a few months!"

"If you're not prepared to marry me, then we can't be mated. But from the first moment I met you, Mel, I recognized you as the only one for me. And I think you felt the same about me, didn't you?"

"I, uh—"

"There's a reason you never dated anyone. Why you'd watch me when you thought I wouldn't notice. Why your scent intensified whenever you were around me."

She blushed. "That's not—"

"It is true. Admit it."

She studied her hands for a moment. "You're right," she whispered. "I felt like we were connected somehow, even though you were pushing me away. But that doesn't change the fact that when you leave here, you might start thinking about how dangerous you are and push me away yet again."

"And you're right too. I haven't been fair to you. You have every reason to think I'll turn away. But if we're mated, I will never leave you again. The animal won't let me. In the wild, panthers don't mate for life, but Changers do. Our connection goes beyond what most humans feel – there's a primal animal bond that ties us with our mate. But I want more than just animal instinct holding us together. Marriage is a human choice, and I choose you."

"I'm not—"

"Do you need time to decide whether you even want to be with me?"

"No. I know how I feel."

"Then what's holding you back?"

"Let me be with you at the next full moon, and then I'll give you an answer."

He drew a startled breath. "I could hurt you."

"You want to make love to me while you're a panther – how is that not more dangerous?" He was silent. "Until you're prepared to be with me as a panther, and believe you can't hurt me, I can't marry you."

"Okay," he said slowly, taking her hand in his. "So if we spend the full moon together you'll marry me?"

"*After* we've spent the full moon together, Lee, I'll be ready to give you an answer one way or another."

"There's only one answer," he said. He leaned closer and skimmed his nose along her cheek before bringing his lips to hers.

CHAPTER 26

Melissa was in her apartment two days later when her phone rang.

"Melissa?" Norm's voice from Quigs came through the line. "Do you have a moment?"

"Yes."

"Lee was just in my office, and he tells me things didn't work out at Mercer."

"That's right," she replied cautiously.

"We need another analyst for a new client we've just signed. Are you interested? It would just be a contract position for the duration of the project."

Melissa drew in a surprised breath. "Yes," she said. "Of course!"

"Good!" She could almost see Norm scribbling notes at his desk. "Can you start Monday?"

"Yes. Yes, thank you!"

Melissa ended the call in a dazed state of elation. It wasn't a permanent position, but at least it gave her something in the meantime. She sent Lee a quick message: *Just spoke to Norm. Thank you!*

Her phone buzzed a moment later. *I just mentioned you were looking. It's your skills that got you the job.*

She smiled. *Then thank you for mentioning.*

Monday morning dawned cold and gray, and Melissa pulled her thick, woolen scarf to her chin as she made her way to the bus stop. She and Lee had agreed that they needed to be discreet in the office about their relationship, and she wondered as she rode the bus how she was going to manage to keep her feelings secret.

She stepped through the double glass doors of Quigs half an hour later, and Mary waved from behind the reception desk.

"Glad you're back, Melissa," she said with a smile.

Melissa nodded, but her attention was on the man standing at the far end of the office. His back was to her, but he lifted his head as she entered, then turned to face her. His eyes burned into hers over the span of the office, and she turned away with difficulty when Norm came over.

"Melissa! So glad you're back. We have a desk set up for you with the other analysts." She followed him as he led her to a desk near the kitchen. "I'm sure Lee will fill you in on your next project as soon as you're settled." She was working with Lee – he hadn't mentioned that to her. "Come see me when you have a moment," Norm continued, "there's a pile of paperwork that needs to be completed."

"Thanks, Norm," she said. Except for her new desk, it

felt as though she had never left Quigs. Nothing had changed – everyone still sat where they had sat before, and Tracy and Caro were still gossiping at their desks. Kasper came over as she hung up her coat.

"So you're back."

"I am. Good to see you, Kasper."

"Lee was just over here. He wants you working with him."

"Yes," she said as she switched on her computer. "Norm told me."

"I thought you two didn't get on," Kasper said. "Why would he want you on his team?"

"Maybe you should ask *him* that," she said.

"What I really want to know is why you came back. And why Lee and Norm allowed you to. It's not what I expected from *you*."

"It's not like that, Kasper."

"Whatever," he said as he stalked away.

She frowned as she logged on to the computer with the password Norm had left at her desk. She had hoped for a better reaction from Kasper. A message from Lee popped up on the screen: *Please come by when you have a moment.* She checked her other messages and printed off some forms that needed to be completed, then headed over to Lee's office.

He rose as she entered and came around his desk as she shut the door firmly behind her. "Good morning," he said, running a finger over her hand.

"You didn't mention I would be on your team." she said. "Are you a masochist?"

He smiled. "Maybe. Or maybe I just think you're a very good analyst."

"I don't know how good I'll be if I have to work with

you," she said pointedly.

"We'll have to find out, won't we?"

She gave a small laugh. "Will they fire me if I leap at you across the table?"

"I may be the one leaping, and then they'll definitely fire me, since I'll be covered in black fur!"

"I don't know if I can do this."

He placed his hands on her shoulders. "Of course you can. We've worked together before, and we can do it again."

"That was different. I thought you hated me."

"You can still pretend I do." He scowled dramatically. "Get me those numbers, Ms. Hewitt, and some coffee while you're at it."

She laughed. "That's not going to happen."

"Well, I tried!"

She grew serious. "Things can't be as they were before, Lee. I understand why you pushed me away, but your reasons are no longer relevant. You wanted me on your team for my analytical skills, and you have to respect me as your colleague."

"You're right."

"I'm glad you can see that." She smiled.

"Speaking of self-improvement, I've been doing some thinking over the last few days."

"That sounds dangerous."

"All these years I've seen what I am as a curse. But when I rescued Emma, it felt … good, as if I could do something worthwhile in the world."

"It was more than good. You saved her, Lee."

"Which made me think that maybe you're right. It's not a curse, but a gift. Instead of hating what I am, maybe I can use it to do good."

"What are you saying?"

"I'm not completely sure yet. But I was thinking that people get lost all the time. Perhaps I could develop a way to help track them down."

"Like a private detection agency?"

"Yes, something like that. I haven't figured it all out, but if being what I am can bring some good, then it will all make sense."

She took his hands in hers. "I think it's a fantastic idea. But let me make one thing clear. You've already done good, Leander Garrett. You've saved two lives now – mine and Emma's."

"Actually, I think it was you who saved me," he said, bending down to kiss her. He drew back a moment later. "Now, down to business." He took a pile of papers from his desk and handed them to her. "Our next project will be with Canadian Energy Consulting. We have a team meeting in an hour, so you should familiarize yourself with their goals and requirements." He moved around his desk and sat down. "I'll see you later, Ms. Hewitt."

The morning team meeting proved less difficult than Melissa expected it to be, and Lee was very good at hiding his feelings – he'd been doing it for years, after all. He was talking to Kasper when Melissa entered the room and took her seat, and although he glanced at her, he paid her no more attention than he had in the old days. Once the other team members arrived, the discussion was purely about work. It was only as they were leaving the room that Melissa felt Lee's fingers brush against hers, and her breath caught in her throat. She didn't look at him, but she smiled when she heard him inhaling softly.

She didn't see him again until it was almost time to leave the office for the evening. He walked over to her station and leaned against her desk.

"How was your first day back?" he asked. In the background she could see Kasper watching them with interest.

"It was okay," she said.

"Just okay?"

"Yep. I've got this really demanding team leader who's quite an ass to work for."

His eyebrows lifted. "An ass?"

"Yes." She responded with what she hoped was a wicked smile. "A real beast."

He crossed his arms and leaned closer, his eyes holding hers. "Then perhaps he'll lick you into shape," he said. She felt herself blushing. "Dinner with me tonight?"

"Of course."

"I'll wait for you in the lobby."

The next team meeting was a few days later, and Melissa hurried into the room, the last one to arrive. Lee glanced up as she entered, then looked around the table.

"Okay, where are we with running the data?" he said. He turned to Kasper. "Do you have the senior management information I was looking for?"

Kasper looked at Melissa. "You were going to run those. Do you have the information?"

Melissa pulled out a sheet. "Right here," she said. She handed it to Lee, who scanned it with a frown.

"There's something wrong with these numbers," he said.

"I assure you, I double checked everything."

"Let me see," Kasper said, taking the sheet from Lee. He studied it, then said to Melissa, "What positions did you include in here?"

"Management, as you asked."

"No," Kasper said slowly. "I said senior management only."

Melissa frowned as she took the sheet back from Kasper. "I'm sorry. I misheard, but I can easily rerun the data."

"You know," Kasper continued, "You may only have been back a few days, but if you took the time to go through the work we've already done, you'd know that Caro ran those numbers a few weeks ago. You can't just come back and expect a free ride."

Melissa glanced at Lee. His arms were crossed, his expression blank. She looked back at Kasper. "I'm not expecting a free ride," she said. "I've been back, what? Three days? You're right, I haven't gone through all the project notes, but I said I would rerun the data."

"Kasper's right," Lee said, leaning forward. Melissa shot him an angry look. "You should've familiarized yourself with everything by now."

She clenched her fists beneath the table and took in a deep breath. "Very well," she said, proud of her even tone, "I will cancel my plans for this evening and spend the time going through the file." She met his narrowed gaze angrily, then looked away. She sat in silence for the rest of the meeting, and rose as soon as it was done.

"Ms. Hewitt, a word," Lee said from behind her.

Tracy gave her a sympathetic look. "Good luck," she whispered as she walked past.

After the others had filed out, Melissa looked at Lee. He was still seated at the table. "Close the door," he said.

She hesitated a moment, debating whether she should walk away, before doing as he instructed.

"What was that, Mel?"

"That's a good question, Mr. Garrett," she said angrily. "Kasper, my colleague, criticizes me in a team meeting, and you support him."

"You know you have my support. But Kasper made a good point."

"The point may have been valid, but he used it as a criticism. And it's not as though I've been sitting on my backside doing nothing, Lee. You shouldn't have let him speak that way to me."

"You think I should show you favoritism?"

"Would you have allowed Kasper to speak like that to Caro?" she shot back. She yanked the door open when he remained silent and stormed from the room.

She was almost at her desk when she saw Kasper. "Happy? You made me look like an idiot."

"You waltz back in here as if you were never gone, and everyone is happy to see you, even Lee who's never even liked you! Well, wake up and smell the roses, Melissa. Lee still doesn't like you, and if you want to prove yourself, then you'll have to work your ass off to make sure you aren't holding the rest of us back."

"Holding you back? I ran one wrong report!"

"And how many more mistakes are you going to make? You think you're special, but you're not." He strode away as Melissa stared after him in disbelief. As she turned back to her desk, she saw Lee standing beside the wall, watching her. She clenched her jaw and sat down.

It was five o'clock by the time Melissa had completed her work and rerun the correct report. She had not seen Lee all day, although she was aware of his presence in the office. It had been difficult to concentrate on her work after the meeting, seething as she was. She felt as though Lee had thrown her under the proverbial bus – it was better when he just ignored her. She had finally managed to get some work done, but her annoyance still had not abated.

As the other analysts began to leave for the day, she pulled out the pile of project notes and began reading though the pages. She was already familiar with the overall project goals, having read through them on her first day, but now she went through each report and data analysis, making notes on the work already completed. By six o'clock the office had emptied and she sat alone at her desk. Outside the window the sky was already black, with a few pinpricks of light from the stars. The moon hung low on the horizon, a thin crescent of light. She stared at it across the room, then scowled when she saw Lee's reflection appear in the window.

"Go away," she said, returning to the pile of papers before her.

He didn't respond, but she felt him walk closer. He pulled up a chair and sat down. "You want some help sorting through the data?"

"What I want," she said, keeping her eye on the page, "is for you to leave me alone."

"Do you mean that?" he asked softly.

She looked up at him. "This isn't going to work, Lee. What you pulled earlier was not cool. If you need to tell me to do something, or if I've run the incorrect data, then fine. But to allow Kasper to speak to another team member like that was wrong."

"You're right," he said. "I handled it poorly, and I'm sorry."

"So what are you going to do about it?"

"I've already spoken to Kasper and told him that we want our team to be built on respect."

She looked at him in surprise. "What did he say?"

"He was angry, at first, but then agreed." He leaned forward. "This is new territory for me, Mel. And for you too. But I'm sorry."

"This can't keep happening. You can't keeping turning on me."

"You're right. I was worried about showing you too much partiality, and ended up going to the opposite extreme. I've never loved anyone before, but I'm learning. So please be patient with me."

She studied her nails for a moment. She had no guarantees that he wouldn't act like an idiot again, but then, life never came with guarantees. "Okay," she said, meeting his gaze. "If you're prepared to try, then I'll be patient." He smiled. "So now what?"

He took her fingers in his own. "Now you let me kiss and make up."

She pulled back. "That's way too easy. You need to do more groveling."

"How about if I bring you some food?"

"What kind?"

"I've already ordered Chinese." He moved his chair closer so their knees were touching, and ran his fingers over her hands.

"You have? That's a good start."

"And I went out earlier and bought a tub of ice cream. It's in the kitchen."

"Ice cream?" Without thinking, she moved closer to him, and his hand went to her neck. His face was only inches from hers as he caressed the back of her head.

"And if you don't let me kiss you, I'll have it all myself. You know how much I eat." His breath fell against her lips.

"That's bribery," she whispered.

"Absolutely," he said as his lips touched hers. She closed her eyes and lifted her hands to his chest.

"Mr. Garrett," she breathed when they broke the kiss, "I'm not sure this is appropriate office behavior."

"To hell with appropriate behavior," he said before kissing her again.

Chapter 27

"So I've been thinking about the idea of tracking and detection services," Lee said the following week. They were in a small sandwich shop a few blocks from the office, grabbing a bite for lunch.

"And what are you thinking?" Melissa asked before taking a bite of her tuna wrap. Lee had a ham sandwich, with enough ham between the bread to make a dozen sandwiches.

"I've some money put away that I can use to start a small business. It will take a while to build up a reputation, of course, so I won't be earning an income for some time. Even then, it probably won't be much."

"What about your work at Quigs?"

"I'll resign. But there's no reason why I can't do some consulting on my own."

"That makes sense. Earn some money to tide you over

while you build up the tracking services."

"Yes, exactly. But this decision doesn't only affect me. It affects you too."

"Oh?"

"Once you agree to become my wife, whatever I do will affect you."

"Aren't you getting ahead of yourself? You still haven't proven yourself to me. Maybe I'll refuse your proposal."

"Oh, I don't think you will. After all, you've already told me you want to be my mate."

Her breath caught in her throat when she saw his eyes begin to lighten and glow. "It's nearly the full moon," she whispered.

"Yes."

"Am I going to see you?"

"Sure you want to do that? It could be quite a risk, you know."

"How so?"

"I might just want a taste of you." He reached across the table and trailed his fingers down her cheek. "And not just some of you," he added, his voice low, "but all of you."

"So I get to be with you, then?"

He pulled away. "The moon will be at its fullest on Wednesday night, so I'm going to work at home on Tuesday and Wednesday, but you can come around in the evening."

"Why will you work at home?"

"Mel, you already know the effect you have on me. I don't think the employees at Quigs will be thrilled to have a panther prowling their midst."

"Do you usually work at home when the moon's full?" When she worked at Quigs before, she hadn't paid attention to Lee's absences and the moon phases.

"No. Until I allowed you into my life, it wasn't a problem. As long as I kept my distance from you I could control the pull. But now that I'm spending so much time with you, I can no longer control it. I'll stay away from the office – and you – while the moon's at its strongest. But be warned – as soon as I'm near you, the pull will be too strong to resist. I'll change in a matter of minutes."

"Will it always be like that? I mean, if I agree to marry you."

"Once we've been through the mating cycle, it will get easier." He paused. "You know, you don't have to come if you don't want to."

"Lee!"

"I know. It's just that I've never shown myself to anyone like that – except Caleb, of course, but I didn't hang out with him. I confess, I'm rather nervous. I don't want you to be scared of me."

"You have to trust me, Lee."

"I do. Which is why a small part of me is also rather excited. I want you to know me – know what I truly am. I've been holding back for so long. I don't want to hold back from you any longer." He smiled. "Which is why I want to ask you to come to Kamloops with me for Christmas. I want my parents to meet the woman I'm going to marry."

"Do they know about me?"

"No." Lee rubbed a finger over his forehead. "It's been a while since I last spoke to them."

"You're going to spring a girlfriend on them?"

"Fiancée. And yes, it really is the best way."

"I'm not sure I like this plan."

"The only plan is that we'll spend Christmas together."

"Please don't spring it on them. At least let them know

you're bringing a girlfriend."

He hesitated. "Okay, if that's what you want, I'll let them know I'm not coming alone."

She smiled. "Then I'd love to spend Christmas with you, Lee."

She took the car to work on Tuesday morning, wincing at the ridiculous parking fees. It was not the first time she'd been at work without Lee, but it was strange to think he was at home, waiting to turn into a wild cat. Leaving the office early, she headed out of downtown in the direction of his apartment. The traffic was slow moving out of the city, and she drummed the steering wheel impatiently as she crept forward inch by inch.

She arrived at his apartment block an hour later and found a parking spot. As the elevator doors opened, Lee was standing right there, waiting for her. His chest was bare and his eyes were completely feline, his pupils slightly elongated, with not a hint of white showing. He reached for her, but she stopped him when her eyes fell on the tattoo on his arm. With her finger, she traced the snarling panther, then looked up at him. In an instant, his lips were on hers, and when he kissed her hungrily, she could feel the sharpness of his teeth.

"I've missed you," he breathed as his hands ranged over her. His voice was low and ragged. "I can only hold myself back for a few minutes." He brought his lips back to hers and kissed her again. A soft rumbling vibrated through his chest and into her, and she pulled him closer. His hands moved to her face, and she could feel the new roughness of his palms as he cradled her cheeks. The air around him began to shimmer, and he stepped back hurriedly, pulling his clothes off in one fluid motion. His spine arched backward as the air became charged, and then he was falling to the floor. He landed on his four paws with feline grace and looked up at her.

She stared at him for a long moment, before slowly stepping forward and running her fingers through his thick, gleaming fur. She walked his length, watching his tail swish through the air. He was a marvelous creature, with a sleek body and powerful muscles that rippled as he moved. Every inch of him was as black as pitch, except his green eyes, which gazed at her intently as he followed her every move. She had seen he was magnificent at the zoo, but then he had been injured, his flank shaved and stitched. But seeing him like this, strong and healthy, he was even more incredible than she remembered. He came to her waist when she was standing, and as she sank to her knees, he towered over her. He lowered his head and slowly rasped his tongue along her neck before resting his chin on her shoulder. His whiskers tickled her cheek as she cradled his head, and she smiled when she felt his ears twitch.

They stayed like that for a moment until her legs began to cramp, and she rose to her feet. She headed to the kitchen, Lee at her heels, where she saw the full pot of coffee and a packaged salad beside it. "Thank you," she said. "Where do I find the cat food?"

He growled, a loud, rumbling sound, and she laughed as she poured herself some coffee.

"Since you can't tell me about your day, I guess I'll just have to tell you about mine," she said. She opened the salad and found a fork. "I finished the analysis you wanted. I emailed it to you just before I left. And Kasper wanted to know if you'd finally come to your senses and kicked me off your team," she said. He bared his teeth in a snarl, and she smiled. "He's jealous, you know. He thinks he's being overlooked, somehow." She took a bite of salad and moved to the living room. Lee jumped onto the couch beside her as she sat down.

"Cynthia called today. You remember her? Her husband is the one who shot you."

Lee looked alert.

"She wondered what had happened to you. I told her you were living wild and free." She buried her fingers into his fur and caressed his neck. A deep rumbling vibrated through his chest. "Are you purring?" she said in amusement. He looked up at her, then slowly and deliberately ran his tongue up her neck and into the nape, lifting her hair. It was a while before she returned to her salad. She turned on the TV when she was done, flicking through the channels until she found a film worth watching. She scooted down on the couch beside Lee, and he wrapped his paw around her as they watched. She drifted off sometime during the movie, waking when Lee nudged her gently with his head. She sat up and rubbed her eyes. It was only ten o'clock.

"I'll call you in the morning," she said. She cradled his face and kissed the top of his head. "Love you."

She was at her car when her phone dinged with a message. She pulled it out and smiled when she saw Lee's name. *Love you*, it read. *Sleep well.*

When Melissa drove to Lee's apartment the next evening, the moon was shining bright and full in the cold winter sky. It was a strange thing to be driven by the moon, she thought. As he had been the previous evening, Lee was waiting for her as soon as she stepped off the elevator. His eyes were glowing, and his five o'clock shadow was darker than usual. He pulled her into his arms, wrapped his hands around her head, and kissed her with a desperate urgency. "Not long enough," he said raggedly. The air around him was already shimmering as he slid his hands down her back, pulling her closer, and Melissa could feel the charge building in the air, like the ozone before a storm. She gasped when he released her and flew backward into the air, twisting, then landed on his four paws. She stared at him as she had the night before, taking in the magnificent creature standing before her, then followed him into the dining room as the smell of something savory and delicious wafted through the air. She stopped when she saw the baked lasagna on the table with a large bowl of Caesar salad and a glass of wine neatly positioned beside a single place setting. A vase of roses sat in the center of the table with a card resting against the vase.

I hope you had a wonderful day. Please tell me all about it. Enjoy the meal, Lee.

She smiled. "Thank you."

As she sat at the table, he lay down beside her, his thick fur pressing against her legs. The table faced a wall of glass, and through it the full moon hung in the sky like a giant silver disk. She trailed her fingers through Lee's hair as she stared at it.

"There's not much to tell you today," she said as she picked up the serving spoon. "Pat Ramsbottom was in the office to meet with Norm, but you probably already know that. And Caro was upset that Kasper didn't have a report ready for her. So as you see, pretty much a day like any other!"

She finished eating and crossed over to the couch, but Lee walked over to the huge glass wall and stared out.

"It calls you, doesn't it?" He looked at her, then crossed the room to lay his head in her lap. She pushed her fingers into his fur. "If I wasn't here, would you be out there? Running with the moon?" He looked up at her. "It's okay. You can go. I want you to trust me, but I don't want to hold you back." He rasped his tongue over her hand, and she smiled. "I'll see you tomorrow." She rose, took her purse, and went to the elevator. She glanced at the majestic creature once more, then stepped inside and closed the doors.

She reached her car a few moments later, but instead of leaving, she sat in the driver's seat, thinking about Lee. She wondered what it must be like, to be governed so much by the moon. Lee had told her once that his animal instincts were stronger when he was in animal form. Did he long to run through the trees and hunt down his prey? He'd looked so beautiful and majestic, standing at the window, his fur shining silver in the moonlight, while his tail had swished from side to side.

The elevator dinged, and Lee stepped out in his human form and headed to his truck. He had almost reached it when he stopped in his tracks and stared directly at her. Their gazes held for a moment, before he turned back to his truck. A moment later a message popped up on her phone. *Thank you*, he wrote.

She smiled, then started her car and headed out of the parking garage. His black truck tailed her as she turned onto the street and drove home. He followed her into her parking lot, then circled around and headed back onto the street, disappearing into the night.

CHAPTER 28

Lee was back in the office on Thursday. Melissa was just switching on her computer when Caro walked past. "Lee wants to see you," she said.

Taking a pen and notebook, Melissa headed to Lee's office. "Should I be concerned that Caro was just with you?" she said as she entered.

"Caro has nothing on you."

"Except you've slept with her."

Lee looked a little embarrassed. "It meant nothing."

"You've never slept with me."

"True. When we make love for the first time, it'll start the mating cycle."

"And you want to be married for that?"

"I do. But that's only partly the reason. As you've so eloquently pointed out, I've slept with other women, but it was purely physical. None of them meant anything to me.

I don't want things to be like that with us. I want to wait for you, Mel. Like waiting for a Christmas present. If you open it too early, you ruin the joy of Christmas morning. I want the anticipation! And I know it sounds old-fashioned, but when we make love, I want to know that we're pledged for forever, not just physically, but in an intimate, spiritual sense. So marry me. You promised to make a decision after you'd seen me change, and now you've seen it." She opened her mouth, but he placed his fingers over her lips. "Wait. Don't say anything now. The reason I wanted to see you was to ask you if you'd go out to dinner with me."

She smiled. "Is this a date?"

"Oh yes. Most definitely."

"Then I accept, Lee Garrett." She slipped from his hands and headed out the door.

The restaurant where Lee had made reservations was in an old converted house not far from Melissa's apartment. It was cozy and intimate, and she scrutinized him across the candlelight. Voices and soft music hummed around them as she opened the menu and made her choice.

"I was thinking about what you said earlier," she said after the waiter had taken their order.

"What did I say earlier?"

"About waiting."

"Ah, *that* earlier!"

"I'm probably crazy for saying this, but I want to wait too."

"You do?" He smiled. "Does that mean there's something to wait for?"

She opened her napkin and placed it on her lap. "Yes," she said primly. She looked up and met his gaze. "I'll marry you, Lee Garrett."

He smiled, but it faded a moment later. "Are you sure?" he said. "Being with me won't be simple."

She threw up her hands in exasperation. "You've been trying to get me to say yes, and when I do, you warn me off again. It's hard to know what you want." She shook her head. "I'll say one thing – simple is boring. Just as long as you promise to always love me, nothing you do can chase me away."

"I'll never stop loving you," he promised. "And once we're mated, our connection will be even deeper. Even now, the animal in me wants nothing more than to wrap himself around you and consume you. Not literally," he quickly added when her eyes widened.

She shivered. "Are you going to bite my neck and claw my arms as we make love?"

He leaned forward and dropped his voice. "Oh yes, I'll definitely do that."

The food arrived a short while later; Lee's, as always, was piled high with undercooked meat. Or was that uncooked meat?

"So how was the hunting last night?"

"I was distracted. All I could think of was you."

"So you didn't hunt?"

"I didn't say that. It just wasn't as pleasurable as usual."

"So what did you catch?"

"A small deer."

She looked at him incredulously. "And you're still going to eat all that?"

He shrugged. "I've told you before. Fast metabolism."

"I'll say."

They were lingering over coffee when Lee pulled a small box from his pocket and placed it on the table in front of her. "I have something for you," he said.

"Is that what I think it is?"

"I don't know? What do you think it is?" he asked teasingly, but a moment later turned serious. "Nothing I give you could ever measure the value you have for me, but I hope this will go a small way to showing you how much you mean to me."

He opened the box, and she gasped. Nestled within a bed of velvet was a huge, multi-faceted oval emerald set in a platinum band, surrounded by dozens of tiny diamonds. More diamonds were set into the band, halfway down on either side.

"It's beautiful," she breathed.

He took the ring from the box and looked at her inquiringly. She held out her hand and he slipped the ring onto her finger.

"Perfect," he said with an air of satisfaction.

"You've been wanting to do that for a while," she said with a laugh.

"Six years," he said.

They lingered over coffee before Lee dropped Melissa off at her apartment with a kiss that left her staggering. She leaned against the wall for a moment, gathering her breath, before taking her phone to her bedroom. She dialed Lauren's number.

"Melissa! What's wrong? Why are you calling so late?"

"Nothing's wrong. I have something to tell you."

"You've been hurt! Are you in hospital? Do I need to come out?"

"What? No! I'm fine. More than fine, actually."

"Then what is it?" Lauren's tone was heavy with suspicion. "Wait? Does this have something to do with that guy? Lee, was it?"

Melissa could not repress the giggle that rose to her throat. "Yes."

"You sound like a schoolgirl."

"I know. He asked me to marry him."

"Marry him? How long have you known him?"

"I worked with him for years, Lauren."

"And this is the guy with commitment issues."

"It's more complicated than that."

"Oh, I'm sure it is. So when is the wedding?"

"Well – we haven't set a date yet. But probably in the next few months."

"Next few months?" Lauren screeched. "Are you pregnant?"

"No!"

"Then what's the rush?"

"We just don't want to wait."

"I see. Well, before you start planning this wedding, I have to meet this guy. Hang on." There was a muffled noise over the line as Lauren spoke to Nick. She was back a moment later. "I'm flying out this weekend."

"This weekend?"

"Is that a problem?"

"No, uh, of course not."

"I'll be there Friday evening."

Melissa stared at the phone in bemusement as it went dead, then typed a message to Lee. *My sister's coming out this weekend to check you out*, she wrote. Lee called a moment later.

"Your sister wants to check me out?" he said when she answered the call. She could tell he was more amused than alarmed.

"I'm afraid so."

"And will she approve?"

"I think she might."

"And if she doesn't?"

"We won't invite her to the wedding!"

He laughed. "I'll be on my best behavior," he promised. "No biting, no growling, no snarling. Anything else?"

"No shedding."

"I don't shed!" he said, feigning offense.

"And no sniffing."

"Not even you?"

"Nope! Not unless we're alone."

"And then I can smell you all I want?"

"Yes," she said with a shiver. Lee was silent. "What are you doing?" she whispered.

"Your scent is on my couch. I'm imagining you're here with me."

She laughed, a little shakily. "I'll see you in the morning, Lee."

"Goodnight, Mel."

Melissa stood in her room the next morning, staring at the ring on her finger as it sparkled in the light of the lamp. After a moment of contemplation, she slipped it from her left hand and replaced it on her right. It didn't fit as well, and it also felt wrong, but she had no illusions that the ring would go unnoticed by her colleagues.

In a team meeting later that morning, sure enough, Caro noticed the ring immediately.

"Good lord, look at that bauble!" she said, gasping. She grabbed Melissa's hand, causing her to stumble. "Are those *real*?"

"No way," Tracy said, moving to peer over her shoulder. "Those can't be real! A real ring like that would cost ten or fifteen thousand, at least."

Melissa looked at Lee.

"They're real," he said.

"How do you know?"

Lee held his hand out toward Melissa. "May I?" She tugged off the ring and placed it in his palm, and he gently breathed on the stones. "Real diamonds don't fog up," he said. "And if we look, we'll find the metal stamp. They'd only use fakes with cheap metal." He held the ring up to the light. "Look – right there."

Tracy leaned closer and squinted. "PT," she read. "Platinum?"

"Yes." He reached for Melissa's hand, but instead of taking her right hand, he grabbed her left and slipped the ring onto her ring finger, grinning as he did so.

"Wow, Mel, where did you get such an expensive ring?" Caro said.

"It was a gift."

"From who?"

"Come on people, let's get down to work," Lee said.

Melissa breathed a sigh of relief as she reached for her notebook.

It was a short meeting, and an hour later, Lee closed his notes. "Good work, everyone." Chairs scraped as they rose to leave.

"Hey guys," Caro said, "it's Friday. We going for a drink after work?"

"I have to pick up my sister from the airport," Melissa said.

"Lee? What about you?"

"I have other plans," he said.

"Bring her with," Kasper joked.

Lee was silent, and all eyes turned to him. "I would," he said slowly, "but she's meeting her sister at the airport."

There was a long moment of silence as they stared at him.

"You and *Melissa*?" Tracy finally said.

"No way," Kasper said.

Lee looked at him. "You thought I didn't care about her, but now you know that I do."

"The ring is from *you*?" Caro gasped as Melissa sank back into her chair.

"Yes," he said. "Melissa and I are getting married."

"No. Way." Tracy said.

Lee flashed her a wry smile. "I'll assume your shock is because I'm getting married. Not my choice of bride."

"Everyone knows what you're like. You have a different woman every month."

"That's not true!" Caro said. She smirked. "Sometimes he comes back for seconds."

Melissa glanced at the desk, her cheeks burning.

"Enough," Lee said, rising. "Let me make it very clear that I love Melissa. And none of your spiteful comments will change that."

Tracy looked abashed. "I'm sorry, Lee," she said. "It's just a surprise."

"Does she know about *us*?" Caro said.

Lee turned to her with a hard look. "There never was an 'us.' We fooled around a bit. We both know it meant nothing."

"Nothing? For you, maybe."

Lee spoke evenly. "Please don't push it, Caro. Don't play the injured party when we both know I was nothing but a distraction from, what was his name? Henry?"

Caro glared at Lee as Melissa rose and headed to the door.

"Melissa, wait!" Lee said.

She paused, but didn't turn around. "I need some air. I'll see you later." She opened the door and stepped out of the room.

"Melissa!" Lee caught up with her as she reached the elevator.

She turned to face him. "Lee, I love you, and I believe you when you say that Caro or any of the other women you've been with meant nothing, but that was completely humiliating."

"I know," he said softly. "And I'm sorry."

"Just give me some space. I need to think."

"I love you," he said, before taking a step back.

"I know."

She made her way to the river and walked along the paved path that ran alongside, her mind spinning. Maybe she was being a fool, thinking she alone could hold Lee's heart. After all, how long had she really known him? It was as if there were two Lees – the one she was in love with, and the stranger who held her at arm's length and fooled around with anyone who was willing. Which one was the real Lee? She dropped to a park bench along the path. A thin layer of snow lay on the ground, and patches of bare ground peeked through the white. Something rustled against her foot and she looked down to see a candy wrapper that had blown beneath the bench. She picked it up, intending to throw it in the garbage, and looked at it thoughtfully. It was bright green – the color Lee's eyes turned when the moon was full. And the color of her ring. She examined it, dazzling in its beauty and such a match for Lee's eyes.

She thought hard. No one else affected Lee the way she did. She alone held his secret. And she was the only one he loved – she knew it instinctively. She started back to the office, pausing to throw the wrapper in the garbage. The air had grown colder, and she wrapped her coat more tightly around herself as she walked. She could deal with Caro and her snide comments, and whatever else she had to go through, because none of it mattered. All that mattered was Lee and the love he held for her. Although she could do without any further humiliations.

Melissa was near the reception desk when her arm was grabbed from behind and she was pulled into a corner.

"You've been gone for over an hour," Lee said in her ear.

"Did you think I'd fallen into the river?" she asked in amusement.

"The thought crossed my mind," he said sourly. "I hate thinking you might not want to be with me anymore."

"I want to be with you," she said. "I just didn't know if I could trust that you wanted to be with me. I needed time to think and sort through things."

"And?"

"And I think we should set a date for the wedding."

He smiled. "Really?"

"Yes. I want to spend the rest of my life with you."

"I'm so sorry you had to endure that humiliation."

"I know. You could have been a bit more discreet."

"I've been such an idiot. I knew from the first time I met you that you were the only one for me, but I pushed you away. I thought I was protecting us both. But it's only when I'm with you and can drop the mask that I can truly find peace."

"Have you stopped running?"

"I'm tired of running. It's time to come home."

"Then let's go home, Lee."

He wrapped his arms around her and buried his face in

her hair. "I am home. You are my home." They stayed like that until the dinging of the elevator made Lee step back. "After you left, things were in an uproar."

"I'll bet," she said. "What happened?"

"Norm demanded to know what I was thinking, getting involved with a colleague."

"I guess he didn't know about you and Caro," she said wryly. He looked away. "So what did you say?"

"I resigned. The next thing I knew, Patrick was on the phone, trying to convince me to stay. 'We can work this out,' he said."

"And?"

"I'll leave at the end of January."

"So soon? Will you manage?"

"I have enough to tide me over, and a few connections that will come in handy if I want to do some freelance consulting."

"Are you sure?"

"The only thing I'm sure of is you, but this feels like the right thing to do."

"Then I'm with you all the way."

He left her outside his office, and she went to her desk. Caro and Kasper were talking in hushed tones as she approached, and Kasper turned to her with a scowl.

"I guess you're pretty pleased with yourself," Kasper said.

"What do you mean?"

"Oh, please! Lee barely even spoke to you before you left, and now he's marrying you! What are you offering him, Mel? It can't be just the sex since he clearly has plenty of offers! So what is your hold on him?"

"How dare you," she said, shocked at the attack.

"And then you come waltzing back into your old job,"

he continued, ignoring her. "And to top it all off, Lee demands that you be on his team."

She was about to speak, when a voice cut her off from behind. "Melissa does have something on me," Lee said, his voice trembling with anger. "She has my heart. And the only reason she was offered her old job back is because she's good at what she does. It has nothing to do with me."

"Lee, please, I've got this," Melissa said, but Lee and Kasper were glaring at each other.

"Yeah? Well, what about me? I'm also good at my job," Kasper shot back.

"Which is why you still have it. But if you say one more word about Melissa, then it will be yours no longer."

"Lee!" Melissa stepped in front of him, forcing him to meet her eyes. "I can fight my own battles."

"We're a team," he said, his voice a growl. "Your battles are mine."

She gave an exaggerated sigh and turned to Kasper. "I don't know why you're so angry with me, Kasper. We used to be friends!"

"You *left*, Mel. I was the one who had to put in extra hours to make up for you. And then you come back as though nothing had happened."

"I'm sorry you were left with everything. I really am. But I would have done the same for you – you know it."

"Yeah, well, you didn't. And I did."

He stormed off, and she turned to see that Lee was no longer behind her. Really, she thought as she dropped into her chair, he was behaving like a wild cat growling over a piece of meat. No wonder there was a policy against office relationships!

CHAPTER 29

Melissa stood at arrivals waiting for Lauren to come through the frosted glass doors. Each time they slid open, she tried to peer through, hoping to catch a glimpse of her sister, but they closed too quickly.

Another twenty minutes passed before Lauren finally stepped into the hall, looking tired and harassed. Her expression lifted when she saw Melissa, and she ran to her with her arms open. "Mel," she yelled, pulling her into a tight embrace. "You look well," she said after they broke apart. She turned Melissa's head from side to side with her hands.

"What are you doing?"

"Just seeing how you look."

"You're not checking me for bruises, are you?" Melissa asked incredulously.

Lauren gave a sheepish smile. "I just want to make sure

you're okay."

"I'm fine," Melissa said, sighing. "More than fine. In fact I'm very, very happy!"

"Good! So when do I get to meet him?"

"Tonight. He's coming over for supper." She linked her arm through Lauren's as they headed for the exit. "So I was wondering, will you be my matron of honor?"

Lauren stopped and flung her arms around Melissa. "Of course I will. I thought you'd never ask."

Melissa laughed. "Who else would I ask, you silly goose?"

After battling rush-hour traffic for an hour, they reached Melissa's apartment and went into the kitchen.

"I thought it was just Lee coming over," Lauren said when she saw the pile of steaks Melissa took from the fridge.

"It is."

"Then—" Lauren began, but the ringing buzzer cut her short. She waited in the kitchen as Melissa went to open the door. Lee's green eyes met hers in amusement.

"You heard that, didn't you?" she said.

"I did," he said. "I take it your sister arrived okay."

"Yes. She's anxious to meet you."

She led him into the kitchen and introduced them. Lauren's smile faltered slightly as she took in Lee's build.

"Pleased to meet you," he said, holding out his hand. Lauren sent her sister a wide-eyed look before taking the extended hand and shaking it.

"Uh, yes, you too."

Lee held up a bottle. "I brought some wine. I'll go get some glasses."

"You didn't tell me he was so hot," Lauren whispered as Lee went for glasses from the cabinet in the living room.

"You didn't ask."

"So what's he like – you know – in bed."

Melissa had figured this might be coming and tried to make her shrug look nonchalant. "No idea."

"You mean—"

"He wants to wait."

"What?" Lauren looked shocked. "Is he … a virgin?"

"Hardly. That's why he wants to wait. He wants it to be different for us."

"That's … that's actually kinda sweet."

Melissa looked away as Lee came into the room, but not before she saw his raised eyebrows. Of course he'd heard every word. He handed her a glass of wine and held out another to Lauren.

"So, uh, Lee, have you always lived in Calgary?" Lauren asked as she took the drink.

"Born and bred," he replied, "but the mountains are my natural home."

"Oh. You both love the mountains. That's good. And you work with Mel?"

"That's right. It's how we first met."

Melissa tossed a salad as they chatted. Lee passed her the steaks and she placed them in the sizzling pan, then immediately flipped all but one over.

"Don't you need to leave those in a bit longer?" Lauren said, peering over her shoulder.

"Lee likes them, uh, rare." She placed the steaks on a plate and handed them to him. She flipped the last one and waited as it sizzled.

"Those aren't rare, they're raw!" Lauren said with a gasp. "And surely you're not eating all that?"

Lee glanced at Melissa. "I'm on a strict protein diet. You know, training." He waved his hand vaguely. "So how do you enjoy living in Vancouver?"

Melissa cut the remaining steak in half and dished it onto two plates, placing one before Lauren, who was watching in horror as Lee cut into the bloody steaks on his plate.

"That's truly disgusting," she said after a moment. She piled her plate with salad, and carefully speared a tomato.

"So are you ready to go shopping tomorrow?" Melissa cut off a small piece of meat and bit into it.

"Shopping?" Lauren was having trouble pulling her eyes away from Lee's food.

"For a wedding dress?"

Her sister grinned. "Yes!"

"And we need to find something for the matron of honor."

"Do I get to come?" Lee asked.

"Absolutely not!" Lauren said. Melissa smiled at Lee's mock surprise. "Have you set a date yet?" Lauren asked, turning back to Melissa.

"We've just decided – it'll be January 28th."

"So soon? But … that's not even enough time to get a dress made. You'll have to get something off the rack."

"I guess I will. Is that a problem?"

"Of course not. It's just, well, I suppose I'd thought we'd take the time to plan the perfect wedding for you."

Melissa looked at Lee with a smile. "As long as the groom is standing at the altar, it will be perfect," she said.

Reaching for her hand, he brought it to his nose and slid it across his cheek before kissing it. "I'll be there," he said as his eyes turned a slightly lighter shade of green.

"So, what do you think of Lee?" Melissa asked Lauren later that evening.

"Are you sure you're ready for this, Mel?"

"What do you mean?"

"It's just – well, he scares me a little. There's something wild, almost untamed about him. I don't want you getting hurt."

Melissa smiled wryly. "The only way he can hurt me is in his misguided attempts *not* to hurt me." They were sitting on the couch, and she leaned her head against her sister's shoulder. "But I'm very sure about marrying him. It sounds cliché, I know, but I can honestly say that he and I were meant to be together, and without him, my life would be poorer."

Lauren wrapped her arms around her sister. "Then I'm happy for you. And even though there's not much time, this wedding is going to be amazing."

They spent the next day going from one wedding boutique to the next, until, late in the afternoon, they found the perfect gown. Made of silver lace, it flared in soft folds at the waist that fell gracefully to the floor. She held it against herself and turned to Lauren.

"Yes! That's gorgeous."

They were on their way back to the car when Lauren paused to admire a picture in the window of an art gallery. Melissa stopped as well, and a picture at the back of the store caught her eye.

Taking Lauren's hand, she dragged her into the building. A tall woman with long gray hair pulled into a ponytail sat at a desk near the door, and she glanced up as they entered. Melissa led Lauren to the back of the gallery and stopped at a painting of a panther, as black as night, standing protectively over a sleeping child.

"I love it," Melissa said. She turned to the woman at the

desk. "What's the price?"

"I'll have to look it up," she said.

"It's nice," Lauren said. "Not what I'd want in my home, but nice."

The woman walked over and named a price. Melissa gulped, and the woman gave her an appraising look. "I've had this piece for nearly a year, with very little interest," she said. "I happen to know the artist is anxious to sell. If you're interested, I'll take a third off the price."

"Oh! I, uh …"

"Shall I give you a moment to consider it?" Melissa nodded and she moved away.

"What are you doing?" Lauren said softly. "You're not actually thinking of buying this, are you?"

"I was thinking of buying it for Lee. For Christmas."

"Lee?" Lauren's surprise was evident. "Well, you'd know if he'd like it. Can you afford it?"

Melissa turned back to the painting. The panther's fur shimmered in midnight blues and raven black against a sea of greens. It was staring into the distance, alert to some unseen threat, its teeth drawn back in a half-snarl, while the child lay peacefully at its feet. She turned back to the sales lady.

"I'll take it," she said.

"Excellent!" The woman lifted it from the wall. "I'll just get it packaged up for you."

They left the gallery half an hour later, Melissa carrying the package under arm as they headed to her car as Lauren looked at her skeptically.

"What are you staring at?"

"A panther and a child? I don't know Lee, but I wouldn't have pegged him for that kind of guy."

Melissa smiled. "Actually, it's perfect."

They had arranged to meet Lee at a restaurant at seven o'clock, and they pushed their way through the crowded doorway at five minutes to. "I hope he made a reservation," Lauren said as they found a corner to stand and wait.

"He did."

"Melissa!" At the sound of her name, Melissa turned to see Cynthia standing a few feet away with Richard at her side. "How are you?"

"Cynthia! Imagine seeing you here."

"We're meeting friends. Mike and his new girlfriend, actually."

"Lesley?"

"No. They didn't work out. So how are you doing?"

"Fine. You remember my sister, Lauren?"

"Of course." Cynthia smiled. "You came to visit Mel on campus once. You waiting for a table?"

"Actually, we're waiting for my fiancé," Melissa said.

Cynthia's eyebrows rose. "Your fiancé! You didn't tell me you were seeing someone."

"Well," Melissa hedged. The door opened behind them, bringing in a blast of cold air, and Melissa glanced over her shoulder to see Lee pushing his way toward them.

"Hi," he said, bending to kiss her. His hand slipped into hers. "I have a reservation. Why are you standing here?"

"We ran into a friend. This is Cynthia. And her husband, Richard."

Lee smiled at Cynthia, then turned to Richard, his hand outstretched. "Richard," he said as the man took his hand, "aren't you the guy who tried to kill Melissa?"

"Lee!" Melissa said sharply. Richard's face was turning pale as Lee tightened his grip. "Stop!"

Lee looked at Melissa with a feral smile. "He almost killed you!"

"But he didn't. You know it was an accident."

Lee dropped Richard's hand, which he immediately brought to his chest. "What the hell?" he sputtered.

Lee took a step closer, his eyes glinting. "Your careless mistake almost cost Melissa her life, and then you wanted to kill the panther that saved her. You're lucky it hasn't hunted you down itself."

"What the hell are you talking about? As Melissa said, it was an accident! And the cougar, or whatever it was, had been injured. Any responsible hunter would've destroyed an injured animal." He looked pointedly at Melissa. "We all know what you did. You set that creature free so it could attack someone."

"Melissa, what's going on?" Cynthia said, frowning at her friend.

"Lee can be a bit protective." She could feel the fury building in him, and she tightened her hand around his. "Ignore him," she said under her breath. "It's not worth it."

Lee turned to look at her, his expression incredulous. "Not worth it?"

"No. He didn't know what he was doing. But you do." She ran her hand up his arm. "You know I'm right."

Lee released a long, slow breath. "Fine." To Cynthia he said, "My apologies. I know you're Melissa's friend. The fact that Mel could have died makes me a little crazy."

"Uh … of course," Cynthia said, before following Richard as he stormed away.

"I don't suppose they'll come to the wedding now," Melissa said as they retreated. Beside him, Lauren was staring at him, wide-eyed.

"I'm sorry, Mel," Lee said, but his tone was far from contrite. Gripping his hand, she dragged him into a corner.

"What was that? I know you're upset about being shot _"

"You think this was about me? This was about *you.* You could have been injured or even killed!"

"But I wasn't. You should go and apologize to Richard."

"You're not serious?"

"Cynthia's my friend, Lee, and Richard is her husband. After that performance, I doubt she'd ever want to see me again."

"It's not you she won't want to see. Just me." Melissa lifted her eyebrows, and he threw his hands in the air. "Fine. I'll apologize. But that doesn't mean I can forgive Richard for what happened. I'm doing this for you."

She watched as Lee wound through the crowd to where Cynthia and Richard were standing and said a few words. Richard didn't look very happy, but after a moment's hesitation, he shook Lee's hand. Lee made his way back a few moments later.

"Let's get our table," he said somberly.

CHAPTER 30

"Are you packed?" Lee asked as he entered Melissa's apartment. It was three days before Christmas, and they were driving to Kamloops to stay with his parents.

"I am." She pointed at her suitcase standing by the door. "You can carry that," she said, picking up a long, flat box, "and I'll carry this."

"What is it?"

She smiled. "Well, you'll just have to wait to find out."

"Is it for me?"

She kissed him as she walked through the door. "Maybe. Or maybe it's for Caleb."

"You have something for Caleb?" he asked as he closed the door behind him.

"Of course! He's going to be my brother."

The city was soon behind them and they headed toward the mountains. Kamloops was a seven-hour drive through the treacherous Rockies, and even though the weather was clear, more than one car had slid on the ice that clung to the highway and slipped into the shoulder or ditch, making the journey even slower.

It was late afternoon when they finally pulled into Kamloops and came to a stop outside a brick-faced house.

"You ready?" Lee asked.

"Yep," she said. "You?"

He wrapped his hand around her neck and kissed her, drawing away a moment later. "Now I'm ready," he said.

They stepped out of the truck and he took her hand as they walked to the front door. His grip was tight around hers as he rang the front doorbell, but he relaxed a moment later when the door was pulled open by a woman smiling widely.

"Mom," Lee said. He turned to Melissa. "This is my mom, Judith."

"I'm glad to meet you, Melissa," she said with a smile. "Any friend of Lee's is welcome here."

Judith looked to be in her early sixties. Her face was lined and careworn, and her smile didn't quite reach her eyes, but as she turned back to her son, her face softened, and Melissa could see that she had once been an attractive woman. She wiped her hands over her dress as she stepped back.

"Come in, come in," she said. She reached out a hand to touch Lee as he brushed past her, then dropped it before reaching him.

"You must be exhausted from the drive. I'm sure you'd like something to drink."

"Coffee, please," Lee said.

"I'll have the same," said Melissa.

She watched as Judith bustled away, then turned to Lee

LINDA K. HOPKINS

with a frown. "Friend? You didn't tell them about me, did you?" she demanded.

"It seemed better to tell them in person."

"We're getting married, and you haven't even let them know you have a girlfriend? How do you think that makes me feel?" She tapped her foot on the floor as she crossed her arms.

"It's complicated, Mel."

"Complicated?" She laughed bitterly. "So when do you plan to tell them?"

Judith returned to the room, her eyes flicking between them as Lee fell silent. She carried a tray with two steaming mugs which Lee took from her and placed on the coffee table. He added some milk to one and handed it to Mel.

"So, how was the trip?" Judith asked as they sat down.

"Slow," Lee said. "Lots of holiday traffic, and the roads were icy. The mountain highway was glorious but dangerous. But we're here now."

She peered at Melissa. "And how do you know each other?" she asked.

"I'm Lee's girlfriend," Melissa said without hesitation. She heard Lee sigh beside her. Serves him right, she thought. Judith's eyes fell on the ring on Melissa's finger, then flew to Lee's.

"I see." Her shoulders slumped. "Your father will be here soon."

Melissa looked between them, wondering at the unspoken communication that weighed down the room.

"My parents believe I'm too much a monster to marry," Lee said, his eyes fixed on his mother.

"That's not true, dear," Judith protested feebly. Melissa's chest tightened as shock rushed through her. Suddenly, Lee's desire to keep their relationship secret

300

made sense. A door slammed and Lee rose as a man entered the room.

"Dad," Lee said.

"Well, son. You're here."

"As you see."

He looked at Melissa. "And who's this?"

Before Lee had a chance to reply, Melissa got up and stuck out her hand. "Melissa, sir," she said.

Mr. Garrett looked at her outstretched hand, then turned back to Lee. "Who is she?"

"She's Lee's fiancée," Judith said, standing beside her husband. Lee put his arm around Melissa's shoulder and drew her closer.

"Fiancée?" the man exploded. "Are you crazy? Have you completely lost your mind? Does she know what kind of creature you are? What you're capable of?"

Lee's grip tightened. "Melissa knows everything."

"Really?" he shouted. He turned to Melissa, his face mottled and angry as he shook his finger at her. "Do you know what he'll do to you? He's dangerous!"

"No," Lee said, his voice low. "You're wrong."

"Does she know about the boy?" he said. "How you left him to die?"

Melissa looked at Lee in shock as the front door opened and someone else entered the room. Judith turned to face the newcomer.

"Caleb," she said, her relief evident. "Look, Lee's arrived. And he's brought a friend."

"Mel," Caleb said, coming over and kissing her cheek. "Good to see you. Welcome to our lovely home."

"You know her?" Mr. Garrett demanded. "Do you know he plans to marry her?"

Caleb turned to his father. "Yes, I do."

The man's eyes narrowed in rage. "You knew and did nothing to stop it?"

"What was I supposed to do, Dad? They love each other."

"You know what your brother's capable of," his father sneered. "You want to have her blood on your hands?"

Lee's hand slid off Melissa's shoulder and wrapped around her fingers. "We're leaving."

"Please, Lee, don't go," Judith said, stepping in front of him.

"You think I should stay and listen to these insults, Mom? And how do you think it makes Melissa feel, hearing him carrying on this way?"

"I'll go with you," Caleb said.

Lee's expression was grim as he pushed his way past his mother, dragging Melissa behind him. He shoved open the door and pulled her outside.

"I'm sorry," he said, his voice trembling with rage. "I thought ..." He let go of her hand and stalked to a large tree standing in the garden. Snow fell from the branches as he smashed his fist into it. "I'm so stupid," he said. He turned to look at her. "I thought when he saw you ..."

Melissa went to him. "It's okay," she whispered. "I think I understand. And I'm sorry I got upset with you."

He stared down at her, then grabbing her face between his hands, kissed her fiercely. He rested his forehead against hers, and his hands trembled as they held her cheeks.

"I'm an idiot for thinking things would be different."

She placed her hands over his and pulled back to look in his eyes. "Your father's the idiot for not seeing how incredible you are. And nothing you do can change the way I feel about you."

He kissed her again, more gently this time, then turned to Caleb, who was standing at the edge of the garden. "Let's get out of here," he said.

"Where we going?" Caleb asked as they got into the truck.

Lee looked at Melissa. "Hungry?"

"Starving."

They pulled up outside a restaurant a few minutes later, and Lee wrapped his arm around Melissa as they walked in. He was still trembling, and she noticed him glancing at the half crescent moon as they walked. They were shown a table in a corner and took their seats in silence. Lee gripped her hand as they looked at the menu and placed their order.

"What did your father mean when he asked if I knew about the boy?" she asked as they waited for the food to arrive.

Lee's jaw tightened and he pulled his hand from hers as he looked away.

"You need to tell her," Caleb said.

Lee stared into the distance. "It was about six years ago," he said. "Around the time I met you, in fact. I was picking Caleb up from school."

"I was in twelfth grade," Caleb added.

"A group of boys was beating up on my brother," Lee continued. "They had him on the ground and were kicking and punching him. When I saw them, I lost it. I attacked them, and one of them ended up in hospital."

"Was he okay?"

"Not really. His stomach was ripped open and his leg was broken. He was in hospital for three months."

"You were protecting your brother."

"What kind of protection is it when a boy, even a bully,

has to fight for his life? The police came to our house to question Caleb afterward. When my father heard what happened, he went crazy. He'd always been a bit scared of me, I think. But he and my mother moved to Kamloops the next week, leaving Caleb with me in Calgary. I haven't seen them since."

He hadn't seen them in six years? And he'd only come back because of her. "I'm sorry," she whispered, taking his hand beneath the table.

He stiffened for a moment, then wrapped his fingers around hers. "I warned you I was dangerous," he said.

She shook her head. "You'll never hurt me."

"Your faith in me is unbelievable."

"No more than your lack of faith in yourself." The food arrived, and they ate in silence for a few minutes. "Why do you think your father's scared of you?" she finally asked.

Lee gave a slight shrug.

"Because of Grandpa," Caleb said.

Lee looked across the table at his brother. "You might be right," he said after a moment.

"You know I'm right." Caleb turned to Melissa. "Grandpa was like Lee, a Changer. He always used to say only the worthy were chosen to be Changers." He gave a bitter smile.

"You know that's not true," Lee said.

"Whatever. Neither Dad or I are Changers," Caleb said. "Grandpa was always hard on Dad when he was a kid. I think Dad was probably a bit scared of him, so it didn't help when Grandpa turned on him."

"He didn't turn on Dad," Lee protested. "He was helping him."

"Maybe. But Dad sure as hell doesn't think so."

"Dad grew up in the cabin—"

"Your cabin?" Melissa asked.

"Yes. He wasn't allowed to go beyond the clearing, but I guess, like all boys, he liked to wander. He got between a rutting elk and his females. The elk was about to charge when Grandpa reached him and flung him out of the way. Dad hadn't seen the elk, so the first thing he knew was his father, the panther, throwing him through the air. He broke his arm in the fall and had quite a few scratches to show for it. I don't think he ever forgave Grandpa."

"So he thinks all Changers are dangerous?"

"Imagine how he felt when one of his sons turned out to be a wild cat!" Caleb said.

"Still, he should have been there for his son. I've only known Lee for a few years, and I know he'd never hurt me. Your father has known him all his life."

"I know," Caleb said, a hint of sadness in his tone. "And I know Lee would never hurt me, even though he threatened to when we were kids, and he almost attacked us when we rescued him." He winked at Lee, who glowered back. "You wouldn't have, though," he added softly.

"I'm not so sure about that," Lee said, but he gave a faint smile when Melissa squeezed his hand.

"So now what?" she said.

"Mom will be expecting us," Caleb said. "You know how she's been dying to see you."

Lee sighed. "I know. It's just—" His voice trailed off.

"You want to change. Run off your anger," Melissa said.

"No. I'll come back with you."

"It'll be better if I go back with Caleb. You come when you're ready."

"No—" he began, but she pressed her fingers to his lips.

"It's fine," she said. "I'll be fine. Caleb will protect me."
Across the table, Caleb gave her a smirk.

"With my whole body," he said.

"See?"

"Are you sure?" Lee said softly.

Melissa pushed away her doubts. "Yes."

"If things aren't going well, we'll leave," Caleb said.

"Okay. But only if you're completely sure," he said to Melissa.

"I'm sure."

They left the restaurant a short time later and dropped Lee at the edge of the forest. "I'll be back soon," he promised Melissa.

"I'll be waiting."

CHAPTER 31

Melissa's fingers tapped incessantly against the passenger seat as Caleb drove Lee's truck back to his parents' house.

Caleb glanced at her sympathetically. "It'll be okay," he said. "I'll protect you."

She smiled weakly and climbed out of the truck. "I'll hold you to that." She drew in a deep breath, bolstering her strength, and followed Caleb to the door. He pushed it open and they stepped inside as Judith walked into the front room, a floury apron tied around her waist.

"Caleb! You came back. Where's Lee?"

"He needs some time," he said. "But I brought Melissa back with me."

"Good, good. You must think we're terrible people, Melissa," she said. "I hope you can forgive Andrew's outburst." She turned to the kitchen without waiting for a reply. "I was just finishing some baking. Come join me."

Melissa glanced at Caleb, then followed Judith into the kitchen, Caleb a pace behind.

"Some tea?" Judith said. "Coffee? I don't think you finished your cup earlier." She gave a nervous laugh and wiped her hands on her apron. "Andrew's just gone out for a while."

"I'd love some coffee, thank you," Melissa said.

"Sit down, please." Judith placed a mug before her. "Have you eaten?"

"Yep," Caleb said, taking a seat beside Melissa.

The oven beeped and Judith opened it to take out a sheet of shaped cookies before replacing it with another and closing the oven again. "Where did you go?" she asked, nodding when Caleb named the restaurant. "They have good food there."

"And large enough portions to feed a hungry cat," Caleb added wryly. Judith cast a nervous glance at Melissa as Caleb laughed. "Mom, you're as jumpy as a mouse," he said. "Melissa's actually very nice."

"Of course she is." She turned to Melissa. "How did you and Lee meet?"

"We've worked together for years. We started dating a few months ago."

"I see. And he—er—he told you about himself?"

"Actually, he saved my life a few times before I learned what he is."

"It's good that you know now. I didn't know about Andrew's family until after we were married. Of course, he's not a Changer like Lee." She turned to the sink and ran the water.

Melissa watched her for a moment, then, rising from the table, went to stand beside her. "Mrs. Garrett, I want you to know something. Lee says you don't approve of him being with someone. But I love him very much, and I know he'd never do anything that would put me in danger."

"Oh, I know that," Judith said. "No, that isn't what worries me. It's just, well"—she rubbed her hands nervously over her apron—"did Lee tell you what would happen? The mating cycle, I mean?"

"You're worried I won't be able to—"

"Yes." Judith blushed and looked away.

Melissa saw Caleb grinning at her. "I know what's involved," she said, "and it won't be a problem. I won't leave the cycle uncompleted."

"So you're all right with it?"

"I am."

Judith attended to the sink of water but not before Melissa saw the relief cross her face. "Good. I'm glad. I'd hate for Lee—"

"I know. Me too."

They stood quietly for a moment as Judith scrubbed a pan. "You know your children could be like Lee?" she said after a few moments. Melissa was silent. She'd wondered about that. "Andrew told me about his family when I was pregnant with Lee," Judith continued. "You can imagine it was quite a shock. It was even more of a shock when I realized that my son was like his grandfather."

"Were you scared?"

"Not scared of Lee. I loved him from the first moment I saw him. But I was scared I wouldn't know how to raise him. Andrew's relationship with his father had always been ... difficult."

The kitchen door opened, bringing in a blast of cold air as Andrew walked into the house. He stopped when he saw Caleb and Melissa. "You're back," he said to Caleb.

"Where's your brother?"

"Running off some steam."

Andrew snorted as he slipped into a chair at the table. "Bring me some coffee, Judith." She poured him a cup from the machine on the counter and placed it silently in front of him. "So Lee goes off and sends her back here with you. Not very gentlemanly of him, is it?"

"Lee would have come back with me," Melissa said, "but I told him to go."

"I thought it was a good idea for you to get to know your future daughter-in-law," Caleb said, "but we can go if you want."

"Well, you're here now." He looked at Melissa. "You're a fool," he said.

Melissa suppressed an angry retort. "For coming back with Caleb?"

"For agreeing to marry Lee. You may think you know what you're doing, but a Changer can turn on you at any moment."

"I'll take my chances."

Judith removed the apron from around her waist. "Why don't I show you your room, Melissa? Do you have a bag?"

"It's in Lee's truck."

"She wasn't sure she'd be staying here," Caleb added, eyeing his father.

"Of course you must stay here," Judith said. "It's Christmas, and you've come all this way." She led Melissa from the kitchen and up the stairs. "Don't let Andrew upset you. He'll come around."

Melissa was silent as the woman led her into a large room with a queen-sized bed against one wall, covered in a floral cover, and a dresser with a TV. Through an open doorway, Melissa saw a bathroom.

"I hope you're comfortable here," Judith said. She looked around the room, then back at Melissa. "Will Lee be back tonight, do you think?"

"I don't know."

"Of course not. Well, please get settled." At the door, she paused. "Melissa, I'm really glad Lee's found you." She hurried from the room and closed the door before Melissa could respond.

She sat down on the bed with a sigh as a knock sounded on the door and Caleb stepped inside. "I brought this in for you," he said, holding out her bag.

She took it gratefully. "Your father really doesn't like me, does he?"

"It's not you."

"Is that supposed to make it better?"

He sat on the bed beside her. "I suppose not. But Mom likes you."

"She seems nice."

"She is. Sometimes it's hard to notice her when Dad's around, but she's always been there for us." He nudged her shoulder. "And she wants the best for Lee." They sat in silence for a moment until Caleb pointed to the TV. "Want to watch a movie? There's bound to be some cheesy Christmas flick."

"Sure." She laid back on the bed and settled herself against the headrest as Caleb clicked through the channels, finally stopping on *Elf*.

"This good?"

"Can't get much cheesier than that."

They watched *Miracle on 34th Street* when *Elf* was done, and Melissa fell asleep before the movie was finished. Sometime during the night, she felt warm arms wrap around her and hot breath against her neck, and then she sunk back into sleep. She awoke to feel Lee playing with a strand of her hair.

"Good morning," she whispered. "Feeling better?"

He brought his hand to her cheek and kissed her gently. "I always feel better when I'm with you."

She smiled. "Did you enjoy your run last night?"

"My run? Oh yes, it was good. Hunted a bit. Played with some other animals." He laughed when she groaned, then turned serious. "I think I can face him at breakfast. How was your night? I'm sorry I abandoned you, but you're still here, so that must be a good sign."

"You didn't abandon me. And I did have a good night. I chatted with your mom a bit, and Caleb and I watched movies for the rest of the evening."

"Hmm," he said, "it's a good thing I trust him. His scent's all over this bed."

"You're the only one I want."

"What did you and my mom talk about?"

"You. She mentioned us having children, actually. Little Changers."

"Does that worry you?"

She wrapped her hands around his neck and pulled him to her. "Not at all. I'll love them even more because they'll be like you. I just wondered – *will* they be like you?"

"I don't know. Dad's not a Changer, even though his father was. But I think the odds are pretty high."

She thought about that. "How will we know?"

"Mom said I purred whenever she fed me."

Melissa laughed.

"How about some breakfast?" he said. "It smells like my mom's cooking up a feast."

"You know she's cooking for you," Melissa said as she

went into the bathroom. "She's making up for last night."

Lee leaned against the door frame as Melissa brushed her hair. "I know," he said. "I just wish she'd stand up to him more."

"Don't be too hard on her. She loves you."

"Are you the family therapist now?" Lee asked playfully.

"Yes. And if you're not careful, I'll start analyzing you." She held up her hand and checked off with her fingers. "Insecure—"

"I'm not insecure!"

"Scared of being loved—"

"Not by you."

"Sheds."

"I don't shed!" he said as he grabbed her by the waist and threw her on the bed. She squirmed away as he tickled her and fell on the floor with a thud.

"And terribly dangerous," she added.

Hopping from the bed, he hauled her to her feet, catching her against his chest. "And don't you forget it," he said.

They made their way downstairs a few minutes later to find Caleb already seated at the table while Judith stood at the stove. Caleb looked up with a smirk. "Good thing you came home, brother," he said. "I really enjoyed being with your girlfriend last night."

"Hmm, so I gathered." Lee cuffed his brother playfully around the ear. "Where's Dad?" he said to his mother.

"Gone out."

Lee's shoulders relaxed slightly. "What's for breakfast?"

"We have bacon, eggs, some sausage, and pancakes. Also a few muffins, some fruit, yogurt and toast."

"Sounds like a feast," Melissa said.

"I'll have everything except the fruit," Lee said, grabbing a plate as Melissa and Caleb shared an amused glance.

"Sure we can't find you some steaks?" Caleb said.

"I'll make a steak out of you if you're not careful."

Caleb laughed. "I'm shaking in my boots, brother."

Somehow, they managed to get through pre-Christmas activities. Andrew was often out, and when he wasn't, Lee dragged Melissa from the house, or retreated with her to the bedroom.

Still, Judith was very nice, and Melissa was glad of the chance to get to know her soon-to-be mother-in-law. They went to the church down the road on Christmas Eve, then came home to eggnog and card games, while Andrew disappeared to the basement.

Melissa woke on Christmas morning just as the sun was beginning to lighten the sky to see Lee lying beside her. He had been sharing a room with Caleb because, he said, it was too difficult to keep his resolve when he slept at her side. He was watching her as she slept, and smiled when she opened her eyes.

"Good morning," he said softly. "Merry Christmas." He dipped his head and kissed her. "The best Christmas gift ever—spending Christmas with someone I love is a luxury I never thought I'd have."

The gift was really hers, Melissa thought, but she remained silent as she ran her fingers lightly over his cheek. Then she smiled and rolled away. "I have something for you." Hanging over the side of the bed, she pulled the long, flat box from beneath it. "Merry Christmas," she said as she handed it to him.

"So it *is* for me," he said with a grin. He ripped off the paper. A layer of cardboard and packaging tape covered the gift, and he pulled it off to reveal the painting beneath.

"It reminded me of you," Melissa said as he stared at it.

"It's incredible," he said, "thank you." He placed the painting on the covers and slipped off the bed. "Wait here while I get your gift."

He returned a moment later with a cylindrical package. He had carried it with ease, but her hands dropped as she took it from him.

"It weighs a ton."

"Open it," he commanded. She turned the package until she found a piece of tape, and slowly and meticulously undid the wrapping. He tapped a finger impatiently, but remained silent. The cylindrical object was a carton with a lid, and she slid it off and reached inside. Her fingers curled around something solid and she pulled out a bronze sculpture of a crouching panther. She looked up to meet Lee's amused expression. "We had the same idea," he said with a smile.

"It's beautiful," she said as she turned the heavy sculpture in her hand. It wasn't very big, about twenty centimeters in length, but the artist had captured the grace of the creature in his work. She placed it on the table beside the bed, then climbed into Lee's lap and wrapped her arms around him. As she bent to kiss him, she wondered how she was possibly going to wait another month before being with him completely.

They joined the family a short while later as they gathered in the living room to open gifts, and the rest of the day passed with Melissa helping Judith in the kitchen as she made Christmas dinner, while Caleb and Lee lugged skates and hockey sticks to the nearby lake.

Lee and Melissa left Kamloops after breakfast the next morning. Despite the huge meal the night before, Judith had risen early to make another large breakfast.

"I'm so glad I was able to meet you," she said, taking Melissa's hands in her own as they stood at the door saying goodbye. Lee stood beside Melissa, his arm around her.

"We'll see you at the wedding?" Lee said.

"We'd love—"

"No!" Andrew barked from his spot in a living-room chair.

Judith glanced at Andrew, then back at Lee with a plaintive expression. "I'm not sure—"

"It's okay, Mom," Lee said with a sigh. He looked at Andrew. "If you change your mind, Dad, you'd be ... well, it would be great if you could come."

He kissed Judith on the cheek, then took Melissa's hand and led her from the house, punching Caleb on the shoulder on the way out.

"I'll see you in a few weeks, bro," Caleb said. He smiled at Melissa. "Bye, sis."

CHAPTER 32

Melissa stood in the vestibule of a small stone church on a cold Saturday afternoon while Lauren fussed over a few stray strands of hair that had escaped the pins holding her curls in place. She stood back to view her handiwork, then twisted one of the tendrils that framed Melissa's face. Melissa shivered slightly. The day was overcast and gray, and although the door was closed, small flurries of snow swirled through the inch-wide crack between the door and the floor.

"I wish Mom and Dad were here," Melissa said.

"I know." Lauren was silent for a moment. "I saw Lee showing an older couple to their seats – is that his parents?"

"Yes." Judith and Andrew had shown up unannounced at Lee's apartment the previous evening. Apparently, Judith had told Andrew that she was not missing her son's wedding, and when she threatened to go to Calgary without him, he had reluctantly agreed to accompany her. They had spent the night at a hotel, however, despite Lee's invitation to remain at his apartment. Andrew might be willing to attend the wedding, but he sure as hell wasn't staying with Lee.

Music swelled through the church. "Ready?" Lauren handed Melissa a bouquet of pussy willow and paperwhites, wrapped in a wide silver ribbon. She nodded, and Lauren slowly entered the sanctuary. Melissa counted to five, took a deep breath, and followed her sister down the aisle. All eyes were on her, and she flashed a smile at Emma, sitting beside her father, then winked at her niece before gazing at the man waiting for her at the end of the aisle, Caleb at his side. Like a panther, Lee was all in black – a black suit, shirt and tie. His black hair lay short against his skull, except for the small knot at the top of his crown. His eyes, green and intense, met hers as she finished the short walk to the altar. Reaching for her hand, he smiled at her as they faced the minister.

"Dearly beloved," he intoned.

The reception was a simple affair – a meal in a private room of a restaurant – and by ten o'clock, the only remaining guests were family members. Andrew had quickly found the bar and remained there for most of the evening, brooding over his drinks, but Judith had sat at the table and chatted with the other guests. Melissa had been thrilled when Cynthia and Richard accepted the wedding invitation, although she noticed that Richard stayed well away from Lee throughout the evening. Just as well, she thought.

Lee's warm hand crept up her back and she smiled.

"Let's get out of here," he whispered in her ear. They had planned to spend their wedding night at Lee's apartment before flying to Hawaii the next morning. They would spend just a week in the tropical warmth of Kauai before returning home and spending another week – the week of the full moon – at the cabin.

She smiled. "Yes, let's go."

They said their goodbyes amidst tears and hugs, and stepped into Lee's apartment an hour later. As they stepped out of the elevator, Melissa drew a breath of surprise. Candles glittered through the apartment, their reflections dancing in windows darkened by the night sky. White roses scented the air and petals were strewn around the entrance.

"How—?" Melissa began.

"Didn't you notice Caleb leaving before us? He came back to light the candles."

"You arranged all of this?" She turned to him. "It's beautiful."

"Not as beautiful as you." He kissed her gently and slowly before sliding his mouth down the side of her neck. "You look exquisite, but I can't wait to get better acquainted with what's beneath that lovely gown."

He stared at her, his bright green gaze capturing hers. "Your eyes," she whispered, "it's not even close to full moon."

"You're my moon, my darling. My body responds to you." He curled a tendril of her hair around his finger, watching as it unwound, then slowly and deliberately began pulling the pins from her updo and dropping them to the floor as her hair tumbled around her shoulders. "Turn around," he said. A long row of pearl buttons held the gown closed from her neck to the small of her back, and he unclasped them. She shivered slightly as his warm hands brushed her skin. He paused, then bent down and breathed in deeply.

"You're nervous," he said gently. "Are you afraid of me?"

She turned to face him. "Not at all. It's just that ... well ... I don't want to disappoint you."

He looked at her incredulously. "Disappoint me? Melissa, that would be impossible!"

"You've been with so many women. My experience is far more limited."

He stared at her a moment, then took her hands. "My grandfather told me once that sex is all about trust."

"Your grandfather?"

Lee smiled self-consciously. "We were at a checkout counter, and he saw a magazine with a headline about sexual compatibility. He looked at it and said, 'Load of nonsense, boy. Don't read garbage like that! Enjoyable sex is all about trust. You can't be vulnerable without trust, and when you're vulnerable, well that's when the magic begins.'"

"He said that?"

"Yes. Then he looked at me, turned red, and didn't say another word until after we'd arrived home."

"How old were you?"

"Sixteen!" They shared a grin as Lee took a step closer. "So do you trust me? Because you and I, we're going to make magic happen."

"You know the trust goes both ways."

"I know. And you know I've never allowed myself to be vulnerable. But I've already shown you all that I am, and now I'll bare my soul." He turned her around and continued where he'd left off unclasping the buttons. He dropped to his knees and brushed kisses across her lower back. She drew in a breath as his mouth caressed her skin, and when he turned her around and kissed her stomach, she had to grab the wall to keep from falling. Slowly he raised himself once more and brought his lips to hers. The gown fell from her shoulders and he stared at her as it pooled around her feet.

"So beautiful," he murmured. He'd already discarded the jacket and tie he'd worn, and she brought her hands to his chest to remove his shirt. He impatiently helped her unfasten the buttons, then pushed the shirt from his shoulders and pressed her against the wall. His kisses before had been slow and sensuous, but as his mouth touched hers again, urgency overtook them both, and they explored each other with a sense of desperation. She wrapped her hands around him with a moan and pulled him closer. She could feel his desire pressing against her, and she yanked open the zipper of his pants and pushed them down his legs.

His hands slipped to her thighs, and she wrapped her legs around him as he carried her to the bedroom. The bed was cool beneath her back as he laid her down, but his skin was hot as he crawled over her. His eyes were blazing as he dropped his head to her breast and caressed her with his tongue. Her lips parted as she lifted herself up to him, and a deep growl vibrated in his chest as he pressed into her. She couldn't look away from his burning gaze as he filled her. He flicked his tongue, and she gasped as his lips curled backward, revealing sharp feline teeth. His mouth dropped to her neck and he sank his teeth into her flesh. Twin points of pain stabbed through her, but as she struggled against it, the pain dissipated, replaced by a smoldering burn that spread throughout her body. She pressed herself into him and he growled, sinking himself even deeper as he moved and sucked. A wave of heat washed over her, and she grabbed the sheets as he lifted his head. Her blood gleamed on his teeth as he stared at her. "You're mine," he rasped.

"Yours," she said. His eyes flared even brighter as they strove together, soaring into the dark sky and past the moon. She cried out as heat exploded within her and mingled with the roar that tore from him. They collapsed onto the sheet, their arms and legs tangled, covered in a sheen of sweat. They lay panting until the touch of skin against skin aroused them once more, and he lifted himself to kiss her again. Outside the clouds parted to reveal a few shining stars, but they scarcely noticed as they flew past all limits of pleasure and soared to the edge of the universe. They dozed and awoke to a deep awareness of each other, claiming each other again and again until they finally fell into an exhausted sleep, Lee's long legs and arms curled around her.

Melissa woke the next morning to the feathery touch of fingers brushing her skin, and she opened her eyes to see Lee staring down at her.

"Morning, my love."

She tried to rise, then groaned. "I don't think I can move."

He smiled – a smile that was superior and exultant all at once. "Do you remember saying you were nervous last night?"

"Hmm."

He brought his face closer. "You were incredible. I've never known such pleasure."

She smiled. "You were pretty incredible yourself." She stretched a little and felt a twinge in her neck. Running her fingers over two small wounds there, she said, "You bit me."

His eyes flicked to the tiny wounds, his expression a mixture of remorse and triumph. "I'm sorry. I was driven by a need I've never known before. To taste you and mark you."

"Have you done that before?"

"No! Not even close. But you're my mate, and I suppose the animal in me wanted to claim you as my own."

"Will you always do that?"

"I doubt it. It was an instinctive action – the start of the mating cycle." His eyes flicked back to the wounds, changing to a slighter brighter green. "You probably don't want to hear this," he said, his voice low, "but I enjoyed tasting you. And I like seeing my mark on you."

She turned on her side to face him fully, ignoring the ache of her reluctant muscles. She touched her hand to his chest, then dropped it to the tattoo of the snarling, angry panther on his arm. Looking at it for a moment, she said, "I'm yours – and you're mine. I think it's only fair that since you marked me, I mark you too."

"You want to bite me?"

"No. I'm going to score you."

He stared at her a moment. "Okay."

She went to the kitchen, took a knife from the drawer, then scooped some of the dirt from a potted plant into a dish. She returned to the bedroom to see Lee watching her curiously.

"What are you going to do?"

She reached for his tattooed arm. "You told me once that the tattoo is there to remind you of who you are," she said. "But that's not you anymore. Not the angry, wild cat, anyway." She placed the tip of the knife just below the panther's snarling mouth and, pressing deeply, dragged the tip of the knife over his skin as she etched an image. He gritted his teeth as blood welled to the surface, and his eyes turned to a glowing green as he watched her dragging the knife deeper. She rubbed some of the dirt into the wound. "I know you'll just heal," she explained, "and I want you to bear my mark permanently."

"A butterfly?" he said as she worked.

"A butterfly changes, leaving behind its old self and becoming something new, a creature of beauty."

He stared at it for a long moment. "You're the butterfly," he said. "The butterfly and the panther." He pulled her into his lap and she straddled him as he kissed her deeply, and they reminded themselves of all the pleasures they would share.

CHAPTER 33

They arrived in Hawaii in the late afternoon, and as soon as Melissa stepped from the plane she was enveloped in a wave of hot, humid air. She stood in the sunshine for a moment before hurrying after Lee as he made his way to the rental car agency. In a half hour, they were on the road, driving along the highway that twisted around the coast, through forests and over hills, to arrive at a hotel at the very tip of the island. Melissa was awestruck when Lee opened the door to their suite. A large sitting area spread out before her, but it was the view of the ocean that mesmerized her. She crossed the room and stepped onto a large terrace, breathing in the fresh, clean air. "I think I could get used to this," she said.

He joined her at the edge of the terrace and wrapped his arms around her. "It's beautiful, isn't it? But I'll be happy wherever you are."

They left the hotel room a short while later in search of nourishment and enjoyed seafood on the patio of the restaurant, overlooking the ocean. It was dark by the time they were done, and they wandered hand in hand along the path that led to the beach. The sky was clear, with thousands of stars twinkling above them, and the waxing moon shining brightly, glittering on the water. They removed their sandals and meandered along the shoreline as the water lapped at their feet. Melissa leaned into Lee, and he bent down to kiss her. Then he pulled away and began to move slowly to an unheard rhythm.

"Dance with me," he said.

She smiled and lifted her hands to his shoulders, moving in time with him. He hummed a few notes beneath his breath, then began singing Moondance, his low voice sending a shiver down her back as he serenaded her. He touched his forehead to hers, and his breath washed over her skin as they stepped in a slow circle. The water swirled around their feet, sucking Melissa's toes into the sand as they danced through the shallow water, the surf rippling around their ankles.

Melissa watched as Lee tapped his fingers on the wooden surface of the table where they sat, waiting for their meal to be served. It was their last night in Hawaii, and it had been more than incredible. Long, passionate nights had followed days filled with sunshine as they swam in the ocean and strolled along the beach. They had gone scuba diving, hiked through the mountains, picnicked on the beach and watched dolphins and whales frolicking in the ocean before heading back to the hotel room and collapsing in a passionate heap on the bed, if they made it that far.

"I can't believe we're leaving tomorrow," Melissa said, taking a sip of her mai tai.

"Hmm? What? Yes, the time's gone by quickly." Lee gave her a distracted smile and stared at the moon, then pulled his attention away as he slid his finger around the rim of his glass.

"It's calling you, isn't it?" she said softly.

"I'm fine!" he said with a frown. He stared at the ocean as she watched him. "Stop!"

"What?"

"Staring at me. Wondering what's going to happen."

"I'm not—"

He pushed himself away from the table. "I need some air."

"Lee?" She rose to follow him, then dropped back into her seat when she saw the waiter approaching with their plates in his hands. He paused as Lee marched around him, then hurried to the table.

"Should I, uh—?"

"He'll be back in a moment," she said. "Leave his plate there."

An hour later Lee had still not returned. The waiter gave Melissa a sympathetic smile as she asked him to pack up Lee's food, then signed the bill. She walked back to the hotel slowly, hoping Lee was waiting for her, but the room was dark and empty. With a sigh, she dropped onto the couch overlooking the ocean and laid her head on a pillow.

A few hours later, she awoke when Lee lifted her from the couch and carried her to the bed. "I'm sorry," he whispered.

"It's starting, isn't it?"

"Yes." He looked down at her and pushed the hair from her face. "I've never felt the pull this strongly before. And being with you – I just want to let myself go."

"We'll be home tomorrow." He was silent. "Lee, what is it?"

"It's not going to be pretty, Mel. I'll be half human, half animal. You may run away screaming."

Melissa pushed herself up on the bed. "Do you remember our first night when you said the best sex happens when you trust someone and can be vulnerable?"

He smiled grimly. "Yes."

"Trust me, Lee. I love you. You're my husband, my mate. This is new for both of us, but it isn't what you look like on the outside that matters. It's the person you are inside."

He smiled. "I know. I just wish I knew what to expect."

She wrapped her hands around his neck and pulled him closer. "I want you, no matter what you look like. Trust that."

He pulled back to look in her eyes, and then his lips were on hers. A growl rumbled through his chest as she wrapped her legs around him and slipped her hands beneath his shirt.

"Mine," he growled.

"Mine," she said.

Lee parked his truck in front of the cabin shortly before midnight the next night. "We're home," he said.

The ground was deep with snow, and even with the heater on in the truck, Melissa's toes were numb with cold. "Yes, home."

"Let's get inside and get a fire going."

The cabin inside was almost as cold as outside, and Melissa shivered as she stepped over the threshold, pulling her jacket tight around her chest. There was a pile of wood at the door, and within minutes Lee had a fire blazing. She went to stand before it, relaxing as the warmth slowly wrapped around her.

"I'm going to go check everything outside," he said. "You okay if I leave you for a short while?"

She nodded. "Enjoy your run."

Lee was already at the door, but he stopped and returned. "Love you," he said, bending to kiss her. He stripped off his shirt and jeans and was gone a moment later.

Melissa grabbed a blanket and sat down on a chair near the fire. She thought about Lee's words the previous night. It was the not knowing that was so unsettling. She had told him that she wanted him no matter how he looked – she only hoped she had spoken the truth. She closed her eyes as the heat of the fire finally filtered through the cabin, warming her for the first time since leaving Hawaii. When she awoke, it was the next morning, and she was on the bed. She had no recollection of being moved, but she could feel Lee's warmth pressed against her back. She turned slowly and opened her eyes to find him watching her.

"Warmer?" he asked.

"Hmm? I will be soon." She still wore the clothes from the day before, and she draped her jean-clad leg over Lee's bare one. She snuggled against him, and as he kissed her, the stubble on his chin grazed her skin. "You need to shave," she said playfully.

He ran his hand over his face. "I don't think shaving's going to help," he said with a rueful smile. She pulled back to study him more closely. Except for the sprinkling of hair around his mouth, he appeared no different from his usual self.

He climbed from the bed, snagging a pair of jeans from

the chair. "I'm going to make you some breakfast."

When breakfast was done, they set out into the snowy landscape, strapping on snowshoes to make the trek possible. They trudged behind the cabin, in the same direction Melissa had fled so many months before, and skirted along the edge of the forest. Three deer were nibbling on some grass at the base of a tree, but when Melissa and Lee drew near they stopped and sniffed the air then sprang away, bounding into the distance.

"You or me?" Melissa asked, watching them.

"Probably me. Most animals smell a predator."

By the time they had returned to the cabin, Melissa was shivering and she could no longer feel her fingers. Lee seemed unaffected by the cold, and she studied him with a scowl. "Don't you feel the cold at all?"

"A little," he said, taking her hands and rubbing some warmth into them, "just not as much as you. But I'm happy to warm you up," he added, stepping closer.

She could feel the heat from his body as she embraced him. "Yes, please," she said.

Lee went out in the late afternoon, bounding over the snow and disappearing into the trees. Several hours passed before he returned, and when he held Melissa close, she noticed that the hair on his arms was thicker.

Over the next couple of days, Lee showed Melissa his favorite places around the cabin: the frozen lake where they slid across the ice on the soles of their shoes; and the peak of a mountain which they scrambled up to look at the view. One morning he took her to a cave where he and Caleb had played as boys, sometimes camping out for the night. In the corner of the cave was a large plastic crate, and Lee approached it with a smile.

"I can't believe this is still here," he said.

"What's inside?"

"Our camping supplies."

He dropped to his haunches and lifted the lid. Melissa peered over his shoulder to see a sleeping bag stuffed into the box. Dust rose as Lee pulled it out and gave it a shake. He laid it aside and reached inside for a second sleeping bag.

"I can't believe these survived," Lee marveled. He took out a lighter and flicked the wheel, smiling when a flame lit the air. "We used to roast marshmallows in here, and look, we even left a stash behind." He pulled out a half-filled bag of marshmallows and held them out in Melissa's direction. She took a step backward.

"I'm pretty sure they're no longer edible," she said.

He squeezed the marshmallows through the bag. "As hard as rock," he said, dropping it back into the crate. He stuffed the sleeping bags back inside and led her out of the cave.

Every afternoon he left her beside the fire to go out on his own, returning later and later each day. She noticed more changes each time he returned. His skin was paler than before, his nails longer.

By the end of the week, it had started snowing again – thick flakes that fell silently to the blanketed ground. Melissa sat at the window, the crackling fire the only sound as she stared out at the peaceful landscape. Lee had left her soon after their walk that morning and had still not returned. She drew away from the window with a sigh. The next night was the full moon, and the effects on Lee were increasingly evident. His eyes glowed continually now, and his legs were covered in a fine layer of black fur. That morning, he'd fumbled in the kitchen with a mug, cursing when it fell from his fingers, which were no longer long and thin but short and stubby with thick, clawed nails. He'd snarled at her when she knelt down to pick up the pieces, then flung himself outside, returning a short while later to take her in his arms and apologize.

She picked up a book then threw it down again, distracted. She looked out of the window, wondering when he'd be back, then headed into the kitchen to boil some water for tea. She'd just filled the kettle when she heard the front door opening. Leaving the kettle on the stove, she walked back into the sitting room to find Lee standing near the door, wearing a pair of sweat pants. She stopped for a moment when she saw him, then moved closer, taking in the latest changes.

Bright green filled his eyes, swallowing all but the smallest traces of white at the corner of each eye. They were ringed in black, as though someone heavy handed had outlined them with kohl. As she drew closer, she saw that his skin was a light shade of gray. His lips had thinned and were the color of charcoal. He watched her warily as she came to a stop before him. She pushed away her qualms. "Hey," she whispered, "I missed you."

Slowly, he lifted his hand to her face. His fingers were even stubbier than before, and his claws scratched lightly as he ran them down her cheek. She took a step closer and brought her hands to his cheeks. Fur lined the upper tips of his ears and when her hand brushed against them, they twitched. Slipping her hands behind his head, she pulled his face down to hers and kissed him. He kissed her back lightly, then pulled away, leaning against the wall. She moved her hands to his chest, then pushed them beneath the elastic waistband of his pants. Beneath her exploring fingers she felt not hair, but thick fur. She glanced up at him, meeting his troubled gaze, then slipped the pants down his legs and stared at him. From the waist down, there was nothing about Lee that was human at all. The skin was completely smooth and entirely black. His thighs were curved inward, ready to support his weight on all fours, and his legs were covered in thick black fur. His knees – no longer human – were bent forward, and he stood on the balls of his feet. A movement caught her eye, and she looked down to see a thick tail, the end twitching from side to side.

She stared at it a moment. "You have a tail," she whispered. Sliding her hands around his backside, she buried her fingers in the fur until they reached his tail. She closed her hands around the thick, sleek shaft and ran her fingers over it. Lee placed a finger beneath her chin and raised her face to look at him, and then his lips were on hers, hard and demanding as his tongue explored her mouth. His hands slipped to her back, pulling her closer, and she could feel the rough skin of his palms like sandpaper through her shirt.

"Come," she said when they broke apart. "Let's go to the bedroom." He stared down at her, then nodded.

"Go," he said. His voice was low and raspy.

When she paused at the door to look back, he had dropped to all fours and was prowling across the room. She looked away hurriedly and climbed onto the bed, her heart racing as she stared at the doorway. He appeared a moment later, then stopped when he saw her watching him, his eyes intent on hers.

"Come," she said again.

He sprang onto the bed, landing at her feet, and crept closer until his face was above hers. "You sure?" he growled.

"Yes." She pulled him down to her. His body covered

hers and she felt his tail swishing over her legs. "Wait," she said. He moved to the side and watched as she tore off her clothes, and when she laid back down, he covered her and made her his.

A cold wind rattling the windows woke Melissa in the early hours of the morning. Lee lay behind her, one arm draped over her side, his tail wound around her leg. She lay like that for a few minutes, then slowly turned to look at him, drawing in a surprised breath when she saw his glowing green eyes watching her intently.

"You're awake," she whispered.

"I'll go ... soon," he rasped, his voice a low growl.

"No," she said, "please stay."

"Be ... back."

She leaned closer and brought her lips to his. "I love you," she whispered as she kissed him. She slipped a hand around his back and held his tail. He groaned, pulling her closer and kissing her deeply as his tail slid through her hand and up the side of her leg. A rumbling started deep in his chest and vibrated through him as he raised himself over her and wrapped his arms around her. He pulled away slightly to look into her eyes, and she grinned up at him. "You're purring." The purring grew louder as he dropped his head back to hers and rasped his tongue along the side of her neck. She shivered and pulled him closer as he sank into her.

They lay in the bed afterward, staring at each other. He stroked her face with his hand, which was now a paw, then lifted himself and sat back on his haunches. "Must ... go," he growled.

"But you'll be back?"

"Back," he affirmed.

"I'll be waiting." He kissed her lightly on the lips, then turned and sprang off the bed, disappearing through the doorway as Melissa watched. She heard the click of the front door, and turned to watch him as he flew across the moonlit clearing beyond the window.

CHAPTER 34

A pale winter sun was shining through the window when Melissa awoke later that morning. Outside, the snowy landscape was glittering in the sun as though celebrating its return. Above the sky was a deep blue. Shivering, Melissa pulled on some clothes and went to the kitchen to start a pot of coffee. Glancing at the clock, she was startled to see it was already eleven o'clock. She looked out of the window, searching the grounds beyond the cabin for signs of a panther, but all was still. What was Lee doing and when would he be back? Her mind wandered to the previous night. In the dark she hadn't been able to see Lee, but she'd known when she ran her hand over his face that he had almost completely changed. She thought about the black panther stalking through the snow. In the cold light of day, being with a huge predator suddenly didn't seem quite so appealing. She took her coffee to the living room and opened her book to the marked page, but she couldn't focus on the words in front of her. Instead, her thoughts drifted outside, prowling through the snow. Was Lee close by? Could he smell her right now? If she called his name, would he hear her? She put down the book and went to the window again. Did she want to call him? At that moment, she wasn't too sure. She stared out at the trees at the other end of the clearing, once more searching for signs of Lee, but saw nothing to suggest he was there. She returned to the couch with a sigh and tried again to read her book.

The hours passed slowly, and more than once Melissa got up to look outside, but it wasn't until late afternoon that she saw the huge black panther sitting at the edge of the forest, his eyes glittering as he stared at her across the distance. She stared back, waiting for him to come closer, but after a few minutes he rose and stalked back into the trees. She breathed a sigh of relief. Now that the moment was at hand, she was wondering how she had ever thought she could do this. But it needed to be done, she told herself. As fearful as she was feeling, she had made a promise to Lee. A promise that could have infinite repercussions if she didn't follow through. She searched the forest's edge once more. Why was Lee staying away? Even if he sensed her hesitancy, he knew she wouldn't turn him away, didn't he?

Another hour passed before Lee showed up at the edge of the forest again, this time pacing between the trees as he kept glancing her way. He was waiting for her, she realized. Waiting to see if she could fulfil her word. She tried to still the pounding of her heart. The panther form was just a guise, she reminded herself, hiding the man she loved within. She'd taken him into her arms the night before, when he was even more freakish than right now. Could she do it now that he was fully a panther? Did she even have a choice? She drew in a deep breath. The time for wondering was long gone. The panther needed his mate before it was too late.

She went to the kitchen and poured herself a glass of red wine, hoping to find some liquid courage. She finished the glass and poured another, but when that was done she knew she could put off the moment no longer. She pulled on her jacket and snow boots and stepped out the door. In the sky, the moon was a huge silver globe.

Lee had worn down a path with his pacing, but when Melissa stepped out, he stopped and stared at her. She stepped onto the snow and made her way to him as he watched her, his eyes glittering intently. He growled softly and his tail swished from side to side as she drew closer. He turned and started back towards the woods, then stopped at the trees and looked at her, and she followed him. A cold breeze stirred the air, and she pulled her jacket tighter around herself, her hands shaking slightly. He continued stalking through the trees, stopping every few seconds to make sure she was following, and when they broke from the trees, the cave was ahead of them. He prowled in, disappearing into the darkness. She looked up at the moon and steadied her nerves before following him in.

The air was warmer out of the freezing wind, she noticed with relief, but the only light that penetrated the darkness were a few rays of moonlight. At the other end of the cave, green eyes stared at her through the darkness. She walked closer, stretching out her hand, and her fingers sunk into thick fur. A low growl rumbled through the air as Lee wound himself around her legs. She pushed off her boots, and was surprised to feel something soft beneath her toes. A sleeping bag. With shaking fingers she unzipped her jacket and let it slip to the ground as Lee watched her intently. Her eyes were growing used to the dark, and she could make out his shape – black on black. She unzipped her jeans and pushed them down her legs. Despite the warmer air in the cave, it was still freezing, and she shook as she removed her panties. With fumbling fingers, she undid the buttons of her shirt, allowing it hang loosely around her waist. She dropped to her knees on the thick sleeping bag and stared at Lee. His bright green gaze regarded her intently, and in the low light, she could just make out his features. She smiled tentatively, and his lips stretched back in a very human grin. A burst of sudden laughter escaped her at the expression, so incongruous on the huge cat. The smile grew wider, and bringing his snout to her neck, he nuzzled her.

"I love you," she whispered. He lifted his paw to her cheek and with startling gentleness, stroked her face, before dropping it back to the ground. Pulling back, he stared at her for another moment, then slowly began to pace around her. She dropped onto all fours, and Lee ran himself along her length, stroking her body with his own. His tail curled around her, thick and heavy, and she shivered. He sniffed her skin, running his cold nose along her body, and then he was behind her, lifting himself onto her. His paws clutched her and he covered her with his length. His face was at her shoulder, and as he pushed himself into her, he sank his teeth into her neck, making her arch back into him as she cried out. A growl rumbled through his chest as he clung more tightly to her. His teeth left her neck as he lifted his head and roared as he filled her, the sound mingling with her cries as she sank to the ground. After a short time, he rolled off her, leaving her shivering again, but using his teeth, he pulled the second sleeping bag over her, spreading it across her legs and tucking it around her toes with his snout, then lay down beside her and wrapped his warm body around her. Through the cave entrance she could see the moon, huge and full, hanging in the sky. His gaze followed hers, and they stared at the moon as the trees above sighed in the breeze.

She fell asleep with him at her back, snuggled against his warmth. But when she awoke the next morning, it was to the feel of a soft mattress beneath her and warm blankets on top, Lee curling around her from behind as he stroked her with his hand. She turned to look at him, and he smiled.

"Morning, my love," he said, his voice gravelly. His dark green eyes held hers.

"You're back."

"I never left." He ran his fingers down her thigh. He leaned closer to kiss her lightly, then fell back on the pillow. "You were incredible," he said. "When you came out to me, I could sense your fear. But you came anyway."

"You were waiting for me."

"I wanted to come to you, but I couldn't bring myself to do it. I couldn't bear the thought that maybe ..."

"I love you, Lee."

"I love you, too."

She slid her arm slowly down his back. "You still have fur!"

"Yes. And that's not all." Something thick snaked up her leg. She sat up and yanked back the covers, staring at him. His legs and arms looked completely normal, but his buttocks were still covered in black fur, and stretching from between his cheeks was a thick black tail.

She reached out and stroked it. "This is your best feature," she murmured.

He pushed her back on the bed. "I knew you liked it," he said in her ear as the tail curled around her leg.

"How long will it stay?"

"The moon is releasing me slowly, but it'll be gone after my next change."

"Then you'd better not change until you've shown me all the things your tail can do."

He growled softly as he brought his lips to hers and stopped her from saying anything more.

Epilogue

"You ready?" Lee said.

Melissa looked up from the crib with a frown. "You're sure he'll be okay?"

Joining her, Lee looked down at the sleeping baby. "He'll be fine. Mom knows how to handle babies."

"But what if he starts getting angry?" Baby Leo was typically easygoing, but the other day when she'd pried a fork from his hand, he'd yelled his objection in no uncertain terms, while his cute baby nails had begun to thicken and grow into unmistakable claws.

Judith bustled into the room. "We'll be fine, Melissa," she said. Clearly she'd overheard the conversation. She had arrived the evening before, driving on her own from Kamloops, after astounding them all by announcing that, despite Andrew's orders to remain home, she would be coming to Calgary to take care of Leo. She would not, she declared, allow Caleb the luxury of spending time with her grandbaby while she barely saw him at all, and if Andrew had a problem with that – well, too bad. Andrew had not yet seen his grandson, and Lee was fine with that, but Judith was hopeful that with time, Andrew would realize what he was missing and take steps to reconnect with his family.

"I managed to raise Lee without too much damage," Judith added, "and I can take care of your son for a few days. Now go, before you miss your plane!" Her expression softened. "You have a lot to celebrate, so enjoy your trip and don't worry about Leo."

"Okay. But you'll call if you have any questions?"

"Of course I'll call," she said, pushing Melissa from the room.

"And you're sure you have my number?"

"I have your number. And your email. And Lee's number and email as well. And if all else fails, I have the name and number of the hotel."

"Okay, good. And you know he needs two naps?"

"Go, Melissa!" Judith said in exasperation. She looked at Lee desperately, and he took Melissa by the shoulders.

"Look at me, Mel. We've talked about this, and everything will be fine. Leo will be fine, and so will my mom."

"I know," she sighed.

"It's our first anniversary and I want you all to myself, without wondering when Leo's going to demand your attention." He brought his mouth to her ear, and his voice was low. "I want to claim you as my mate again."

She felt a clenching in her stomach, and when he met her gaze, his eyes were a lighter shade than they had been a moment ago.

343

"Ready?" he said.

"Yes." She followed him to the open elevator.

They called goodbye to his mother, and then the doors were closing and his arms went around her. "We have a lot to celebrate," he said as he held her.

She smiled. "I know." Leo had been born three months earlier, almost nine months exactly after the end of the mating cycle. But that wasn't all Lee meant. Once they were back in town, he had begun to advertise his services in helping locate people who'd gone missing. It had taken a few weeks before a woman contacted him to help her find her missing teenaged daughter. She'd run away with her boyfriend, but by the time Lee tracked her down, she was eager to return home. The story had reached the newspapers, and he'd had a steady stream of clients since.

She leaned into him. "Who would have thought when you were ignoring me all those times that we'd end up like this?"

She felt him smile into her hair. "It just seemed like I was ignoring you, but I was actually noticing every move you made."

"Should that make me feel better?" she asked teasingly.

"Maybe not," he said, twisting a strand of her hair around his finger, "but your scent was the first thing I looked for in the morning, and the last thing I thought of each night."

She smiled. "I think a part of me knew even then what you were. From the time I first started working at Quigs, I dreamed of you."

"You dreamed you were being hunted."

"Tracked and pursued. I just hadn't realized I didn't need to be afraid."

The elevator opened and they stepped into the parking

lot. "Are you afraid now?"

"Afraid of a huge black predator that would take me as its mate? Nope."

He laughed. "So you're willing to risk your life by flying with said predator to Hawaii for a second time?"

"Will said predator want to claim me for a second time?"

She slipped into the passenger seat of his truck. He leaned in to her, his eyes glowing brightly.

"Oh, yes. Devour and consume you." He leaned closer and skimmed his nose along her neck. "When you sink your hands into my fur, I'll wrap my tail around you and show you how much the beast can pleasure you."

She shivered. "Mine," she murmured.

He smiled. "Mine."

THE END

Interview with the Author

Q. In the bedroom scene after their marriage, Melissa
uses a knife to cut a butterfly into Lee's arm. Why
did they not just go to the tattoo parlor?

A. Adding the butterfly was more than just to show
that Lee had changed, but was also about Melissa
marking him, as he had done her, which is why it
was important that she do it herself.

Q. You really pushed the line with this book with
Melissa and Lee making love while he was in
panther form. Why did you do this?

A. First of all, let me be very clear that I am
completely and totally opposed to bestiality.
That said, I did not want to shy away from the

risker elements of the story, which clearly this is. I was aware, in writing it, that some people would find this scene offensive, but leaving it out felt dishonest, and the easy way out. It took some soul searching, but I believe I did the right thing keeping this scene in.

For me, the relationship between Lee and Melissa is allegorical. There is no way that we can imagine that a man could actually take on the shape of any animal, but Lee's inner beast can resemble our own inner dragons that we must deal with to be at peace with ourselves. For their love to be true, Melissa needed to accept Lee completely, and making love is the ultimate step of trust.

Also, whether as a man or a panther, Lee is always Lee. He may not be able to speak as a panther, but he remains the same person. As such, although he and Melissa make love while he is in panther form, he is not truly an animal. Of course, both the fact that a man can change into an animal and their making love while he is in that form are purely the result of an overactive imagination!

Q. I was hoping there would be a reconciliation between Lee and his Dad. Is there a reason this didn't happen?

A. Unfortunately, life doesn't always give us the easy solutions we would like. Andrew must deal with his own fears and insecurities before he can learn to accept and ultimately love his son. But as long as there is life, there is hope, so perhaps Andrew will be able to take those steps with Judith's help.

Acknowledgements

Thank you to my family for your love and support as I continue to pursue my dreams. Kristin and Bethany, I love how excited you are for each book I publish. Thank you!

Thank you to my editor, Arlene Prunkl, for all your tips and guidance. I have learnt so much through this process.

And most importantly, I thank God for giving me the gift of writing.

Other Books by Linda K. Hopkins

Books in *The Dragon Archives* series:
Bound by a Dragon
Pursued by a Dragon
Loved by a Dragon
Facing a Dragon: A novella (a free ebook for subscribers only)
Dance with a Dragon
Forever a Dragon
Redeemed (June 2018)

For more information about these books go to www.lindakhopkins.com. Sign up to receive free access to short stories not available anywhere else, updates about new books and a chance to enter into prize draws. You can also connect with Linda on Facebook.

Printed in Great Britain
by Amazon